MINE

To the Dreamers,
the Risk Takers,
the Defenders of the Defenseless,
and all those who do the right thing

NIGHT HIKE

ONE

Joel

THIS WOULD BE the last summer of Camp Red Hawk.

Arguably its glory days as a top-notch summer destination had passed a few years earlier, when the camp's aging owners had turned day-to-day operations over to the competent but far from visionary Karl Eames, Camp Director.

Still, it wasn't a bad place. Most campers returned home after a week or two—or in a few cases, three—smiling and sharing tales about canoe races, water fights on the lake, ghost stories by the campfire, and hikes up Winston Peak, which was really just a tall hill with no official name. When summer 2005 rolled around, no one predicted the doors to the camp would soon be closed forever.

A few campers, mostly kids who'd spent time at Red Hawk in the past, had learned how to exploit the camp's growing weaknesses. They knew they could easily break into the snack shack by removing the loose pins from the hinges, and if they took only a few candy bars and cans of soda a night, no one seemed to notice. They also knew if they didn't want to participate in a particular activity, all they had to do was make an excuse that would get them sent to Nurse Nancy's office. If she was there, they'd be allowed to lie down until they "felt better," and if she wasn't, which was often the case, they could sneak back to their own cabins, where they could play on smuggled-in Game Boys while chowing down the goodies they'd stolen the night before.

These kids also knew that after ten p.m., when the evening campfire was over and the lights had been turned off, the counselors, who were supposed to be keeping an eye on them, gathered in the boathouse to drink beer and smoke pot, providing the perfect opportunity for the kids to sneak into the woods for a little adventure.

On that pleasant mid-July night, Mike Hurst was whispering for the millionth time, "Come on. Come on." His gaze had been glued to the cabin's door since Dooley had snuck out just after curfew.

Antonio Canavo, on the other hand, lay quietly on the bunk above him, glancing through a *Sports Illustrated* magazine with the aid of his head-mounted flashlight.

Joel Madsen also lay on his bed, the lower one of the other bunk. But he wasn't reading anything or watching the door. He was daydreaming about Leah Bautista, one of the other campers. She was in the same activity group he was.

He had tried to talk to her once. The candy-bar incident.

Just thinking about how stupid he'd sounded made him groan. He was so sure he'd botched things that he hadn't said a word to her since.

Tomorrow, he thought. *I'll say hi and then walk away before I add something ridiculous.*

On the other bottom bunk, Mike started in again with a *come on*, but before the words escaped his mouth, the door swung open, causing him to jerk in surprise and whack his head against a crossbeam.

Joel snorted in amusement while Antonio and the just returned Dooley—his last name; he didn't allow anyone to call him George—laughed out loud.

Mike rubbed his skull. "It's not funny."

"Maybe not to you," Antonio said, hanging over the edge of the bed and looking at his bunkmate.

When the laughter died down, Dooley said, "Are you guys ready or what?"

The three boys climbed off their beds, Mike still wincing, then, with Dooley in the lead, they slipped outside.

14

Their cabin was one of twelve designated for male campers. The girls were in an identical set not too far away. Each group faced the trail that led back to Campfire Plaza, a wide grassy area with a gentle rise, ringed with log benches facing the large fire pit. Beyond Campfire Plaza were the cafeteria, snack shack, admin building, counselors' quarters, and the road to the highway.

Dooley, however, led them the other way, toward the bathrooms and showers—a large building between the boys' and girls' areas that was divided into separate spaces for the two groups. Upon reaching it, he signaled for everyone to wait and then hurried toward the girls' cabins.

Joel could hear Mike breathing nervously behind him.

"Relax," he said.

"I *am* relaxed," Mike replied.

Antonio turned and glared at them. "Will you two shut up?"

Mike put a hand over his mouth and nose as if that would quell the noise, but it only made it louder. Joel didn't say anything else, though. Mike could be a little annoying at times but he meant well.

Dooley returned a few moments later in the company of the girls who were joining them on the excursion. It was Joel's turn to exhale nervously. He'd known Courtney and Kayla were coming. They were Dooley's and Antonio's summer girlfriends. What Dooley *hadn't* mentioned was a third girl.

Leah.

Oh, crap. Oh, crap. Oh, crap.

Leah glanced at him as she and the others approached.

Did she just smile at me? Was that a smile? Did I smile back? Oh, crap.

"Until we get to the stream, no talking," Dooley said as they huddled together. He looked at Mike. "That means you, a-hole." A-hole was the nickname Dooley called pretty much everyone when none of the camp staff was around.

"Yeah, yeah. Don't worry about me."

When Dooley first mentioned the idea of an after-curfew

hike to someplace cool in the woods, it wasn't a surprise that Mike hadn't been interested. He was a rule follower, and this kind of outing was definitely forbidden by camp guidelines. What got him to change his mind was the promise of free candy bars for the rest of his stay. Now all he wanted to do was get it over with and return to the cabin.

They headed down the trail, Dooley holding Courtney's hand and Kayla tucked in tight to Antonio's side. Leah glanced at the two couples, and then looked back at Joel and rolled her eyes. He knew he should have probably rolled his, too, but a sudden warmth in his cheeks caused him to look quickly away.

After they passed the stables, the path narrowed, forcing them to walk single file, and didn't widen again until they reached the bank of the stream.

"Anyone need a rest?" Dooley asked.

"I gotta pee," Mike said.

"Gross," Kayla said.

"What? Everybody pees."

Dooley pointed into the woods. "What are you waiting for? Hurry up."

Trying to hide his embarrassment, Mike disappeared between the pines.

"Anyone else?" Dooley asked.

There were no takers.

"So how much farther?" Leah asked.

Dooley made a show of looking across the river and assessing the trail. "I'd say about twenty minutes."

"Now you going to tell us where we're going?" Joel asked.

"Dude, trust me. You're going to be glad you came." If it weren't for *a-hole*, then *dude* would have been Dooley's favorite word.

Antonio opened his backpack. "Anybody hungry? I got Snickers, Kit Kats, a couple Almond Joys…"

Kayla and Courtney swarmed him, making oohs and aahs as they hunted through the bag. By the time they made their selections, Mike had reemerged from the forest.

"Let's get moving," Dooley said, "or we'll be out here all night."

A series of stones created a makeshift bridge across the water. Joel would have made it without getting wet if Leah, who was in front of him, hadn't slipped. Without thinking, he jumped into the stream and caught her before she hit the water.

"Thanks," she said as he helped her back up.

He wanted to say, "No problem," but whatever came out of his mouth had little connection to the English language.

"Quit goofing off," Dooley yelled back at them. "Let's pick up the pace."

A little way beyond the stream they passed through a clearing and the night sky came into full view. Joel couldn't believe how many more stars could be seen here than back home on the outskirts of Denver. It was just…wow.

"Hey, a-hole, what's the holdup?"

Joel suddenly realized he'd stopped in the meadow while the others had kept going. They'd almost reached the trees on the other side.

"Sorry."

The others disappeared into the woods before he caught up. All except for Leah. She waited until he reached her and smiled. "They *are* beautiful, aren't they," she whispered.

"Huh?"

"The stars. You can barely see them back in Denver."

She was from Denver, too? He should probably ask what part, see if they lived close to each other, but he only smiled and nodded, not trusting his voice.

"Do you know any of the constellations?"

Actually, he did. Thanks to the Science Channel, he knew quite a bit about astronomy, but he worried she was just baiting him to expose him as a geek, a side of his personality he'd fought hard to keep under wraps since arriving at Camp Red Hawk.

When he glanced at her, though, he detected no hidden agenda, so he ventured a tentative, "I know the Big Dipper. And, um, Orion."

"Did you know that if you line up the two end stars of the Dipper's cup they point at the North Star?"

His eyebrows shot up in surprise. "Yeah. Polaris."

Maybe he wasn't the only geek at camp after all.

He tried to come up with something to keep the conversation going, but his mind was a blank. Soon the trail narrowed again and he let Leah move in front of him.

Several minutes later, Mike said, "How far is this thing?"

"Stop whining," Dooley called back. "We're almost there."

After a few more minutes, Joel began to wonder about Dooley's definition of *almost there*, and was opening his mouth to ask him when a fence appeared directly in their path.

"Don't tell me you brought us out here to see *that*," Mike said.

Leah tilted her head up. "That's…pretty tall."

The chain-link fence was at least twelve feet high, and that wasn't even counting the additional few feet created by the strands of barbed wire strung across the top.

"No. Not the fence, a-hole," Dooley said. "This just means we're almost there."

He followed the fence into the darkness, Courtney, Antonio, and Kayla immediately moving after him. Mike, however, hesitated, causing Leah and Joel to do the same.

"Maybe we should head back," Mike said. "I'm tired and it's going to take a while to get to the cabins. And if all this was just for a fence…"

"He already said it wasn't about the fence," Joel said. "Besides, if this thing he wants us to see is as close as he says, we might as well check it out, right?"

When Mike still didn't move, Leah tapped Joel on the arm and nodded after the others. He and Leah moved around Mike and hurried to catch up. Only a few seconds passed before he heard Mike jogging behind them.

As they caught up to the others, Dooley said, "What took you guys so long?"

Joel glanced at Mike and said, "Had to tie my shoe."

Dooley scoffed, but his annoyance changed to excitement as he said, "This is what I wanted to show you."

He shined his light on the fence. Attached near the top was

a weathered and chipped metal sign.

RESTRICTED AREA
NO TRESPASSING
US GOVERNMENT PROPERTY
VIOLATORS WILL BE
DETAINED AND PROSECUTED

At the bottom was a line of smaller print, blotched by rust stains that obscured most of the words.

"Whoa," Mike said. Whatever reluctance he'd been feeling seemed to have momentarily disappeared. "What is this place?"

Dooley shook his head. "No idea. It's not on any map."

"Of course it's on a map," Leah said. "Everything's on a map."

"I checked online myself after I went home last summer," Dooley said. "I even zoomed in on the satellite view. This is all just part of the national forest. Nothing but trees. Not even the fence is visible."

"No roads? No buildings? Nothing?" Leah asked.

"That's what I said, isn't it?"

"That's not possible," Joel said. "You must have missed something."

Dooley's jaw tensed. "Are you calling me a liar?"

"No. I said you must have missed something."

"I didn't *miss* anything."

"Hey, over here!" Antonio's voice came from the darkness farther ahead.

The tense atmosphere forgotten, they jogged toward his voice. Before they reached him, they encountered a tangle of branches and rocks and dirt pushed up against the fence, blocking the way.

"Where are you?" Dooley yelled.

"Here," Antonio answered from the other side of the debris. "Just go around."

As they carefully picked their way past the pile, Joel noticed a swath of scarred and pitted ground stretching as far as he could see back into the woods. He guessed a flash flood had carried the junk through the forest until it smashed into the fence.

As they came around the other side, Leah said, "Oh, wow."

Joel pointed his light ahead. Along with the branches and rocks deposited by the flood were two giant tree trunks. They had slammed into the fence with enough force to rip a wide hole in the chain link.

Antonio was standing in a meadow on the other side, Kayla looking at him through the gap.

"You shouldn't be in there," Mike said nervously.

Antonio laughed. "Who's going to know?"

Dooley worked his way up one of the logs to the rip and paused. "What do you see?"

"Pretty much the same as that side." Antonio swung his light around, illuminating a small meadow and several trees. "I'll go in a little farther and see if there's anything interesting."

"I don't think that's a good idea," Mike said. "The sign said RESTRICTED AREA."

"Don't be a jerk," Dooley chided him as he stepped through the hole.

"Should we come with you?" Courtney asked.

"Just stay there for a minute while we check things out," Dooley told her.

"Be a good little woman," Leah whispered so only Joel could hear. "Let the big tough men handle this."

It was all Joel could do to keep from laughing out loud.

They all watched as Dooley and Antonio crossed the meadow and disappeared into the woods. For a while the two boys' lights bounced off trees here and there, but soon the beams vanished.

"Should...we go look for them?" Kayla asked a minute later.

"I'm not going in there," Mike said. "I-I-I'm not getting arrested."

"We'll give them a few more minutes," Joel said. "I'm sure they're fine."

"You scared, too?" Courtney asked.

"No, of course not." While that wasn't a lie, the restricted sign had definitely given him pause.

Half a minute shy of when Joel would have given in and gone searching for them, a light flickered in the woods. A few moments later, they heard the crunch of footsteps on pine needles.

When Dooley stepped out from the trees alone, Kayla took a step through the opening. "Where's Antonio?"

"You got to see this. Come on!" Dooley waved for them to follow and then vanished back into the woods.

Courtney joined Kayla on the other side.

"Don't you even know what restricted means?" Mike said. "We're not supposed to be in there!"

"If they were really concerned, the government would have patched this up long ago, don't you think?" Courtney said before the two girls hurried after Dooley.

"Restricted means no trespassing!" Mike called after her. "*I'm* not going in."

"Then stay there, chicken," Kayla called back.

Flustered, Mike looked at Leah and Joel. "You two are staying with me, right?"

If he'd been alone, Joel might have let Mike persuade him, but when Leah gave him a sly smile and said, "Let's check it out," he followed her through the rip.

TWO

JOEL AND LEAH jogged over to the spot where Dooley and the others had disappeared between the trees. Before they entered the woods, Joel glanced back toward the fence and could just make out Mike's silhouette on the other side.

A panic hit him. What if Mike was right? What if they did get caught? What if they were *arrested*? Would they get kicked out of camp? Wait, would he have to complete middle school in jail? Maybe even high school? What would his parents say?

Something rubbed across his palm. He glanced down and saw Leah had grabbed his hand.

"Come on," she said. "We don't want to lose them."

He nodded and smiled, his fears forgotten.

The path—or what passed for one—led them through the trees and bushes to the widest meadow they'd yet encountered. Right at the edge was another fence. It was in considerably worse condition than the one with the sign on it, and didn't need the aid of a flash flood to punch a hole through it. Most of the chain-link fencing had slumped to the ground, where it lay in a rusting heap.

Dooley, Courtney, and Kayla stood on the other side.

"Where's Antonio?" Kayla asked.

Dooley pointed his flashlight to the right, at a hill on the edge of the meadow. "There."

The hill was fifty feet to the summit at most, but it boasted the unusual feature of a wide rocky overhang with a one-story building tucked beneath it. Though the structure had a closed door, the easy way in was through the large hole in the wall near the right front corner, inside which stood a smiling

Antonio.

"What is that?" Courtney asked. "A house?"

"An office, I think," Dooley said, "but I'm not sure. I just took a quick look inside before I came back for you guys. Let's check it out."

As they approached the building, Antonio said, "The maid didn't come today so it's a little messy."

One by one, he helped everyone through the hole. Once inside, the first thing Joel noticed was the odor of dust and rotting wood. He moved his flashlight beam across the floor and saw that while some linoleum tiles remained, mostly it was exposed concrete splintered by dozens of weed-filled cracks.

He moved his light to the walls. Whatever color they'd once been had turned into a water-stained tan. Here and there nails stuck out where something had once hung. Along the opposite wall was a partially opened door.

Three desks sat in the room, big metal things with rounded corners. They looked like they were from one of those old detective movies Joel's dad would sometimes watch on TV. Behind each were the crumpled remains of a wooden chair.

"Look at this," Leah said.

She picked a landline telephone off the floor. It was the super ancient kind, complete with rotary dial and buttons across the bottom. A thick, cracked cable ran out the back and into the wall.

Dooley walked over and grabbed it out of her hands. "This is awesome. I call dibs."

"No one has dibs on anything," Leah said. "We're already trespassing. We're not going to steal, too."

"It's not stealing. No one's using it."

As Dooley started yanking on the cable, Joel said, "Leah's right. Just leave it."

For a moment, it looked like Dooley was going to shove Joel, but then he shrugged and dropped the phone on the floor. "A piece of junk anyway."

After he walked off, Leah whispered, "I'll bet he comes back tomorrow night to get it."

Joel nodded.

The search continued into the next room. It was the same size as the first, but instead of desks, there were a couple of round, water-warped tables circled by four chairs each. The chairs were metal and once had padded seats and backrests covered in a green plastic material. Most of the material had rotted away, leaving only bits and pieces as reminders.

"What's in the next room?" Kayla asked Antonio, indicating the closed door.

"Didn't make it that far back yet," Antonio said.

He started for the door but Dooley pushed him aside. "This one's mine."

Dooley turned the knob, clearly expecting the door to open. Instead, it moved only an inch before jamming to a halt. Unable to stop himself in time, Dooley smashed into the metal surface with a loud grunt.

"Dammit!" he said, grabbing his nose. "Am I bleeding? I am, aren't I?"

Courtney shined her light on his face. "Move your hands."

"Get that out of my eyes."

"How am I supposed to see without it?" She grabbed one of his hands and pulled it way.

Vibrant red blood ran from his nostrils, glistening in the beam.

"Tilt your head back," she said. "Does anyone have a tissue or a rag or something?"

When no one responded, Courtney said to Dooley, "Pull your T-shirt up and hold it over your nose."

"I'm not going to mess up my shirt."

"It's already messed up."

He looked down and groaned when he saw the bloodstains around the collar. "Ah, man." Reluctantly he pulled up his T-shirt.

"You should probably lie down," Kayla suggested.

"I don't need to lie down. I'll be fine."

Leah pulled a chair from one of the tables and scooted it over to him. "At least sit down."

Dooley made no objections this time and did as she suggested, tilting his head over the backrest.

With Dooley out of commission, Antonio tried his hand at the door.

"Hey, I said it was my turn," Dooley shouted when he realized what was going on.

Antonio snorted. "You screwed up your chance."

He pressed his shoulder against the door and pushed. A loud scraping sound came from the other side, but the door moved only a few more inches before stopping again.

"Madsen, give me a hand."

As Joel joined him, he felt cold air drifting through the small gap.

"On three," Antonio said. "One, two, *three.*"

Again the door put up resistance, but the two boys were able to keep it moving until there was a gap wide enough to pass through.

More cold air wafted over the threshold.

"What's in there?" Kayla asked. "A freezer?"

Antonio played his light through the opening. "Nah, just another room." He slipped inside and disappeared.

Likely fearing his own toughness would be questioned if he stayed where he was, Dooley shot out of the chair, T-shirt still over his nose, and hurried after his friend. Courtney and Kayla were a bit more reluctant this time, but still followed after their boyfriends.

"Should we join them?" Leah asked, not nearly as confident as she'd sounded earlier.

"I don't hear any screams."

Leah chuckled. "So you're saying we might as well?"

"We'll never hear the end of it if we don't."

"Joel, you coming?" Antonio called.

Joel looked at Leah. After a moment, she whispered, "Okay."

"Yeah," he replied to Antonio, and then stepped into the cold room.

THREE

Mike

NEAR THE TOP of the debris pile, Mike found a spot stable enough to sit on. From there, he could see over the fence and into the woods where the others had gone.

He kept hoping to catch a glimpse of one of their flashlight beams, but thirty minutes came and went without even a hint they were coming back. Every minute that passed added to his growing belief that something had happened to them, and whatever that something was would soon race out of the woods and deliver to him the same fate.

Dammit, what's taking them so long?

Though he'd initially decided he would head back to camp after twenty minutes, that was never going to happen. Even if a bear or a wolf or Bigfoot didn't make him its dinner, he knew he'd end up lost. As his mom was fond of saying, he wouldn't be able to find his way out of the Chapel Hills Mall—a place he'd been a thousand times—if his life depended on it.

The woods made him uneasy enough during the day. They downright terrified him at night, even more so because he was alone. The whistle of the wind in the trees and the hoots of owls were unsettling, but he could deal with them. It was the occasional crack of a twig or the thud of something falling to the ground that freaked him out.

He'd been regretting not going with the others since the moment they disappeared. Sure, that would have meant the possibility of breaking the law, but better life in prison than dying from fright as a law-abiding citizen.

He checked his watch again. Forty minutes.

Where are you guys?

A piece of wood snapped nearby. He froze, waiting for the sound to repeat. When it didn't, he took a breath and returned his gaze to the forest beyond the fence.

Where are *you?*

FOUR

Joel

UNLIKE THE OTHER two rooms they'd explored, this third space contained only the heavy bookcase that had been moved against the door.

"Well, this is boring," Courtney said, shivering.

Antonio played his light over the far wall. No exit. "I guess we reached the end."

Joel looked back the way they'd come, then at the doorless wall. "That's weird. I'm pretty sure the building's longer than this."

Leah nodded in agreement. "Maybe there's an outside entrance on the other end."

Dooley kicked at a piece of loose flooring. "There's nothing here worth checking. Might as well go see if you're right." He headed back toward the exit.

Joel turned to follow, but stopped. "Hold on."

"What is it?" Leah asked. The others paused and looked back.

"If the only way in and out of this room is through that door, then how did the bookcase get pushed against it?"

Leah's brow furrowed. "Excellent question."

"Whoever left last probably pulled it into place as they went out," Antonio said with a shrug.

"And how would they have done that?" Leah asked him. "It was on the other side of a door that was *closed*."

"I don't know," he said. "It had to get there somehow, right? There's nothing here. Let's go outside and see if the other half is more interesting."

But when he started walking again, the only one who followed him was Kayla.

"Genius boy's got a point," Dooley said. "Maybe there's a hidden door or something. That would be pretty interesting, wouldn't it?"

"Yeah. I guess."

They spread out through the room, Joel and Leah playing their lights along the baseboard of the meadow-facing wall. Joel was thinking they might find an emergency exit, maybe a panel or something that popped out of the wall for quick access to the outside, but they didn't even find a crack. At Leah's suggestion, they checked the ceiling for a hatch, but again nothing looked out of the ordinary.

They were about to examine the floor when Kayla said, "This is weird."

All lights turned toward her voice.

"The air's moving." She was several feet from the wall that abutted the hill, her hands, palm flat, hovering knee high above the floor. Antonio placed his hand beside hers.

"You're right."

Dooley, his upper lip smeared with the remnants of his bloody nose, joined them. "Ha!" he blurted out and began running his hands over the floor.

"What are you doing?" Kayla asked.

"What do you think I'm doing? I'm looking for a trapdoor. That air has to come from somewhere, right?"

Leah glanced at Joel and nodded toward the others. A moment later they were also kneeling next to Kayla, their hands out. The airflow was there, all right. As Joel lowered his hand into the stream, though, he realized Dooley wasn't going to find any door. The air wasn't moving up through unseen cracks in the floor, but passing horizontally through the room toward the back wall.

That wasn't even the oddest part. The stream had...dimension. Joel estimated it to be about six inches wide by four high, like it was a column of air running through a rectangular duct. Only there was no duct.

Joel turned to Leah.

From the confused looked on her face, he knew she'd made the same discovery. By unspoken agreement, they followed the stream away from the wall, hoping to discover the source.

When Joel reached the center of the room, he jumped back.

Dooley glanced over. "What is it?"

"Um, nothing. I, uh, I almost stepped on a nail," he lied.

Leah discovered what he had found a moment later. Though she didn't jump, she did jerk her hand back like she'd touched a live wire.

Once more, they shared a look, and then together reached forward again. At the exact center of the room, the air stream took a ninety-degree upward turn, like it had hit an invisible wall.

The ceiling was too high for them to follow the flow all the way up, so Joel pointed toward the back wall. He and Leah circled around their camp mates and followed the stream in the other direction.

About a foot before they reached the wall, the stream angled downward and gradually condensed until it was no more than half an inch thick, just wide enough to pass through a thin opening at the bottom of the baseboard.

"How does it do that?" Leah whispered.

If she expected him to know the answer, she was going to be disappointed.

He pushed on the baseboard but it stayed rock still.

"Try sliding it up," she suggested.

He pressed his fingers against it and attempted to lift it away from the floor. There was a moment of resistance, and then it began to move upward until the gap was about two inches wide.

"What are you guys doing?" Courtney asked.

Joel moved to the side so the others could see the opening. "The air's going in here."

"What are you talking about?" Dooley said, strutting over as if to prove them wrong. "That's impossible." When he felt the flow, however, his smug smile disappeared. He followed the stream back to the point in the center of the room where it angled up. "It's got to be some kind of trick."

"It's some kind of something all right," Leah said.

While Courtney, Kayla, and Antonio felt the strange flow, Dooley returned to the wall and shined his light through the gap along the baseboard. "It's gotta be another room." He stood back and examined the wall. "Which means this must be the door."

He ran his fingers over the surface, pushing inward every few inches to see if he could find the way through.

"Why don't we just try this?" Leah said.

She cupped her hands around the baseboard opening and pulled. There was a *pop* not unlike that of a house settling, and then another, and finally a groan as a five-foot-wide section of the wall swung out.

Though the door looked heavy, it appeared to move fairly easily, as if it had some kind of counterweight or specialized hinge system.

When it was all the way open, Dooley played his flashlight across the backside of the door. "Whoa."

The others moved in for a closer look. Not only was the door made of metal, it was at least four inches thick. Like a door in a bank vault, Joel thought.

Antonio looked into the new space. "There's another door."

Joel pointed his flashlight into the space. "That kind of looks like an elevator door, doesn't it?"

Dooley pushed past the others and moved through the doorway, obviously trying to make up for being aced out of entering the cold room first. About twenty feet in, right before the elevator door, the hall took an elbow turn to the left.

Dooley disappeared around the corner and then yelled back, "There's some stairs here, too."

Up until the moment Joel had discovered the strange behavior of the airstream, investigating the building had been kind of fun. Not any longer. "Maybe we should head back. We've been gone a long time, and Mike's probably already returned to camp. If a counselor catches him, he'll give us up in a second."

Dooley stuck his head around the corner. "Are you kidding? This is getting good."

"We can always come back tomorrow night," Joel suggested, though there was no way he'd be joining any repeat expedition. Something was *wrong* about this place.

Dooley snorted and disappeared again.

"I'll go in if you go," Courtney said to Kayla.

"Come on," Antonio said, grabbing Kayla's hand and pulling her inside. She smiled back at Courtney, who followed.

"Maybe we can just take a quick look," Leah suggested to Joel. "And then if you want to go back, I'll go with you."

Bad idea, bad idea, bad idea. Though the warning blasted in his mind, Joel's hormones overrode it. He nodded and stepped over the threshold.

Immediately they both began shivering. It was as if the doorframe was a barrier separating the cold room from the frigid hall. The air—all of it, not just a confined stream—moved down the short corridor like an icy breeze.

With courage he didn't realize he had, he put his arm around Leah to warm her up. Much to his surprise and pleasure, she leaned into him.

The others had all disappeared around the corner. When Joel and Leah arrived at the turn, they saw that the stairs started only a few feet away and descended into darkness. They could hear their friends working their way down the steps but couldn't see them.

"I really don't want to go down," Leah whispered.

"Good, because I don't, either."

Joel gave the hallway a good look. Unlike the rooms they had come through, this space appeared as if it could have been built yesterday. The off-white walls were unmarked. No stains, no cracks, not even any dust. The clear coated concrete floor glistened in the flashlight beam like it had been poured only days before.

The elevator door was the only item that seemed old, though not because of any deterioration. Age-wise, it was as new looking as everything else, but its design seemed to come from a different era, very similar to that of the desks in the first room.

Not expecting anything to happen, he pushed the call button. It lit up and a second later the door slid open.

"Son of a…" he muttered.

The car was larger than he expected, room for at least twenty people. It had metal walls and a ceiling of white opaque material that hid interior lights.

"We could take it down," he said. "Meet them at the bottom."

"Do you…want to do that?"

He stepped back from the opening. "Not really. Why don't we wa—"

A scream echoed up the stairwell from far below.

FIVE

Mike

MIKE STARED AT his watch as the second hand moved past the six and started toward the top again. When it finally hit twelve, he lowered his wrist.

That was it. His friends had been gone exactly an hour, three times longer than he'd expected. He'd made a deal with himself that if they weren't back when the sixty minutes were up, he would do something. Since he'd been sure they'd have returned by now, he'd put no thought into what that something would be.

He knew the smart move was to stay where he was, but the stress of waiting was driving him crazy.

God, you guys are really pissing me off!

Perhaps if he went just a little way beyond the fence, maybe to the point where he'd last seen their lights, he'd be okay. If that was as far as he went, there would be no way for him to miss them in the dark. And if he didn't see any sign of them there, he could come back and wait.

Yeah, that's a good plan. I can do that. No problem.

It took a few more words of encouragement to himself before he finally scaled down the debris. When he reached the break in the fence, he paused. Once he'd crossed it, he would be a lawbreaker like the others.

Make it quick and you'll be back before anyone knows.

He hesitated a moment longer and then stepped through the gap.

Six

Joel

JOEL'S FIRST INSTINCT was to get out of the building and not stop running until they reached the camp, where they could get adult help. But if the screamer was hurt, the delay might mean the difference between life and death.

"I'll-I'll go check," he said. "You can stay here."

Leah slid her hand into his. "No way. We'll go together."

He glanced at the elevator and then back at Leah. Her face mirrored his fear of the confined space. "The stairs will be safer."

She nodded, relieved, and they headed down, flashlights illuminating the way.

The stairwell curved gently to the right. It wasn't until they'd completed a couple of rotations that Joel realized they were going around the elevator shaft.

"Do you feel that?" Leah asked. "The air?"

He nodded. The cold wind seemed to be picking up speed the farther down they went, as if urging them to move faster. A few more times around and they had to lean back against it to keep from toppling down the steps.

A terrified whimper came from below.

"Hold on, we're coming!" Leah shouted.

One more turn around the wall and they finally reached the bottom. Their lights could cut only a short path into the darkness, but it appeared they were at the end of a hallway. The air was really racing now, moaning as it crammed itself into the corridor.

For a moment, Joel wondered if the scream hadn't been a

scream at all but the sound of the wind. Then he heard the whimper again.

"Dooley?" he called.

A startled cry, and then, "Oh, God. Oh, God. Help me!"

The voice was most definitely not Dooley's.

"Courtney?" Leah said.

"Please, help me!" Courtney screamed.

The wind nearly shoved Joel and Leah to the ground as they took a step forward. Joel leaned against the wall in an attempt to stay upright, and his hip knocked against something jutting from the surface. He redirected his light and saw several metal pipes running horizontally down the corridor. He pointed them out to Leah and they both grabbed on.

Stepping carefully, they moved down the hall, Joel in front.

They'd gone no more than a dozen feet when Leah gasped.

Joel spun around, thinking she'd fallen, but she was still behind him. Her gaze was fixed on something in front of her, her face pale.

He turned back the other way and added his flashlight beam to hers. He expected to see Courtney crumpled on the ground, but the walkway was clear. He was about to ask Leah what she'd seen when movement caught his eye.

"Please, help me!" Courtney cried.

She was there all right, but not on the ground. She was clinging to an unlit light fixture attached to the center of the ceiling, her body flapping behind her like a ripped sail in a storm.

Joel staggered backward in surprise and bumped into Leah, dislodging her grip on the pipes. Instantly the wind whipped her around him toward the open hallway.

"Joel!" she yelled.

Without thinking, he dropped his flashlight and threw out a hand, trying to grab her as she slipped past. He thought he'd missed her but then felt her fingers clamp onto his wrist. He did the same with hers and hauled her toward him, not letting go until she was pressed once more against the wall.

His light, however, was gone. He could see the beam

twirling around and around as the flashlight was sucked farther down the passageway.

"Turn your light on," he said.

"I can't. I dropped it."

Joel thought he could actually feel the pitch black of the corridor pressing in on them.

"Please!" Courtney's voice was weakening.

"Can you climb down?" Joel called. Even as he said it, he knew it was a crazy question. There were plenty of pipes on both walls, but except for the fixture that anchored Courtney, the ceiling was smooth.

"Help me!"

"The wind has to stop soon!" Leah said. "When it does, we can get you down. Just hang on!"

"I can't...hold..."

A bang, and then the sound of flapping fabric growing fainter and fainter.

"Courtney?" Leah asked.

The wind moaned.

"Courtney?"

Nothing.

"Courtney!"

SEVEN

Mike

MIKE KNEW HE was going to die in the forest.

He was lost.

Big surprise.

He'd predicted that would happen, hadn't he? It didn't matter that his plan had been sound, it was bound to fail in the execution.

Things had started off fine. He'd headed along the same path he'd seen his friends take. He'd then carefully made his way to what he estimated was the farthest point he'd seen their lights. Of course he found no one. He hung around for a few minutes, hoping to hear them coming his way, but the woods had remained quiet so he'd headed back toward the fence.

That's when everything fell apart.

When he didn't reach the fence by the time he thought he should have, he retraced his steps to the place where he'd stopped to listen. When he couldn't find that, either, he officially freaked out and began hunting around for anything familiar.

A tiny voice in the back of his mind kept reminding him of what he and his friends had been taught at camp: "If you ever get lost, stay where you are and we'll find you." It might have been the right thing to do, but he was too scared to stop moving.

His panicked search eventually led him past a deteriorating fence and into a meadow he had not seen before. Above him the stars blazed across the sky. If only he could use them to get home.

Wait. He'd overheard Joel and Leah saying something

about constellations, how you could connect some of the stars to find the…north star? He searched the heavens, but quickly realized he had no idea what he was looking for.

As his gaze dropped back down, he spotted a small hill at the edge of the clearing. There was something odd about it, something at its base in what appeared to be a giant cave opening. In the starlight it was hard to discern, but the shape was too regular to be anything but manmade.

A building. *Yes*! Maybe someone there could help him. With renewed hope, he raced across the meadow.

As he drew closer he realized it was more overhang than cave entrance, but he didn't care. It *was* a building.

"Thank God!" he puffed between breaths. *Someone's got to be there. Someone's got to—*

One moment he was running, and the next he was flying over the meadow in one direction, his flashlight in another. He hit the ground with an *oomph* and lay there stunned for a moment.

When he finally did sit up, he started to cry. He knew he shouldn't. He was thirteen, and thirteen-year old boys didn't cry, especially when other boys were around. Around somewhere, anyway. But he couldn't help himself. The fall had been the last straw.

He should have stayed in his bunk and let them go without him. Now he was going to die because he'd liked the idea of having a Twix bar whenever he wanted one. Now he never wanted to see another Twix bar in his life.

He should have said no. He should have been asleep in his bed right now. He should have—

The building. He'd momentarily forgotten about it.

There was still hope.

Wiping the tears from his eyes, he jumped to his feet and looked around for his flashlight. The beam had switched off when the device hit the ground, so he had to fumble around for it. He was almost ready to give up when his foot bumped into the casing.

When he pushed the button and it lit up, he sighed in relief. Maybe his luck was changing.

Taking better care of where he stepped, he continued toward the building. It wasn't too long before he realized he probably wouldn't find anyone there. Whatever the place had once housed, it looked abandoned now.

Trying to keep from spiraling back into despair, he told himself there could be a phone inside. And even if there wasn't, the building would provide shelter until the sun came up. He could then climb the hill for a look around and hopefully figure out where he was.

The structure was creepy, though. He hoped nobody had ever died inside. He always said he didn't believe in ghosts, but really, how could anyone be sure whether they existed or not?

He slowly approached the break in the wall, ready to run at the first sign of supernatural activity, but all remained still. In a way, that was almost worse. He could easily picture a monster standing just inside, waiting to spring its trap.

"There are no such things as monsters," he whispered. "There are no such things."

He half believed that.

Well, maybe a quarter.

He shined his light through the opening and was relieved when no eyes glowed back at him. From the stains on the walls and a few old desks, he confirmed the building was deserted.

He played his light across the floor and noticed footprints in the dust. Several sets.

He was no professional tracker, but the prints looked fresh.

Were his friends inside?

He tried to remember the shoes they were wearing.

Antonio had on boots. And Joel had some kind of sneakers on. Mike couldn't remember what anyone else wore.

He aimed his light at the prints closest to the door, but they were all grouped on top of each other and he couldn't distinguish anything. As much as he didn't want to, he pulled himself inside and followed the prints into the room.

The first isolated set left chunky marks that he thought could have been created by boots. And there, off to the left, a diamond-pattern print that he was pretty sure came from a pair of Converses.

Yeah, that's right. Joel is wearing Converses. The tension eased from his shoulders. *It has to be them.*

The prints led through a doorway into another room. Since they all headed in and none back out, he guessed his friends were either still inside somewhere or had found a different exit. He listened for sounds but didn't hear anything.

The place was already making his skin crawl, so going any farther seemed like a bad idea. What he could do was go back outside and look for that possible other exit. If there was none, he could wait in the meadow until his friends came out.

As he turned toward the hole in the wall, he finally allowed himself to fully believe everything would be all right.

That was when he heard the noise.

EIGHT

Joel

JOEL SHUFFLED HIS feet forward in small increments so that when he reached the stairs, his toe tapped the riser instead of slamming into it. He and Leah had agreed that going after Courtney without their lights was a bad idea. Their plan now was to return to camp and get help.

On the ascent, they stayed to the outside where the treads were wider. At first, the wind whipped against them, forcing them to keep their pace slow to avoid falling backward, but its strength diminished as they climbed, allowing them to gradually increase their speed.

There was no warning when they finally reached ground level. Joel lifted his foot to take another step but his shoe banged down on the floor.

"Watch it," he warned to prevent Leah from making the same mistake. "We made it."

Holding her with one hand and keeping his other on the wall, he guided her past the elevator door and into the cold room. The space was as dark as the stairs had been. He tried to remember the layout, but misjudged the position of the bookcase that had been holding the door closed, and collided with it.

"Are you okay?" Leah asked.

Wincing, Joel rolled his shoulder up and down. It stung but the pain wasn't that bad. "Yeah. I'm fine."

He felt his way around the bookcase into the next room. There they finally saw dim light coming from the opposite door. Since they'd been in pitch black for so long, it was more than enough for them to see where they had to go.

Joel squeezed Leah's hand.

They were safe.

NINE

Mike

THE LOUD BANG echoed through the open door behind Mike.

He turned toward it, but then—with visions of razor-toothed monsters and deranged ghosts spinning through his head—just as quickly twisted back toward the hole and ran.

He successfully hopped over the lip but landed awkwardly and tumbled to the ground.

He thought he heard a voice, but that might have been the panicked blood rushing past his ears.

When he pushed himself up, however, he heard another noise.

But it was *not* a voice.

TEN

Joel

As JOEL MOVED into the last room, he saw someone leap out through the rip in the wall. Though he couldn't see the person's face, he recognized the shape.

"Hey, Mike. It's me," he yelled.

He ran toward the hole in the wall and opened his mouth to shout again.

But before the words had even formed in his throat, an intense high-pitched hum he could both hear and *feel* slammed into him.

He slapped his hands over his ears, but the noise was so overpowering that his knees buckled and he fell to the floor. Twisting around, he looked for Leah and saw that she too had been knocked from her feet and had her palms against her ears.

He tried to yell that they needed to get outside, but he couldn't even hear himself over the hum.

He stretched as far as he could and tapped her elbow with his foot. When she looked at him, eyes squinting in pain, he nodded toward the hole and then struggled onto his knees and elbows to crawl out.

That was as far as he got before a pulse of energy shot through every cell in his body and turned his entire world white.

ELEVEN

The Reclaimer

THE DECISION OF who should serve her on the outside was an easy one. Data from previous events indicated those farthest from the beam's epicenter stood the least chance of being permanently damaged. True to form, brain scans of the three chosen revealed this to be the case. As for those who had been closer, she had other uses for them.

Requirements satisfied, she moved on to stage two.

The fact that she had three subjects pleased her. If one were lost in the preparation phase, it would not endanger the project. And if all three made it through, then her timetable could be moved up.

Though the creatures were primitive compared to the Originators, their minds did contain some complexity so the procedure would take a delicate touch.

One by one she worked through the three, adjusting their minds to suit her needs, creating pathways that never would have existed on their own, and adding the bits of code that would fine-tune the subjects and build the bridges of communication.

From previous tests, she knew there would be a high probability of side effects due to her tinkering, the transferences of traits possessed by her creators via the embedded code. But none of that mattered. It was the data that was important. Nothing else.

When she finished the last of the procedures, she noted in her logs that all three subjects continued to be viable. She then assigned each creature the tasks most suitable for it, and sent the trio back into the world.

Soon the information would flow.

TWELVE

Joel

JOEL GRADUALLY BECAME aware of the sun. From its angle, it was probably a couple of hours either side of noon. He noted the paved road to his right, and the dirt shoulder below him. He wasn't lying on it, or sitting, or even standing still.

He was walking. One foot in front of the other, in front of the other, in front of the other.

Sounds followed him. Footsteps. One set…no, two.

He looked over his shoulder and saw Leah and Mike trailing him, their faces expressionless. Somewhere deep inside, he knew something wasn't right, but it was another minute before the fog encasing his mind pulled away enough for him to order his feet to stop.

"Joel?" Leah said uncertainly.

He turned and saw she had also "woken." Mike, however, appeared to still be in a trance.

Joel grabbed his friend's shoulders as Mike started to walk past him. "Whoa. Are you okay?"

While Mike's feet stopped moving, he made no indication he'd heard anything.

"What's going on?" Leah asked. "Where are we?"

"I…I don't know."

"How did we get here?"

"I don't know that, either."

What was the last thing he remembered?

The woods. They had gone on a…on a…secret night hike. He and Leah and Mike…and…and…

He looked around again. "Where are the others?"

Leah scrunched her nose. "What others?"

When he tried to answer, he couldn't remember their names. "The *others*. There were others with us, weren't there?"

"With us where?"

"We went on a hike. Dooley…"

That's right, Dooley. He was one of the others. Whatever Joel was going to say about him, though, was instantly forgotten when a deep, elongated whisper filled his mind.

Learn. Transmit. Mine.

He twisted around, looking for whoever had spoken, but no one was there except the three of them.

"Did you hear that?"

"Hear what?" Leah asked.

"That voice."

Her brow furrowed. "What voice?"

Again the answer to her question eluded him. He knew he'd just asked her about it, but he didn't know why.

A few seconds later, she asked, "Is this the road back to camp?"

"I don't know."

"What are we doing here?"

"I-I don't know."

Thirteen

Deputy Ness

ROUNDING THE CORNER in his sheriff's car, Deputy William Ness took another sip of his coffee, hoping the caffeine would kick in soon. As lead investigator of the team searching for the missing teenagers, he hadn't slept much.

So when he came out of a dip in the road and saw three kids walking along the shoulder ahead, he at first thought his mind was playing tricks on him. After several blinks, though, they were still there.

He stopped on the shoulder about twenty feet in front of them. On the seat next to him were pictures of the missing campers, but he didn't need to look at them. He'd memorized all seven faces and the teens in his rearview mirror were part of the group.

He climbed out of the car and smiled at the boy in front. "You're Joel Madsen, aren't you?"

The kid looked surprised.

"And Leah Bautista and Mike Hurst," Ness said. "Am I right?"

"Um, yes," Joel said.

"So glad I found you. Are you all okay?"

"We-we could use a ride," Leah said. "We're from Camp Red Hawk. Do you know where that is?"

Ness paused before saying anything more. The kids' responses were slow, and they didn't appear nearly as relieved at being found as he thought they would. Drugs? Or shell-shocked? He decided to play things cool. "Sure, I know exactly where that is. I'm heading in that direction right now. Happy to give you a lift."

"Really?" Joel said.

The other boy, Mike, hadn't reacted at all when Ness got out of his car, but a confused look was starting to cloud his face. "Joel? Leah?"

Joel glanced at Ness and then stepped over to Mike and whispered something to him.

"Is it just the three of you?" Ness asked.

"Uh-huh," Joel said.

"No others with you?"

"There were," Leah said, "but…"

"But we got separated," Joel finished for her.

Ness plastered a big smile on his face to hide his concern. "Hop in, and let's get you back to camp."

FOURTEEN

THE PARKING LOT at Camp Red Hawk was jam-packed when Ness arrived with the kids. Nearly all the vehicles belonged either to the sheriff's department or the park service. Ness had radioed ahead so a lot of people were waiting when he pulled up near the cafeteria. At the front of the group stood the worried parents of each of the kids.

As soon as his passengers climbed out, they were smothered in hugs and tears.

"Why are you here?" Joel asked his parents the moment he could get a word in.

"Why are we here?" his mother repeated. "Oh, honey, we've been so worried about you."

That was all the reunion Ness was privy to before he was waved over by Dan Rawlings, senior forest ranger for the area. With him were several other members of the search coordination team.

"Where'd you find them?" Rawlings asked when Ness joined them. His expression, like those of the others, was a mix of surprise and relief.

"I was driving down Route 17 on the way back here and there they were," Ness said.

"What about the other four?" Marina Hassan, another ranger, asked.

"One of the kids said they got separated."

The group's mood dimmed.

"Did they at least know where they saw them last?"

Ness grimaced. "They seem pretty dazed. Thought it best to get them here before asking too many questions. For now, we should have the teams focus on the area east of Ryder's Bend. That's the direction they were coming from." He looked at the two sheriff's deputies who were part of the group. "Separate the kids into three different rooms. Not next to each other, either. I'm not sure, but they may have been scared into saying nothing. It should be easier to get them to talk individually."

The two men nodded and the meeting broke up.

FIFTEEN

Joel

THE KIDS AND their parents were led over to cabins in the girls' area, where they were separated by family into three different buildings.

Joel was confused when he walked in. Though the cabin's layout was exactly the same as in his cabin, the mattresses were bare and there were no personal items anywhere. The thing was, he knew for a fact that all cabins—both boys' and girls'—were being used. The director had said as much at the opening night campfire. It then dawned on Joel he hadn't seen any other campers since he and Leah and Mike had returned.

"Where is everybody?" he asked.

His mother, her arm still around him, said, "What do you mean, sweetheart?"

"The other kids. The ones who were staying here. They were here last night."

His father looked surprised. "Last night? You were *here* last night?"

"Well, not in this cabin," Joel said.

Before the conversation could continue, someone cleared his throat. Joel looked over at the doorway and saw the deputy who'd driven him and his friends back to camp.

"Did I hear that right?" the man said as he entered the cabin. "Did you say you were here last night?"

"No. Not *here*," Joel said. "My cabin."

"Your cabin?"

"Boys' number four."

"And this was last night?"

"Yeah. Where else would I be?"

"Did you see any other campers?"

Joel's bewilderment increased. "Not after the campfire. Just the kids I share the cabin with."

The adults now looked even more perplexed than Joel felt. For a long moment, no one said anything.

It was Joel's dad who finally broke the silence. "Joel, what day do you think it is?"

"Thursday."

The adults looked at each other.

"So last night," the deputy said, "you were at the campfire, and then you went to your cabin and then…?"

This was the moment Joel had been dreading. He didn't want to admit they'd broken the rules, but what choice did he have? "We, uh, we waited until we knew the counselors were busy and then snuck out to take a hike."

"Last night," the deputy said.

"Uh-huh."

Another shared look among the adults.

"What?" Joel asked. "What's going on?"

"Sweetie," his mother said. "Today isn't Thursday. It's Tuesday."

"Tuesday? What are you talking about?"

His father said, "You've been gone six days."

Joel stared at him. "That's not funny."

"He's not joking," his mom said. "We've been here since Thursday afternoon. All the other kids were picked up by Friday. There's been an army of people looking for you."

Joel shook his head. "No way. We left last night."

The deputy sat down on one of the bunks. "Why don't you tell us what happened Wednesday night?"

"*Last* night," Joel said.

The deputy smiled but said nothing.

SIXTEEN

The Three Who Returned

LATER, IN THE dark of night, as they each drifted off to sleep, Leah and Joel heard the voice.

::LEARN.

::TRANSMIT.

::MINE.

Mike heard the voice, too, but his message was not quite the same.

By morning, they had forgotten all about it.

SEVENTEEN

Excerpt from the official report on the Camp Red Hawk disappearances
Primary Investigator: Deputy William Ness

Joel Madsen, Leah Bautista, and Mike Hurst were asked to repeat their stories several times to different members of the investigation team. The accounts remained factually unchanged and were consistent with one another, while having enough deviations for investigators to form the opinion that they did not plan their responses in advance.

All three children are convinced they were gone only one night. They all remember leaving camp and heading into the woods. But none could recall which direction they had gone. Their next memory after that was of walking down the road where I found them.

When asked if there had been a specific destination they were hiking to, none could remember, or if whether or not the destination had been reached. They also have absolutely no idea what happened to the other four teens who'd been with them. Each seemed to have a hard time remembering the names of the still missing campers, and in many instances needed to be prompted.

The three were taken to Children's Hospital in

Denver for observation, where doctors were unable to find any physical reasons for the collective memory loss. Wide-ranging tox screens were taken but all returned negative.

Each child underwent several sessions with a child psychiatrist who specializes in trauma. Unfortunately, the doctor was unsuccessful in jarring loose anything that might have led us to their four camp mates.

At this point Courtney Reed, Kayla Witten, George Dooley, and Antonio Canavo are still listed as missing.

Bruiser

& THE

Fastest Girl

IN THE

World

EIGHTEEN

Joel

EIGHTH GRADE STARTED no differently for Joel than it did for most kids—full of awkward hormonal spikes and a growing desire for independence, sprinkled with fleeting moments of hope that the security of childhood would last forever.

The occasional petty outburst brought on by nothing at all was also common for his age, as was the strange feeling that clenched his chest at the sight of girls he'd grown up with and never thought twice about before.

It was no surprise, then, that as winter approached, his parents and his teachers failed to notice there was more going on with him than the standard teenage tribulations. They'd seen it all before, so who could blame them for thinking they were seeing the same again?

That he was doing better academically than ever was written off by everyone as the natural progression of a bright kid coming into his own. That he'd sprouted up three inches between August and the end of the year, shooting past his father's height, seemed natural, too. He was at an age when that kind of thing happened.

But getting into two fights during the fall term and another in the spring, something he'd never done before—that was troubling. It was found, however, that in each incident, he'd been sticking up for someone being bullied, so no one thought of him as a problem kid. He was simply at a point in life when his emotions got the better of him.

Still, there were consequences for resorting to violence.

In a private meeting with Joel and his father after the third fight, Principal Manning said, "As much as I wish I didn't have to do this, school policy dictates a two-day suspension." He looked at Joel. "This is off the record, just me speaking as a person, not as your principal. I don't blame you for what you did. I would hope I'd have done the same in your shoes. But this *is* your third fight, Joel, and if it happens again I won't be able to help you. You'll receive a week's suspension, with the very real possibility of expulsion. I know that neither you nor your parents want that."

"Don't worry," Joel's dad said. "It's not going to happen again, is it, Joel?"

Joel mumbled, "No."

"I can't hear you."

"No," Joel said, louder. "It won't happen again."

He hoped he wasn't lying, because he knew if he saw another jerk beating up someone simply because he could, he wouldn't be able to look the other way. It was how his brain worked now. Anytime he saw someone being taken advantage of, he'd forget whatever he'd been doing or thinking about, and all he could focus on was the situation before him.

As if reading his mind, Principal Manning said, "If you do come across any more…incidents, I urge you to find a teacher or one of the quad staff and let them handle it."

That sounded good in theory, but Joel knew if he did as the principal suggested, the perpetrator would likely be long gone by the time an adult arrived. But he said, "Yes, sir," to help bring the conversation to an end.

Thankfully, there were no more fights before the school year finished. This had nothing to do with Joel avoiding confrontations, however. His growing reputation as a more than capable defender of the defenseless kept him from making a return trip to the principal's office.

On the first day of summer vacation, when his eyes opened that morning, his first thought was of Camp Red Hawk.

This was unexpected. The camp hadn't crossed his mind since the previous fall. Now that it had, any joy he should have been feeling about the days of freedom before him failed to materialize.

He knew Red Hawk had been permanently closed, and that its director and owners had been charged with negligence and other crimes in connection with what had happened the previous July. What happened after that, though, he had no idea. Once he'd given videotaped testimony about what he remembered, which wasn't much, he'd put the summer behind him, hoping never to think about it again.

And yet here it was, once more fresh in his mind.

Of course he knew the reason why. For the three previous years, his parents had sent him to summer camp, a different one each time. Though they hadn't said anything yet about this summer, he assumed he'd be told soon enough where he was going.

The thing was, Joel didn't want to go to camp again. He had no desire to be anywhere remotely similar again.

He waited a week, expecting his folks to pull out one of those glossy brochures and show him the "fun" they'd arranged for him to have, but each night passed without the topic coming up.

He was getting so anxious about it that at dinner on the eighth night after school had ended, he broke down and asked, "So what camp am I going to this year?"

Joel's mother, who had been in the midst of dishing out salad, stopped, tongs in the air. "Camp? Don't you remember? You're not going this summer. We're visiting Nana and Papa in St. Louis."

"We are?"

"I told you that months ago, sweetie."

He didn't remember, but that was okay. He wasn't going to camp.

Just like that, the dread that had wrapped itself around him like a straightjacket vanished.

WHILE JOEL OCCASIONALLY accepted invitations from friends to go over to their house and play video games or swim or just hang out, more often than not he found himself drawn to the library.

That was something new. For most of his life, his reading

habits had been limited to comic books and the occasional sci-fi novel, but now he devoured books on dozens of different topics—biographies, science texts, histories, how-to manuals, even books on sociology and psychology, two topics he'd known almost nothing about before that summer. It felt like he couldn't stop devouring knowledge even if he wanted to.

And he *didn't* want to.

"Joel?"

It was a Wednesday morning in late June, and he was deep in a book about the American legal system, entranced by a section on tort law.

"Joel?" This time there was a touch on his shoulder.

He finished the paragraph he was on before looking up. The instant he saw the girl's face, his mind spit out:

> Jasmine Hammond, aka Jaz
> 7th Grade Just Completed
> Lives Three Blocks from School
> Excels at Math

Instant information such as this had gradually been appearing more and more in his head. Assuming everyone had the same ability, he'd come to expect it rather than be surprised by it.

"Hi, Jaz."

His knowing her name seemed to both please and fluster her. She glanced at the book he was reading. "Is that a textbook? Are you in summer school?"

He shook his head but said nothing.

She glanced at the floor and then back at him. "I just…I…um…I never thanked you."

She was talking about fight number two. A couple of idiots had cornered her by the lockers outside the science lab. Unfortunately for them, Joel happened to be walking to his locker nearby.

"No reason you need to," he said.

"Of course there is."

"It wasn't a big deal. Don't worry about it."

Joel wasn't ashamed about what he'd done to her tormentors, but he didn't see the point in discussing it.

"It was a big deal to me."

He didn't know what to say, so he gave her a quick smile and returned his attention to the book.

For several seconds, he could feel her there, still staring at him, before she finally whispered, "Thank you," and hurried away.

NINETEEN

THE DREAM CAME in the wee hours of the morning.

It featured two of Joel's friends from camp the previous summer. The guy and girl he'd been found with by the road. Mike and, um…Leah.

Right, Leah. How could I forget?

Though he hadn't seen either of them since they'd left the hospital after camp, their features were surprisingly fresh in his mind, as if they'd just spent the day together. Which was strange because when he was awake, he could barely remember them at all.

The other four in the dream were out of focus, so it took a few moments before it dawned on him that they must have been the ones who hadn't come back from the hike. The missing kids.

He attempted to remember their names, too, but the best he could come up with was Dudley and Carrie. Neither was right, he knew. As for the names of the other two, he had nothing at all.

At the beginning of the dream the seven of them were surrounded by trees. Then images began piling on top of one another, rapid fire. A room dank and dreary, with three desks. A staircase spiraling round and round and round, filled with the howl of a storm. A passageway, even darker than the other places, the noise of wind so loud nothing else could be heard.

And flying down the middle, the spinning beam of a flashlight.

Walls and floor and ceiling.

And walls and floor and ceiling.

And walls and floor and—

"Help me."

The sound but a whisper, and yet he could somehow hear it above the howling wind. The speaker was a girl, her face out of focus, pressed against the ceiling of the tunnel as if gravity had reversed.

"Help me."

Joel gasped as his eyes shot open, his heart thumping like it wanted to leap from his chest.

The first hint of morning light was seeping around his curtains. He looked at his clock—5:15 a.m.

What the hell was—

All thought flew from his mind as blinding pain shot up from the little toe of his left foot.

He threw his covers back and sat forward to inspect it. A black and green bruise covered his toe, and continued a good half inch onto his foot. When he touched it, the pain returned with a vengeance, causing him to fall back against the bed, gritting his teeth.

"Mom!"

His door flew open seconds later and his mother rushed in.

"Honey, what's wrong?"

"Are you all right?" his father said, a few steps behind her.

Grimacing, Joel said, "It's my toe! It…"

He paused. The pain was gone.

His mother scanned his feet. "Which toe?"

Joel pushed back up. Not only was the pain gone, but the bruise had vanished, too.

He touched it, tentatively at first, and then pushed at it, harder and harder.

Nothing. No hint that it had just looked and felt like it had been run over by a truck.

"Joel?" his dad said.

"I, um, I thought I'd hurt it."

His mom gently raised his foot and touched his little toe. "This one?"

He nodded.

She wiggled it back and forth. "Any pain?"

"No. Feels fine."

"Must have been just a dream."

"Or a cramp," his father suggested. "I used to get those all the time at your age. Hurt like a mother—"

"Hey!" Joel's mom said.

"They hurt a lot," Joel's father said.

Joel's mom gave Joel's foot a loving squeeze and set it back on the bed. "Well, I might as well get some coffee going."

After his parents were gone, Joel examined his toe again. It had *not* been a cramp. No cramp had ever left a bruise. And no bruise had ever disappeared so quickly.

So maybe I did dream it.

He shook his head and whispered, "I saw it."

He repeated the words and was pretty sure he was right.

When he said them for a third time, though, he began to wonder what had really happened.

Sleep took him again, dreamless this time, and when he woke, it was half past nine. He dressed in a blue T-shirt and baggy gray shorts, and headed downstairs to grab some breakfast.

This was the first summer he'd been allowed to stay home alone, so his parents had already gone off to work. To gain this independence, though, he'd had to agree to call his mother every few hours, and if he were to go anywhere, he had to check in with their next-door neighbor, Mrs. Valdez.

He grabbed an untoasted Pop-Tart, shoved it in his mouth, and dropped onto the couch to pull on his Converses. It wasn't until he was slipping his left foot inside his sneaker that he remembered the toe.

It doesn't matter how real it felt, it must have been part of that strange dream, he decided, because it certainly wasn't bothering him now.

Not long after ten a.m., he wheeled his bike out of the garage, made the prerequisite stop at Mrs. Valdez's place, and headed off. His friend Justin had called the night before and they'd arranged to meet at the arcade. Joel's plan was to give Justin maybe an hour of his time and then head to the library.

As he rode, the other parts of the dream came back to him. The room and the stairway and the tunnel all were somehow familiar, and yet he had no recollection of ever seeing any of them before. Could they have had something to do with the four kids who'd disappeared? Or was this more of his mind playing tricks on him?

When he'd returned to school the previous fall, there had been some talk about the Red Hawk Four, as the missing kids had been labeled by the local news. Joel had been very careful to not reveal he had been there, too, and, as one of the Three Who Returned, had been smack in the middle of the drama.

Justin's bike was chained to the stand outside the arcade when Joel arrived. Joel found his friend inside feeding dollar bills into the token machine, and soon they were standing side by side in front of the classic Ultimate Mortal Kombat 3 machine.

Joel had spent much of the previous summer, before he'd headed to Camp Red Hawk, next to Justin in that very spot, improving to the point where he and Justin had been pretty evenly matched. This was the first time he'd played since then. In fact, he was only there because Justin had kept after him until Joel ran out of excuses for not getting together.

His rustiness fell quickly away, though, as he recalled timings and control combinations, and then started employing them in ways he'd never tried in the past. Justin landed a few initial lucky strikes, but that was it. Eight losing games later, Joel's friend shoved the machine with a frustrated grunt and walked away.

"So I guess we're done?" Joel said.

"I want to try something else. That game sucks anyway."

Thirteen-year old Joel would have said, "You're the one who sucks," but fourteen-year old Joel didn't talk that way anymore. He shrugged and followed his friend.

The place was already half full, so a lot of the games were taken. There was even a line for the dance game where you had to jump on arrows in a specific pattern. Most of those waiting at the moment were girls. Joel had always thought the game was stupid, but that had been when he was several inches shorter and girls weren't important. Now…

"How about that?" he said, nodding toward the line.

Justin looked over and scowled. "Are you kidding me?"

"What's wrong with it?"

"It's *dancing*."

"So?"

"So nothing. We're not dancing. Come on."

It turned out all the games Justin wanted to try were also occupied.

"If we're not going to play something, then I've got things to do," Joel said.

"We just got here. Besides, what could you possibly have to do?"

Given Justin's reaction to *Dance Dance Revolution*, Joel had no intention of mentioning the library. "Things."

"What things?"

Joel frowned. "Errands…for my parents."

With a scoff, Justin said, "You can do those anytime."

He looked around, his gaze stopping on the railed-off area at the back where the "big kid" games were kept: pool tables, air hockey, and—

A cheek-splitting smile appeared on Justin's face. "The ping-pong table's open!"

Joel reluctantly followed him to the back.

The ping-pong table, like most of the other games in the place, had seen better days. The net sagged in the middle, and the white lines around the outside of the table were faded and chipped.

"Volley for serve," Justin said.

"You can just serve."

"Come on, man, we volley. Those are the rules."

Joel wasn't sure if that was true or not, but if it got this over with faster, then fine. "Okay. Volley, then."

Justin picked up the ball. "It's got to go back and forth three times before it counts."

He hit the ball nice and easy. Joel returned it, and then Justin smashed the ball at an angle that would be hard to reach for most players, but Joel got there with enough time to tap the ball so that it barely cleared the net. Justin dove forward, but he knocked his hip against the side of the table and missed the ball.

"Dammit!"

"You all right?" Joel asked.

Justin motioned at Joel with his paddle. "Yeah, yeah. Just serve."

"Okay. Zero-zero."

The first game ended 11-2 in Joel's favor. In the second, Justin managed to double his previous game total.

"Best three out of five," he said.

"I really gotta go."

"Three out of five. Come on. It's summer, for God's sake. No one needs to go anywhere."

Joel hesitated before nodding. "Three out of five. But then I'm out of here, okay?"

"Sure, sure. Whatever."

Joel decided to back off a little to give his friend a chance to save some face. Justin, for his part, put up a much better fight in game three than he had previously, and was able to take the lead at 10-8.

"For the win," he said, as he prepared to serve the next ball.

Joel had already decided to give him the game, but he didn't want Justin to suspect that, so he kept the volley going as he waited for the opportunity of a convincing miss.

Justin returned a shot that forced Joel to back away from the table several feet. Joel thought for sure his return would fall short, but it clipped the top of the net and passed over, bouncing off the table an inch from the edge. Justin was in position, though, and with a gleam in his eye, he tapped the ball so that it gently flew back onto Joel's side.

Joel charged forward, flailing for the ball, and bumped against the table.

With a loud snap, the table leg on Justin's side collapsed and the table fell, corner first. Justin had no time to get out of the way, and the look of triumph that had started spreading across his face turned into anguish.

He screamed so loudly, even those playing *Dance Dance Revolution* looked over.

Joel ran around to where his friend had dropped to the floor. The corner of the table sat squarely on Justin's left foot. Joel grabbed an edge and moved it off.

"I'm so sorry," he said.

Justin writhed on the floor, his hands over his shoe.

One of the two teenage arcade employees hurried over. "What the hell happened? What did you do to the table?"

"It broke and fell on him," Joel said.

"Well, you're going to have to pay for that."

Justin moaned.

Ignoring the a-hole—*who was it who used to say that word?*—Joel reached for Justin's foot.

"Don't!" Justin yelled.

"We need to take a look. See if you're okay."

"I'm *not* okay!"

Several other customers started gathering around.

"What happened?"

"Was it a fight?"

"Did he sit on the table or something?"

Justin eyed them, then whispered to Joel, "Okay. Take it off. But careful."

Justin squeezed his eyes shut as Joel worked the shoe and sock off.

"Oh, geez," someone behind Joel said.

"Eww," at least two of the onlookers threw in.

Another added, "That doesn't look good."

Joel stared at Justin's left foot, more specifically at his friend's little toe. He knew without a doubt it was broken, and that in the coming days the bruise that was already starting to form would encompass the whole toe and part of the foot. He also knew exactly what his friend's pain felt like, for he had experienced it himself that very morning.

It can't be. That was a dream. This is...this is...a coincidence.

"He should go to the hospital," someone said.

Joel held out his hand to his friend. "Let's get you up."

When Justin was standing on his good foot, Joel put an arm around his back to support him. "Does anybody have a car?"

Most of the other kids looked about his age, so Joel turned his attention to the arcade employee who looked old enough to have a driver's license.

"I'm working, man," the guy said. "I can't just leave."

Information suddenly flashed in Joel's mind.

Police station.
A block and a half away.

"Come on," he said to Justin, and started walking him toward the front door.

"Hey," the employee called. "I need your names. My boss is going to want to know who's going to take care of this."

Without looking back, Joel said, "Tell your boss he should be more worried about being sued for faulty maintenance than who's going to fix his stupid ping-pong table."

"Wait. Sued?"

The police were more than happy to transport Justin to the hospital, where it was confirmed he had broken a toe. The officers were also interested in how the accident had occurred, and sent someone down to the arcade to take pictures of the "unsafe" table and ask questions.

Joel didn't make it to the library that day. After Justin's mom arrived at the hospital, he returned to the arcade for his bike and headed home.

Once he was alone in his bedroom, he removed his left shoe. The bruise he'd seen that morning had not returned. He touched the spot and felt the bone under the skin.

Everything was fine.

A dream, that's all.

There was no way his experience had anything to do with Justin's accident.

No way.

Except for the fact the injuries were identical, down to the smallest detail.

Yeah, except for that.

He lay back on the bed and stared at the ceiling, hoping for answers. It wasn't long before his eyelids grew heavy and he started to fall asleep.

In the gray world before he slipped all the way under, a low voice whispered in his head.

Mine.

TWENTY

AFTER RETURING HOME from Camp Red Hawk, Leah's parents restricted her to the house for the rest of the summer, allowing her to go out only if one of them was with her. Since her mother was a teacher, she also had summers off and was always around.

Though Leah was allowed to spend as much time as she wanted with her friends, they had to come to her place. And if it was a friend Leah's mom and dad hadn't met, they would insist on talking to the person's parents first.

"It's like you're in prison," Tracy Eastman said one day as they sat in Leah's bedroom. "I mean, it's not like you killed anyone, right?"

Leah smiled and shrugged and changed the subject.

The story of the missing children from Camp Red Hawk was a big deal that summer—in the paper, on the Internet, and even on the local TV news. The only details missing from the story were the names of the Three Who Returned. Out of fear that whoever had taken her would find out where she lived and come for her again, Leah's parents had forbidden her from telling anyone she was one of the three.

On another day a different friend, Melinda Waters, brought up the Red Hawk disappearances and asked, "Wasn't that the camp you went to?"

Leah shook her head. "Camp Bicknell." It was the one her brother had attended.

"Really? I thought you said Red Hawk."

"My parents were thinking about it but decided on

Bicknell."

"Whoa, then you were lucky, huh?"

"Yeah, I guess."

"I wonder what happened to those kids?"

Another shrug and another change of subject.

The truth was, Leah wondered about that, too. She wondered about all of her time at Camp Red Hawk. Her memories of those days were becoming harder to recall and she didn't understand why. She could remember Joel and that other kid—the rule follower...what was his name? Mark? Something like that. The others, though? She couldn't even picture what they looked like, let alone remember their names.

She tried to talk to her parents about it once, but they shut her down immediately. They had even at first refused the sheriff's request for an additional interview with Leah before reluctantly giving in, with the caveat that the discussion would be terminated if Leah seemed at all disturbed.

Her parents' fears were unfounded, however. Leah wasn't disturbed at all, because she had nothing to add to what the officers already knew. She couldn't even remember some of the things they said she'd told them before, though she'd kept that to herself. She believed the deputies had left thinking the interview had been a waste of time.

The rest of her summer was spent with more visits from friends and a surprising amount of time reading books from her parents' collection. Their taste was pedestrian at best, however, and on more than one occasion, she had begged her mother to take her to the library, where she checked out books that were considerably more challenging.

To say she was excited on the first day of eighth grade would have been a colossal understatement, especially since it was touch and go for a while as to whether or not her parents would homeschool her. She'd nearly turned blue protesting the possibility, and had even locked herself in her room, refusing to come out for a full day.

Fortunately, when it became clear what the realities of homeschooling meant financially, her parents had accepted the fact that Leah needed to go back out into the world.

Being away from home without her parents was possibly the most liberating thing she'd ever experienced. She felt so good that even her schoolwork seemed fun and easy. At the end of the first semester—and for the first time in her life—she achieved straight As. She did it again in the spring. She was surprised, though, that her academic improvement came with an unexpected cost. Several girls who had been close friends began avoiding her, intimidated and confused by the change in what they'd come to expect from her.

Determined that the same thing wouldn't happen as she started her freshman year at Verde High School, she worked diligently to maintain a low A average, even letting one of her classes—History—dip to a C+. To say this was easy would have been a lie. She knew all the answers and understood all the concepts, most of the time even better than her teachers. Acting dumb was painful.

While struggling with her growing intelligence, she also began changing in physical ways. Though no one would call her a giant, she had already grown taller than her mother—a respectable five foot six—and was closing in on her dad, who stood at five foot ten.

With size came strength, but in Leah's case, her increase in strength wasn't commensurate with her increase in height. It was far greater. Thankfully, the first person to notice this was Leah herself. Though she couldn't hide her height, especially from the basketball coach who kept hounding her to try out, she was able to downplay her strength by never doing anything to put it on display.

Though her growing intelligence may have confused her, her new physical abilities scared the hell out of her. Leah had no doubt that she, a mere freshman, could outrun anyone at Verde High, girl or boy, and likely outperform most of the school's best athletes at their chosen sports, too.

How any of this was possible, she didn't know. Her family was not particularly athletic, and the only real physical activity she partook in was the mandated hour of PE each school day. At least her arms and legs weren't bulging with muscle. There would have been no way to hide that during gym class.

Another change, perhaps the strangest of all, made its first appearance the tenth week of high school.

Lunch period—the time of the natural sorting of the student body.

The cliques of the cool and the outcasts and those caught in between spread across the quad in territories each had laid claim to at some point. There were the athletes and the cheerleaders, the band, the choir, the brains, the theater geeks, the losers, the druggies, and so on. Those who didn't fit into any of these tried to stay out of the way of everyone else.

The Venn diagram of Leah included several groups: the brains, of course, though their pedantic conversations bored the life out of her; the band because she played oboe, much better this year than she ever had; the theater geeks because she knew several of them from her grade-school days; and the norms because that's where she wanted to fit in most, though if they knew the real her, they would not have thought she belonged.

It was toward this last group, which claimed the corner bench near entrance F, that she headed that day with her friends Amanda and Molly. Their path took them past the annex storage building and across a grassy strip behind the cafeteria. At one end of the grass was the drama tree, bare now in anticipation of winter. Apparently it had been serving as the meeting point for the theater geeks for years.

"Leah," Paul Markle called out as she walked by. "Come feast with us."

Leah could hear Molly groan as Amanda whispered, "Weirdos."

"Can't today," Leah said. "Already have plans."

"Tomorrow, then, perhaps. We'd be honored with your presence."

"Sure, maybe tomorrow," was what she was about to say, but she was stopped by a *whooshing* sound, faint but growing louder. Looking over her shoulder, she saw a cup flying through the air, white with a yellow arched M on the side. It had already passed its apex and was in a downward arc that would land it directly in the middle of the theater geeks.

Leah didn't need to see inside the cup to know it contained

a milkshake. These bombardments had been happening since the first week of school. Everyone knew who was behind it, a couple of a-holes who'd been kicked off the football team for behavioral issues. Though administration had brought them in to question them about the attacks, little could be done without an eyewitness stepping forward.

At the moment, however, the identity of the thrower wasn't important. The cup was coming down, and when it hit, it was going to splatter everyone.

She swiveled around, shoving her bottle of iced tea under her arm and squeezing it to her ribcage. Behind her she could hear the first sound of someone noticing the incoming cup and the start of a yelled out warning. It was way too late, though. Few, if any, would be able to get out of the way in time.

Leah made a quick adjustment to her position, and then, as the cup was about to sail past her, she plucked it from the air and spun around to decelerate the momentum and keep the contents from spilling out.

The voices behind her silenced, and when she looked up from the cup, everyone within sight was staring at her.

"Whoa," Jayson Chu said. "That was *awesome*!"

"Leah," Molly said. "What the hell?"

Leah had to fight the urge to send the shake back to where it came from. She could do it, too. Instead she walked over to the nearby trash can, tossed the cup inside, and said to her friends, "Come on. I'm hungry."

News of her act spread, and for a few days she became a minor celebrity, with people she'd never even talked to coming up and asking her questions. Thankfully the attention didn't last long.

After the incident, Leah began noticing other things that added to her suspicion that something beyond her improved strength and intellect was going on. Little things like snatching a pencil that rolled off a desk before it dropped an inch, rising from her chair a split second before any of her classmates reacted to the bell, stealing the ball in a PE game of soccer from the best player on the girls' team. Not once. Not twice. But over and over.

The only way she could explain it was that she felt as if she were *ahead* of everyone else. Not by much, but enough to be noticed—by her anyway.

This, too, she knew she had to keep secret. Perhaps more than anything else.

TWENTY-ONE

Joel

BEFORE JOEL REACHED the halfway point of ninth grade, it became apparent to all those concerned that James Madison High could not provide the level of education he required, and remaining at the school would be a colossal waste of his time.

What was left unsaid was that the school's administration and faculty were scared of him, both of his mind and his growing strength. When he'd left middle school, he'd been approaching six feet and one hundred and eighty pounds, but by the time he started his freshman year two months later, he was six-three and nearly two-twenty.

Though there had been no repeats of the fights that had occurred in eighth grade, everyone was sure it was only a matter of time. Just like at the end of middle school, the students who might have drawn Joel's attention were even more scared of him than the staff was.

So everyone was relieved when Joel took the GED one spring morning and was out the door by lunchtime with his high-school equivalency certificate in his hand. Two weeks later he took the SATs and scored a perfect 2400.

Joel didn't have to apply to college. Universities came looking for him, all offering full scholarships and living expenses. He chose Stanford based on careful research, and then settled in for a final summer at home.

TWENTY-TWO

Leah

IN JULY BETWEEN her freshman and sophomore years of high school, Leah returned to summer camp.

Not Camp Red Hawk, of course. It had never reopened. Her destination was Camp Cedar Woods.

When she had initially brought up the idea, her parents had refused to even consider it. But she wanted to go back, had to go back. She needed to put the summer camp demon behind her. So she applied for a job as a counselor and when she was accepted, she presented it to them with the argument that if they didn't let her go, they'd be giving in to fear and allowing what had happened at Camp Red Hawk to control their lives. She was throwing back at her father a principle he had taught her when she was younger. The tactic worked, and with their reluctant consent, she returned to the mountains.

Camp counselors were brought up to Cedar Woods five days ahead of the first group of campers. Leah felt no sense of nervousness, until the bus carrying her and the other teen staff members came around a curve not far from their destination. As she looked out the front window, she could have sworn for a moment that she saw a girl and two boys walking along the shoulder. But when she blinked, they were gone.

"Are you all right?" Renee, the girl sitting next to her, asked.

Leah forced herself to nod. "Yeah, I'm fine."

"Car sick?"

A pause. "Maybe a little."

"Need a barf bag?" Renee started digging through her

stuff.

"No. I'm okay. Really."

Renee studied her for a moment. "Well, if you do, let me know. I've got plenty."

"Thanks. I think I'll just rest for a moment."

Leah leaned back and closed her eyes. While that cut off any further conversation, she could once again see the image of the three kids walking.

She knew who the girl was—her, only smaller and younger, her weird transformations not yet begun.

And the boys, she knew them, too.

Her friends. The smart and kind one with the green eyes flecked with hazel that sparkled whenever she looked at them. She'd held hands with him, she suddenly remembered. She'd reached out and taken his palm into hers. She'd never done that before then.

To this day, it had been the only time she'd ever been that intimate with a boy.

And then there was the other one, the rule follower, nice but a bit scared of the world.

God, what were their names?

She frowned, but try as she might, she'd come up with nothing by the time the bus pulled into Camp Cedar Woods.

A middle-aged man and a guy who couldn't have been much more than twenty stood in the dirt parking area, greeting the counselors as each exited the vehicle.

With a shake of a hand, the older man repeated over and over, "Hi, Blanton Melk. Camp director. Nice to meet you. And you are?"

Each time a counselor said his or her name, the younger man consulted a clipboard and announced a cabin number.

Leah stepped from the bus, and the older man held out his hand. "Hi, Blanton Melk. Camp director. Nice to meet you. And you are?"

As they shook, she said, "Leah Bautista."

"Cabin eleven," the assistant announced, and pointed to his left.

She adjusted her backpack and headed off, the

hallucination of the kids on the road finally fading.

Her first few days at camp were spent participating in activities designed to help the counselors get to know one another better, and in meetings where they learned what was expected of them and the skills they would need to help the campers.

It was easy to pick out who the returning counselors were. They called one another by nicknames and seemed to have an endless supply of inside jokes.

On the third day, three additional counselors showed up— two brothers and a friend. By the way the veterans greeted them, it was clear this was also not their first time at the camp. Leah assumed their parents had dropped them off, but word soon circulated among the new counselors that Terry, the oldest brother, had driven them up himself.

The night before the first set of campers were to arrive, the counselors built a bonfire in the central fire pit and enjoyed a dinner of hamburgers and corn on the cob while the veterans told stories of their past at Cedar Woods.

Without exception, all the tales ended with laughter and smiles and a few calls of, "That's not how it happened!"

After the last of these stories were told, Director Melk stood up. "I'd love to hear from those of you who have spent time at other camps. Any volunteers?"

The newbies glanced at each other nervously, all hoping someone else would speak up.

"No one?" the director said. "How about we start with a show of hands of those of you who *have* attended summer camp before?"

After a few seconds, a hand went up, and then one by one the others followed.

"Six of you," the director said. He checked a sheet of paper that had been in his pocket. "I think someone's holding out on me. Unless you lied on your application." He looked directly at Leah, wearing a knowing grin.

"Oh," she said, and laughed softly as if she'd forgotten. She lifted her hand to join the others.

Satisfied, the director pointed at one of the new boys.

"Which camp were you at?"

"Um, Camp Lewiston."

The director frowned. "Lewiston? I haven't heard of that one."

"It's in Oregon."

"Oregon?"

"My grandparents live there."

The director teased a few more boring details out of him, and then moved on to the next person.

"Camp Bryer Creek," the kid said.

And then the next. "Camp Owens."

"Camp Morning Hill."

"Camp Dakota."

"Camp Riverside."

The descriptions of the camps grew more detailed as each kid gained confidence from the one before. The director added comments here and there about the places he was familiar with, always finding a way of adding that they may have been good but not as good as Camp Cedar Woods.

The director turned to Leah, the only one who hadn't spoken. "And you?"

She could feel everyone's attention shift to her. She wanted to make up a name like she had in the past, but her mind was blank.

"You don't remember?" some kid said. A few of the others snickered.

"Camp…Camp Red Hawk," she finally said, not knowing what else to say.

A hush fell over the pit area. Director Melk looked mortified, obviously having just remembered the particulars of her resume, and realizing why she hadn't initially raised her hand.

One of the veteran boys asked, "When were you there?"

She didn't mean to say it, but the truth…it just came out. "Two summers ago."

"Holy shit."

Another counselor said, "Were you there when—"

"Okay," the director said, "I think it's time to see which

one of you can make the best s'more."

While a few lingered in their seats, glancing at Leah, most were happy to move on to something else and headed over to where the dessert fixings waited.

The director walked over to Leah and whispered, "I'm so sorry. I totally forgot."

"It's fine," she said, giving him a reassuring smile. "Not a problem."

He looked relieved. "Come on. Let's melt some chocolate."

The next day, as the summer staff prepared the camp for the kids who would arrive in a few hours, Leah couldn't help but notice that the other counselors were treating her extra nice. Thankfully, the busier they got, the less they seemed to care about her connection to Camp Red Hawk. Whatever lingering discomfort some of them might have felt disappeared when the buses arrived and the reality of wrangling a bunch of preteens set in. From that point forward, they treated Leah like any other member of the team.

Each counselor was not only responsible for the six kids staying in his or her assigned cabin—which was different from the way things had run at Camp Red Hawk—but was also assigned to one of the daily activities the campers were shuttled through. Leah and three other counselors—Kelvin, Todd, and Maddie—ran the obstacle course. Their job was to familiarize the kids with the course and help them learn the skills they would need to complete it. This would culminate with a combination obstacle course/scavenger hunt pitting all the groups against one another at the end of the week.

Though fun, the job was physically exhausting, and by the end of each day, Leah and her fellow obstacle-course counselors were usually asleep moments after they closed their eyes.

Todd was the younger brother of Terry, the guy who'd driven his own vehicle up to camp. He was a teaser, quick with a joke, and always calling the campers by funny nicknames. Leah wasn't sure about him at first, but he never crossed the line into being mean, and it wasn't long before she was laughing with the others.

It helped that he was kind of cute. Though not as cute as...as...as the boy with the green eyes.

The one she'd held hands with.

The one she'd felt good standing beside.

Though she could picture his face, his name still escaped her, and she couldn't remember a single thing they had said to each other.

Todd was a nice distraction from these fractured memories. On their third day working together, she began to catch him looking in her direction when he thought he was being sly.

"Geez, why don't you two sneak into the woods for a while?" Maddie suggested to Leah one day between groups.

The comment caught Leah off guard. "What are you talking about?"

"The way you two stare at each other? Please." Maddie laughed and walked over to straighten out the rope ladder.

It was then that Leah admitted to herself she had been staring at Todd as much as he'd been staring at her. She tried to play it off as boredom, but that only lasted until she caught herself peeking at him again when he was goofing around on the pull-up bar.

Maddie was right. Leah liked him.

Each group of campers bore the name of an animal. The next group on the course was the Gray Wolves, eight eleven-year-olds divided evenly between boys and girls.

Today was Maddie's turn to be in charge of sending kids off at intervals that would hopefully keep them from piling on top of one another, while Leah, Todd, and Kelvin were scattered along the course to encourage and help out where needed.

Leah's domain included the zigzag balance beams elevated a foot above the ground, and the rope swing over the mud pit. She followed the campers, and as they completed the sections, she clapped and yelled, "You can do it," and "Way to go," and "It's okay, you'll get it next time."

They ran everyone through the course once, gave them a

water break, and then started a second pass. When the fifth camper, a girl named Sidney, approached the zigzag beams, Leah said, "You got this, Sid. No problem."

The girl had misstepped the last time and nearly twisted her ankle when she fell. It was obvious from her look of discomfort that outdoor activities were not her thing. Leah moved in closer than she usually did, but her caution was unnecessary as Sidney completed the zigzag with barely a wobble.

Leah clapped loudly. "Way to go! See? I told you."

The girl looked surprised as she moved on to the rope swing. Since it was a simple matter of holding on, none of the kids—including Sidney—had had any problems with it. Sidney grabbed the rope, still glowing from her success on the beam, and launched herself over the mud.

Leah, positioned next to the pit, watched the rope arc down and up again as Sidney headed toward the other side. Before the girl reached the end of her swing, though, Leah both saw and heard the bracket holding the rope to the crossbar give way.

She leaped into the mud and threw out her arms as Sidney fell, back first, directly toward the dirt lip of the pit. Leah snagged the girl two feet above the ground and took the brunt of the falling bracket against her own back.

Sidney, hyperventilating, wrapped her arms around Leah's neck.

"I got you," Leah said. "You're okay."

"I…almost…fell," Sidney said between breaths.

Not almost, Leah thought as she stepped out of the pit and lowered the girl's feet to the ground.

The other three counselors and the rest of the Gray Wolves rushed over in a stampede of pounding boots.

"Holy sh—" Todd caught himself and then said, "—crap! Are you two all right?"

"I almost fell," Sidney repeated, with even more disbelief than before.

"I saw," Todd said.

Kelvin looked up at the crossbar. "It snapped clean off."

Leah and the others looked up, too. Part of the bracket was still attached to the four-by-four beam, but the section that connected to the rope had cracked along each edge and broken away.

"Leah, your back," Maggie said.

Leah tried to look over her shoulder, and for the first time felt the sting of pain.

"Play some trust-me games," Todd said to Kelvin and Maggie. "I'll take her to the office."

He put his hand on Leah's elbow and guided her away from the course.

"I'm fine," she said. "I'm sure it's nothing."

"Yeah, you're probably right, but we should get that blood cleaned up so you don't scare all the kids."

"Blood?"

He nodded. "You're going to need a new shirt."

She tried to take another look, but her unique changes didn't include the ability to turn her head all the way around—yet—so she couldn't see what he was talking about.

Noreen Dixon, a registered nurse and the assistant camp director, cleaned up Leah's wound and said a few butterfly bandages were all that were needed. When she finished, Leah donned the new camp T-shirt Todd had retrieved from the storeroom. When she finally got a look at her old shirt, she was shocked by the size of the bloodstain. Sure it had hurt when the bracket had hit her, but it hadn't hurt *that* bad, and now it wasn't much more than a dull ache.

"Director Melk said you can take the rest of the day off," Todd told her as they left the office.

"You talked to him?"

"Well, sure. He had to know what happened."

She knew Todd was right but it still bothered her. "I don't need any time off. Besides, Kelvin and Maddie could probably use our help."

"Are you sure? I mean, you can goof off while the rest of us work."

"Sounds boring."

They walked in silence for a few moments before Todd

said, "I don't know how you did that."

"What?" she asked.

"Caught her. I mean, I was looking right at Sidney when the thing broke. Before I even realized what happened, you were waiting under her."

A familiar tingle played along the skin at the back of Leah's neck. She thought about the moment she'd acted. She'd seen the bracket break and had begun to move, that was all. Or was it?

"If you'd been standing where I was, you'd have been able to do the same," she said.

"I don't know. Maybe." He looked far from convinced.

Not wanting him to pursue it any further, she said, "I'll race you back," then sprinted away, making sure she ran just slow enough to let him win.

TWENTY-THREE

CAMP CEDAR WOODS was a strict, one-week-per-group camp. Attendees arrived around one p.m. on Sunday and left at noon the following Saturday. For the counselors, Sunday mornings were spent in preparation for the incoming campers, while Saturday afternoons were free for them to hike or swim or lounge around.

On the Saturday between groups two and three, Leah had planned to return to the spot by the lake she'd found the previous weekend, and spend a quiet afternoon reading. But Todd came looking for her right after the buses left and said, "Terry's taking a few of us to town. Thought you might like to come along. What do you say?"

Technically, any counselor under eighteen was not allowed to leave camp without Director Melk's permission, but the director had hitched a ride on one of the buses back to the city and wouldn't be returning until the next day. For the duration, Nurse Dixon was in charge. She was good at dealing with cuts and bruises but wasn't the most observant person in the world, and it was unlikely she'd notice who left and who stayed.

Though Leah had been looking forward to some reading, getting away for an hour or two—especially with Todd—sounded like fun, so she accepted the offer and off they went.

Town was a twenty-minute drive away, and was really no more than a four-way stop with a gas station/mini-market on one corner and a café called Monty's Eats on the other. Leah and Todd bought slushies and waited outside while Terry and his friend Juko loaded up on snacks and sodas the camp store didn't carry.

When they all piled back into the crew cab of Terry's truck, Leah assumed they'd be returning to Cedar Woods, but that wasn't the direction Terry headed in.

She whispered to Todd, "Where are we going?"

He shrugged. "Just driving around a little."

She had no place to be, so why not? Leaning back in her seat, she sucked down some more of her drink and looked absently out at the forest.

Fifteen minutes later, she suddenly sat up. The view hadn't changed, but for some reason it felt familiar.

A wide turn and then—

I've been here before.

"Where are we going?" This time she asked loudly enough for everyone to hear.

Terry glanced back at his brother via the rearview mirror. "You didn't tell her?"

Todd squirmed in his seat and avoided Leah's gaze.

"Tell me what?" she asked.

When Todd still didn't answer, Terry said, "Camp Red Hawk."

Her eyes widened. "Red Hawk? But…but it's closed."

"Yeah, but the camp's still there." He smiled. "Since you know the place, thought maybe you could show us around."

"No!"

The others looked at her in surprise.

She calmed herself by taking a breath, and then said, "We should go back."

"We're almost there."

"Please. I have things I need to do."

"We won't stay long. I promise."

She wanted to argue, but worried that if she made too much of a fuss, it would cause them to ask questions she didn't want to answer. So she settled silently back in her seat.

A few minutes later, she spotted the camp turnoff. The sign had been painted over in dark brown, but a few of the words were still legible—RED and TURN and HAPPY. She hoped Terry would drive past it, but he slowed the truck in plenty of time and angled onto the entrance road.

It'll be over soon enough, Leah told herself. *Nothing's going to happen. It'll be fine.*

The road to the camp was rougher than she remembered, and much of it now appeared to be covered with wild grass and pine needles. She closed her eyes and hoped like she'd never hoped before that a tree had fallen across the way and would force them to turn back. No such luck. Even a chain that had once been strung across the road before the parking area had been cut and was now lying in the dirt.

Camp Red Hawk shared a similar layout to Camp Cedar Woods'. But whereas Cedar Woods looked clean and bright and inviting, the harsh winters had exacted their toll on Red Hawk. Large patches of shingles were missing from all the buildings, and a whole section of the dining hall's siding had caved in.

Terry parked at the midpoint between the administration building and the dining hall, near the start of the now overgrown pathway to the rest of the camp.

"Oh, wow. This is cool," Juko said as he and Terry hopped out of the cab.

Temporarily alone, Todd whispered, "I'm sorry. I should have told you, but I thought you wouldn't come if I did."

He was right about that, but she said nothing.

"I, um, I just wanted to spend a little time with you."

Whatever warm and fuzzy feelings she may have had for him were gone. Afraid her anger might cause her to actually hurt him, she opened the door and climbed out, leaving Todd inside alone.

Terry and Juko had wandered over to the admin building and were peering into one of the broken windows. Juko stuck his head through the opening and then pulled back out.

"I'm too big," he said.

Terry shouted toward the truck, "Todd, get over here!"

Leah heard the door open behind her and Todd climb out. "What?" he said.

"I need you. Come here."

As Todd jogged over, Terry smiled at Leah. "Bring back

memories?"

"A few," she said, her arms crossed.

If he noticed her foul mood, he gave no indication as he threw out his arms and shouted, "This place is awesome!"

Todd, with a little help from the other two, climbed through the broken window and vanished inside. While Terry and Juko leaned close to the opening so they could see better, Leah wandered toward the dining hall.

Little things began coming back to her—walking to lunch with her cabin mates, spending an hour one afternoon on kitchen duty, eating breakfast and listening to the director read the day's schedule. Pleasant memories that surprised her. She'd forgotten she had fun here. She'd made friends, too. Trudy and Gwen and…and Randi and Sue.

And…

…*John*?

No, that wasn't it, but close.

She meandered over to the path and down to the campfire pit. Here was the big difference between the two camps. Red Hawk's fire pit was surrounded by a small rise that had once been tiered with log benches, though now much of the seating was missing. The campfire area at Cedar Woods was flat.

Leah sat down on one of few remaining logs near the pit and looked down toward the lake that served the camp. Fun times had been had there, too. Canoe races and swim parties and—

"If anyone can make a bigger cannonball splash than me, I'll buy 'em a Snickers bar," the counselor, Brian, had announced. He was a big guy, easily over two hundred pounds, and had a hearty laugh.

"What if I don't like Snickers?" a boy asked. *His name started with a D, didn't it? Not a normal name. Something strange. Du…Du…Dooley! Yes, Dooley.*

"It won't matter because you're not going to beat me," Brian told him. "But all right. Winner gets whatever candy bar they want. How's that?"

Another counselor, Jennifer, was enlisted to act as judge, and the kids lined up to take their turn, Brian going last.

One by one, campers jumped off the end of the dock into the lake, trying to make as big a splash as they could. Leah even made an attempt, but immediately knew her effort, like those of the kids before her, had been far from sufficient to outdo whatever Brian would accomplish.

And then Dooley went. In the words of several of the other boys, his splash was epic. Even Brian seemed impressed.

As more of the kids went, Dooley remained the one to beat. Until the second to last camper.

Not John, but, but, but...God, what was his name?

Before he leapt from the dock, no one would have given him a chance. Most of the kids had put some of their energy into landing a good several feet from the end of the pier, but Not-John put his effort into gaining height before coming down, legs tucked, less than an arm's length from the dock.

If Dooley's splash had been epic, Not-John's had been monumental. It rose at least two feet higher, and the outward splash went far enough to soak the boy who had been waiting to go after him. The other kids erupted into a roar that Leah was sure could be heard all the way back at the cabins.

The final kid's try was less than spectacular, meaning Not-John's splash was the one Brian had to outdo. The counselor made a big show of stretching and preparing, but when all was said and done, Not-John was awarded his choice of candy bars from the camp store.

Had that been when she'd first noticed him?

"Hey, this is cool!"

Terry came down the path toward the fire pit, followed by Juko and Todd. They stopped at the bottom and looked up at the seats.

"Wish we had an amphitheater like this back at Cedar Woods," Juko said.

Terry shrugged. "Wouldn't be too hard. Get a tractor and push some dirt around."

"Maybe you should suggest it."

"Screw that. They can figure it out on their own if they want." Terry looked at Leah. "What kind of camp was it? Theater camp or something?"

"Just regular camp," she said. "Like Cedar Woods."

"Huh."

"So where did everyone stay?" Juko asked.

Leah pointed left into the woods. "That way."

Juko looked at where she indicated. "How do you get there?"

"There's a path." New growth had made it not as obvious as it had once been. She searched for a moment and then pointed. "Right there. By that tree with the broken limb."

"How about you show us?" Terry asked.

Feeling less dread than she had when they first arrived, she said, "I can do that."

She led them to the path and into the forest.

"The stables are out this way, too," she said.

"Stables?" Terry said. "Really? Damn, we don't have any stables."

"It would be so cool to have horses," Juko said.

"There weren't any horses when I was here," she told them. "I think they just used the buildings for storage."

"That must have been disappointing."

When she reached the fork, she automatically took the path to the right. Soon the trees parted and revealed twelve cabins. Like it did elsewhere, nature had started reclaiming the area around the buildings.

"These are the girls' cabins," she said.

Juko moved up to the door of the nearest one and looked inside. "Kinda small. Only two bunk beds?"

"That's it."

"How did this work?" Terry asked. "Couldn't have been a counselor in every cabin."

"Counselors had their own cabins on the other side, by the dining hall. These were just for campers."

Terry and Juko looked at her as if she were trying to pull their leg.

"So no one was watching you guys at night?" Juko asked.

"I'm sure the counselors were supposed to."

"But they didn't."

"Not really."

"Man, you must have had a lot of people sneaking out."

While the boys searched the cabins on the front row, Leah couldn't help but be drawn to one toward the middle. Above the door hung a wooden number six.

My cabin, she thought as she touched the doorframe. She stepped inside.

The mattresses were gone but the frames for the two bunk beds were still there. She had slept...on top of the one...to the...left. Using the crossbeam of the lower bed, she stepped up into the area she had once occupied.

Since she had been the last person to sleep there, she felt that gave her a special ownership of space. But as she looked around, no memories jumped out at her. It was just wood and air and dust and—

She paused, her gaze on a joint between a board running up the wall and the start of the ceiling. It looked as if there was something stuffed into the gap.

She ducked, stepped inside the bed frame, and hopped up on the rail that ran next to the wall. Using the support frame of the top bed, she pulled herself up as far as she could, but still had to stretch to reach the joint. It felt like a piece of paper inside. She teased the corner out until she was able to remove it.

The paper was folded a few times, the visible side white and blank. As she opened it, she saw color on the opposite side. Dark brown. It wasn't until she had it all the way open that she could read the words printed on it.

HERSHEY'S
Milk Chocolate

A candy wrapper.

Why was there...

Memory flood.

Cannonball contest again.

The candy Not-John wanted as his prize had been a Hershey's Milk Chocolate bar. Later, in the free time between the end of the afternoon activities and dinner, Leah had crossed paths with him.

"You had a, um, pretty good jump," he told her. "I-I'd say you came in second."

"It wasn't that good."

"You were in the water. You couldn't see it."

She smiled. "True."

He broke his candy bar in two and held out the half still in the wrapper. "Um, would, um, you like some?"

"Uh, sure. Thanks." She took it and broke off a small piece, then tried to hand back the rest.

"You keep it. I don't need a whole bar anyway."

Before she could insist, he hurried away.

This was that wrapper. She had carefully folded it that night and stuck it into the space between the boards because she couldn't bring herself to throw it away. It had a kind of power.

She rubbed her thumb over the surface.

"Joel," she whispered. *That was his name. Why did I forget?*

As she stepped down from the bed frame, she felt a sudden urge to go back outside, almost as if a thin rope were tied around her waist, tugging her.

Miiiinnnneeee.

A whisper.

The wind in the trees sounding like a voice.

Heading for the doorway, she refolded the candy wrapper and slipped it into her pocket.

She could hear the guys in one of the cabins but didn't join them. Instead, she followed the tug of the invisible rope back to the path. A few minutes later, she was passing the stables and entering the off-limits area of the woods.

She had no recollection of ever going this way before, and yet she knew she had. It wasn't anything she saw that caused her to realize this. It was a feeling, a sense of certainty.

Where she was going and why, she didn't know. But she couldn't stop, nor did she want to. A feeling of calm accompanied the tug, giving her a sense that everything was okay.

Miiiinnnneeee, the wind said again, like a finger brushing against her skin.

If there was an actual path she was following, she couldn't see it. It was the invisible cord that guided her, pulling gently but insistently forward even as the forest pressed in around her like a cloak.

The ghost of a thought that she should be scared passed through her mind, and was just as quickly ushered away. It was like home waited for her ahead, and the sooner she got there, the better things would be.

After a while a fence appeared, high and topped with barbed wire. Not much farther down she spotted a sign hanging on it. She felt no need to read it, though. She'd done that before.

When? She couldn't remember.

What it said? Not important.

The pull of the rope was all she needed.

Not far beyond the sign, she came upon a haphazard pile of branches and tree trunks and garbage and rocks pressing up against the fence.

She remembered this, too, didn't she? The mound of debris?

Yes, but…it was changed. Larger than before, and…and…wider.

Miiiinnnneeee.

The invisible rope tugged her around the rubble to where she suddenly knew she'd find a hole in the fence. But when she reached the other side, she saw the hole was no more. In its place sat a ton of additional deadwood and junk.

The rope yanked at her, wanting her to walk through the fence as if the hole were still there.

Miiiinnnneeee!

Panic growing, she scrambled onto the pile and tried to climb over the debris. But it was too steep, and every attempt ended with her slipping and having to start again.

"No, no, no," she whispered.

She kept at it. Up a few feet and down again.

"No."

Up and down.

"No."
Up and down.
"No. No. No."

TWENTY-FOUR

WHEN LEAH OPENED her eyes, she found herself looking at the back of the driver's seat of Terry's truck, the road *thump-thumping* below her.

"Leah?" Todd's voice.

She turned her head and realized she was lying in his lap. She quickly sat up. "How did...how did I get here?"

"We carried you back after we found you."

Her brow furrowed. "Carried me?"

Juko looked back from the front passenger seat. "How do you feel?"

"My legs sting a little."

"That's not surprising," Todd said. "You scraped yourself up pretty bad."

"I what?"

"How's your head?" Juko asked.

"My head? My head's fine. What happened?"

"We were hoping you could tell us," Terry said from the driver's seat.

"After we checked out the cabins, we went to get you but you were gone," Todd told her.

She grimaced. She'd been in her old cabin, number six. She hadn't gone anywhere.

"Good thing you weren't trying to hide," Todd said. "Your trail was pretty easy to follow."

"My trail?"

"We found you in the woods lying next to a pile of dead trees. We tried to wake you up but..."

She couldn't make sense of what he was saying. In the

woods? No, she had been in cabin six. She'd been looking around, she'd found…

She jammed her hand into her pocket and felt the folded Hershey's wrapper. She almost pulled it out but didn't want to explain it to the others.

"What were you doing out there?" Todd asked.

That was the question of the hour.

She didn't know what the answer was, but had no doubt the side trip was connected to all the other issues she'd been dealing with since the last time she was at the camp. That was something else she wasn't going to share, so she said, "We used to go on hikes in the woods."

"You just decided to go on a hike alone, then?" Juko asked.

"Just a short one," she lied. Or assumed she did.

"You should probably lie back down," Juko said. "You might have a concussion or something."

Ignoring him, she looked out the window. "Where are we?"

"About ten minutes from camp," Terry said. "As soon as we get there, we'll get you to Nurse Dixon so she can take a look at you."

"Pull over," she said.

"What?"

"Pull over. Now."

"Are you going to throw up?"

"Pull over!"

Terry swung the truck onto the shoulder and hit the brakes.

Leah hopped out, the other three following.

"If you're going to puke," Terry said as he came around the front, "try not to get any on my ride."

"Real sensitive there, Terry," Todd said.

"Hey, I'm only trying to—"

"I'm *not* going to throw up," Leah said. "I feel fine."

Terry looked confused. "Then why did you want to stop?"

"Do any of you have water?" she asked.

"Uh, yeah," Todd said. He climbed into the truck, returned with a bottle, and handed it to her.

She took a deep, long drink. As freaked out as she was about her missing time, it was something she could figure out later. Right now, she needed to control the situation.

She looked at the three boys. "Listen very carefully. What happened today stays between us. As far as anyone else is concerned, we never went to Camp Red Hawk and you didn't find me unconscious."

"I'm not sure that's such a good idea," Juko said. "What if—"

Eyes narrowing, she said, "No what-ifs. We stopped by the store and then we went on a hike. We walked through some bushes and that's where I got scraped up. The day was nice but otherwise uneventful. *Nothing* unusual happened. Got it?"

"But what if you *do* have a concussion?" Todd asked.

"I don't," she said.

"You're not a doctor. You can't know that."

Except she could. Other than the cuts, she knew her body was in perfect condition.

She turned to give Todd a dose of her ire, but the genuine look of concern on his face caused her to soften a bit. "I'm not hurt. I promise." It looked like he was going to say something else, so she held up a hand to stop him. "If it turns out I'm wrong, then we'll say I tripped and didn't think anything of it at the time. Okay?"

He looked less than convinced.

"You need to believe me. I *am* fine."

He hesitated a moment longer before nodding.

She knew he didn't buy it, but she was also sure he would do as she asked, so she returned her attention to the other two. "And you guys?"

A look of discomfort passed across Terry's face and then he shrugged. "Yeah. Okay. If that's what you want."

"I'm serious. When we get back into the truck, we don't talk about this *ever* again. And that means even between you guys. Understand?"

He threw up his hands in surrender. "I said okay already."

"I'm not so sure," Juko said.

She took a breath. "If you see any signs that something

might be wrong with me, you can let Nurse Dixon know. Okay?"

"I guess," he said, grimacing. "One problem, though. We did tell a couple of people we were going to Red Hawk."

"Then tell them we changed our plans," she said.

"I guess we can do that."

"Thank you," she said.

The rest of the drive back was made in silence. Nurse Dixon bought the story of the bushes and the hike, and treated Leah's scratches while warning her she needed to be more careful next time. There was no mention of Leah being too young to have left camp without permission.

For the remainder of Leah's time at Cedar Woods, Terry and Juko did all they could to avoid her. Even Todd minimized his interactions with Leah, his crush on her as over as the one she'd been developing for him.

When she returned home the first week of August, her parents did their best to hide their relief that she was back.

"How was it?" they asked.

"Fine."

"What did you do?"

"Worked a lot."

"Did anything exciting happen?"

A pause. "Not really."

TWENTY-FIVE

Joel

FOR THE FIRST time since the incident involving Justin the previous summer, Joel woke to the pain of injury. It occurred two weeks before his and his mother's relocation to California. She was coming with him because, in her words, "you're far too young to be on your own." Once again, the event was preceded by the dream of the fuzzy faces and the dark tunnel filled with wind.

Unlike with his toe, however, he didn't yell when he woke to find himself in pain. This time, a stinging red blotch marked his hand. Sure enough, the irritated spot and the pain soon faded.

Forty minutes later, he was in the kitchen, grabbing a bagel out of the toaster. When he turned toward the table, he bumped into the fresh mug of coffee his mother was carrying. The scalding liquid sloshed over the lip and splashed on her hand.

She sucked in a breath, rushed over to the sink, and plunged her hand into a stream of cold water.

"Are you okay?" he asked, moving in next to her. "I'm so sorry. I didn't realize you were there."

"You have to watch where you're going, sweetie," she said, wincing.

In a broader sense that might have been true, but when Joel saw the exact same red mark on his mom's hand that he'd seen on his own not an hour before, he was sure he couldn't have done anything to prevent this accident.

It happened again three days before the move. On that

morning, he woke to find his jaw throbbing and tender to the touch. Though he had no mirror handy to check, he knew there was a bruise, too. If he had the dream this time, though, he didn't remember it.

In both his mother's case and Justin's, the injuries had been the result of accidents caused by Joel. Thinking he couldn't be a catalyst if he avoided contact with everyone, he stayed in bed until after his father left for work. Unfortunately his mom was home, after having already worked her last day at the local Coldwell Banker real estate office before her transfer to one of the company's branches in Palo Alto. To minimize his interaction with her, he dressed, grabbed his bag, and hurried from his room to the front door, yelling that he needed to go to the library and would be back later. As far as he could tell, she was still uninjured as he stepped outside.

In truth, he had no intention of going to the library. There would be dozens of people there, and far too many chances to cause someone harm. He decided he'd ride around and hoped no one would pay him any attention.

When he spotted the old dirt road that ran into the wilderness behind the Strickland Country Club, he realized it would be the perfect place to pass the day without unintentionally causing injury to anyone.

At Old Kitta Hill, he dismounted and pushed his bike up to the boulders on the west side, where he found a shaded spot he could sit in and read one of the books he'd brought.

He enjoyed an hour of blissful solitude wrapped in a text on theoretical physics, and was so engrossed in the data of a particle accelerator test that he barely noticed the panicked yelp echo over the hill. When it happened a second time, he looked up.

He worked his way to the summit of the hill, where he heard a rustle drift up from the other side, followed by someone pleading, "Don't!"

He weaved his way through the trees toward the sounds. Three quarters of the way down, the gentle slope ended at a vertical drop of approximately twenty feet. Peering over the edge, he saw the back of a man's head.

He quietly moved sideways until he had a better view. The man was kneeling on the chest of another guy, his hand pressed over the prone man's mouth.

Both were dressed in ratty clothes, and looked as if they hadn't taken showers in months. When the kneeling man's head turned enough to reveal his profile, Joel realized he'd seen him before, hanging out in various area parking lots, sometimes begging, sometimes digging through the trash, but more often than not passed out.

The man snarled at the guy on the ground. "Where'd you leave it?"

The prone man's response was garbled by his assaulter's hand.

"Goddammit, where is it?"

Whatever the guy said next was clearly not what the man on top wanted to hear. The aggressor reached around his back and pulled a knife from under his shirt.

Silently, Joel hurried to the bottom of the slope and moved in behind the man, just out of range.

"You should drop that," he said, his voice low and even.

The man whirled around and jumped to his feet when he saw Joel. "Get out of here. This isn't your business!"

The victim began pushing himself away, but the guy with the knife heard the movement and stamped a foot down on the other man's ankle.

"You stay," he said to the guy.

"I told you to put that down," Joel said.

The man swished the knife drunkenly through the air a couple of times, nearly losing his balance in the process. "The hell I will."

Joel stepped forward and swung, knowing where his fist was going to land even before he threw it. The alcohol in the man's system delayed his reaction time so much that he didn't even move to keep Joel's knuckles from slamming into his cheek. Down he went, unconscious before he hit the ground.

The other guy scrambled to his feet and backed away, wide eyed. "Don't hurt me!"

"I don't want to hurt you. I was just—"

"Look what you did to him." He glanced at the man and back at Joel, a crazed look on his face. "Leave me alone!"

"Are you okay?"

"Leave me *alone*!"

The man ran off.

Joel climbed back up the hill to get his stuff, unsure if he'd done any good. There was one thing, though, he no longer had any doubts about.

He was the catalyst of the injuries his body foretold.

TWENTY-SIX

STANFORD PROVIDED JOEL with the first intellectual stimulation he hadn't discovered on his own since seventh grade. His classes weren't particularly challenging—like his aborted first year of high school, he was still earning top grades—but he liked that his courses were more focused, and his professors expected him to dive deeper into subjects.

A consequence of his success came in the form of a nickname that quickly spread across campus—Prodigy.

Joel hated it.

As much as he wanted to learn all he could, he also wanted to fit in. But how could he make friends when everyone had already formed an opinion about him? Even his mother had begun to treat him as if he were different from everyone else, almost like she was afraid of him. At his core, he was still the happy kid he'd once been, a kid who now couldn't understand what had happened to the life he thought he was going to have.

Knowing there was little he could do about the unwanted attention, he poured his energy into learning. It became like a drug. The more he took in, the more he wanted to know. To feed his unquenchable appetite, he signed up for the maximum amount of credits allowed, but it still wasn't enough. So he sat in on as many other classes as he could, mainly choosing lecture courses with large numbers of enrollees so his presence would go unnoticed. While knowing he shouldn't, he couldn't resist taking the tests and turning them in. Even in these classes he wasn't officially taking, he earned top grades.

By the third quarter, at the urging of several professors, the administration granted Joel credit for the extra classes and removed his limit of credits per quarter. This new freedom allowed him to design an educational track that would see him complete his undergrad studies at the same time he should have been graduating from high school, and not with just one degree but two, in physics and pre-med.

As for the phantom injuries, they were absent throughout his freshman year. But they weren't gone forever.

TWENTY-SEVEN

Leah

SCHOOL-WISE, LEAH'S sophomore year was no different from her freshman one. Again she knew she could easily be the number one student in each of her classes, and again that was attention she didn't want. So she continued Project Dumb Down.

This turned out to be harder than it had been in ninth grade, as she'd grown even smarter over the summer. Her mind now struggled with itself every time she purposely screwed up a homework assignment or wrote the wrong answers on a test.

She was well aware it was impossible for someone to get so much smarter in such a short time, and though she didn't know how her intellectual boost occurred, she knew the catalyst was the day trip back to Camp Red Hawk.

The night after that visit she'd begun having what she'd come to think of as enhanced dreams. They were like a whacked-out obstacle course filled with wild-colored landscapes and impossible shapes, and had no use for the rules of physics. At first, she found herself running down twisting ribbons of gold and purple and turquoise. Sometimes she felt pulled by an invisible rope, while other times it seemed as if giant hands pushed her from behind.

The dreams would come approximately every other week. There was no consistent pattern, but she always knew when one was on the way. At some point in the hours before she slept, her shoulders would tingle. The sensation would spread over her back and around her sides by the time she climbed into bed.

Perhaps this should have given her a sense of dread, but

she felt only anticipation. As strange as the dreams were, they comforted her.

When the summer after tenth grade arrived, she didn't request to return to camp, and her parents certainly didn't suggest it. Leah busied herself between a job at the public library and spending time with her friends.

Through the first half of her junior year, she continued along the familiar groove of pretending to be an above average but not brilliant student.

Her deception, however, would not make it through the second half.

ON THE AFTERNOON of the Valentine's Day dance, Leah's shoulders began tingling, letting her know another dream would be coming that night. But as much as she would have liked to go to bed right after dinner, she'd made a deal with her friend Monica that if no one asked either of them to the dance, they'd go together. Surprise, surprise, Monica's boyfriend broke up with her at the end of January, and Leah was forced to honor their bargain.

They spent the first hour of the event with a few other girls who'd come alone, occasionally dancing as a group but mostly sitting around and gossiping about other students. As Leah's mom had predicted, only a few boys came dateless. That was fine. Leah was having a good time with the girls, and would have happily stayed until the last song if not for the tug.

At first she thought someone had pulled on her dress. But no one was behind her. She assumed she'd imagined it, but then the pull returned. Not a gentle tug this time, but a yank.

It was like in the dreams, only she wasn't asleep. This was the first time she'd ever felt it awake.

Wait, no, she thought. *It isn't the first time, is it?*

A fog lifted in her mind. Two summers ago. The return to Camp Red Hawk.

The blank spot in her memory was not blank anymore. She'd felt the tug that afternoon, too. That's how she had ended up in the forest.

Like back then, she was overwhelmed by the desire to

follow the pull.

"I'll be right back," she said.

"Where are you going?" Monica asked.

"Um, restroom."

"Oh, great. I've got to go, too."

Telling Monica she wanted to go alone would have sounded strange, so Leah smiled and they headed across the multipurpose room together.

The restrooms were outside to the left. As they moved into the central hallway, Leah said, "I should call home. Promised my mom. You know, check in? I'll catch up with you in a minute."

"Sure," Monica said, continuing on to the bathroom.

As soon as her friend was out of sight, Leah made a beeline for the room where everyone had left their coats, found hers, and once more gave in to the invisible rope.

It guided her out the main exit, down the steps, into the parking lot to her car, and then went slack. Getting the message, she hopped in and backed out of her parking spot. As soon as she put the car into drive, the rope reasserted itself.

Her curiosity about where she was being taken soon turned to concern as she realized she was being led home. Was something wrong? Had something happened to her parents?

Squeezing the wheel, she increased her speed. When she turned onto her street, she expected to see emergency vehicles parked in front of her house, lights flashing, but all was quiet. And when she pulled into the driveway, she could see the TV flickering off the living room wall.

She rushed up the steps, unlocked the door, and hurried inside.

Her parents looked over from the couch, startled.

"Hi, honey," her father said. "Is everything all right?"

"Oh, um, yeah. Fine." She channeled her relief into a smile.

"I thought you weren't going to be home until ten."

"I, um, got bored."

"Well, it was a Valentine's Day dance," her mother said. "I told you, always better to have a date."

"Thanks, Mom. I'll remember next time." Before they could ask another question, Leah said, "I've got homework to do, so I'll, uh, see you in the morning."

"Good night, sweetie," her mother said.

"Sleep well," her dad said. "And sorry about the dance."

As Leah said, "No biggie," the rope yanked again, pulling her up the stairs.

Once she was in her bedroom, it led her to her bed. She finally realized what was going on. The dream wanted her, and it wanted her now.

She fought the urge to lie down, and said out loud, "Hold on. I'm not sleeping in this."

In record time she was out of her nice dress, into her nightgown, and under the covers with the lights off. She stared at the ceiling, certain she was too worked up to fall asleep anytime soon, but she was wrong. Within moments she was out.

The dream was different this time.

There were no ribbons, no bright colors, nothing to indicate she was in one of the imaginary landscapes she'd spent so much time in.

The scene before her was real world, nighttime. A suburban lane with houses and apartment buildings and street lamps and cars. A street in a big town or maybe a city.

Yes, a city. She could hear sounds in the distance—buses and the drone of a nearby freeway…and people. Thousands and thousands of people.

The air was moist, which meant she must be near a body of water, a lake or maybe a river. It was cool, but not cold like it was currently in Colorado. Yet she *knew* this was the same night as when she'd been awake.

She took a breath, and when she felt the coolness enter her lungs, she realized she was actually there, standing on the sidewalk.

As vivid as the other dreams had been, they were nothing compared to this.

She heard voices and laughter behind her. Turning, she spotted a large group of people in front of one of the buildings.

A gathering of some kind.

She started to turn away, but the pull stopped her. It wasn't like the rope this time, not nearly that forceful. This was more like a thread attached to the center of her chest, thin and weak yet unbreakable.

It wanted her to walk toward the people, so she did. As she neared, the din of voices separated into fourteen different conversations. If she focused on any particular one, she could bring it forward and hear what was being said, like tuning in to different stations on a radio.

The thread continued to pull her forward, through the group and toward the building's entrance. She had to twist and turn to avoid running into anyone, though no one appeared to notice her.

She was there and she wasn't.

She moved into the building and up a set of stairs. As she passed the second floor, she heard more mumbling conversations. The third floor, however, was quiet. Upon reaching the landing, two gentle tugs guided her to the left and down the hall.

Both sides were lined by closed doors, each with metal numbers mounted to it. But the numbers on apartment 319, unlike the others, pulsed with a blue-white light she knew only she could see. It was no surprise, then, that the tug guided her there.

The moment she put her hand on the knob, the world went black. When she could see again, she was standing in a cramped living room.

A single pull sent her down a hallway and into a dim, unoccupied bedroom. She waited, assuming she'd get tugged again, but the thread remained slack.

An empty room in a strange apartment? What could possibly be—

A flash of light, brighter than any she'd ever seen, forced her to jam her eyes shut.

"You can lie down in here. When you feel better, we'll get you home."

Leah eased open her eyelids, and was surprised to find that

her vision had been unaffected by the flash.

She was still in the room, only now the overhead light was on and two young guys were helping a girl over to the bed. All three appeared to have been drinking. The girl was the worst off, though. If not for the arms around her, she would have surely fallen.

"Now?" one of guys asked after they laid her down.

The other guy shook his head. "Ten minutes. That should be plenty of time."

Before Leah could wonder what they meant, the searing light flashed again.

TWENTY-EIGHT

Joel

EVEN BY JOEL'S standards, it had been a grueling day.

Four daytime classes and an evening astronomy lecture on the relationship of Pluto and Charon. It was well after nine o'clock when his mother picked him up and drove them back to their two-bedroom apartment, five blocks from campus.

As always, she prepared a late-night snack and asked if maybe he was taking on too much at once. After that, there were stories from her day about houses she'd seen and the ridiculous expectations some of her clients had. She was not a big fan of California, though she did like her commissions on the overpriced homes. What she longed for, though never said, was to move back to Denver to be with Joel's dad instead of seeing him only on one of their quick back and forth visits. Joel suspected a small part of her hated him for choosing a college so far from their life in Colorado.

He nibbled at his sandwich to be polite before saying, "I'm kind of tired. I'll see you in the morning."

"What time would you like breakfast?"

Though his schedule never changed, this was yet another thing she always asked.

He'd been annoyed by her unnecessary questions for a few months, but knew it was her way of staying involved in his life and justifying why she was still living with him. The truth was, despite Joel's age, he didn't need her help anymore. They both knew it, but neither ever mentioned it.

"Seven's fine," he said.

She gave him a hug. "Goodnight, honey."

Joel was asleep no more than a minute after his head hit his pillow. At first his dreams were filled with a mix of molecules and equations and planets and the girl in his anatomy class who sat a few rows in front of him.

And then the wind began to howl.

And the dark closed in.

And a dim light appeared down a long tunnel, spinning around and around, flashing off walls like a strobe.

"Help me!"

A blurry-faced girl clung to the ceiling, her legs whipping behind her in the gale.

"Help me!" The yell coming from oh so far away.

He wanted to call to her, to ask what he could do, but like each time he'd had this dream, his voice remained mute.

A hand touched his arm and he looked over in surprise. He'd always thought he'd been standing there alone, but there was a girl with him now, someone who'd always been there, he realized.

And her face was not obscured.

He both knew her and had no idea who she was.

She looked at him, frightened and confused, mirroring his own feelings. With a gasp, she turned her attention back down the tunnel. He followed her gaze.

The girl on the ceiling wasn't there anymore.

"Help me! Help me! Help..." Her yell faded in the distance.

Suddenly, the twirling beam of light shined on her as she said a final, whispered, "Help me!"

Joel took a step forward. If the girl beside him hadn't gripped his arm, the wind would have sucked him up and flung him down the tube. She yanked him back, and....

Joel woke with a start. For a moment he remained wrapped in the terror of the dream, but then a pain more intense than anything he'd ever experienced raged through him. He fought hard to keep from screaming. He hurt nearly *everywhere*—his shoulder, his ribs, arms, nose, his jaw.

He tried to tilt his head to take a look at himself, but even the slightest movement sent searing shockwaves racing in every direction. From the corner of his eye, he could see something was wrong with his right shoulder. It looked off, out of place.

Dislocated.

What was the cause? A car accident?

Though he knew the pain would last only seconds, it felt like forever before it began to recede. Once he was whole again, he sat up and looked at his shoulder. As always, the damage was gone.

What was surprising was that unlike all the other times he'd experienced a premonition, it was still dark outside.

He looked at the clock—11:17 p.m. He'd been in bed for barely thirty minutes.

Confused, he lay back down. The other events had all come in the morning.

Why was this one different?

What in God's name was going on?

TWENTY-NINE

WHEN THE FLASH dissipated, Leah found she was still in the bedroom, the unconscious girl still on the bed. But now the girl's clothes were gone.

Three others were present, all guys. One stood on each side of the bed, the guy farthest away holding a palm-sized video camera, and the guy nearest her holding a smartphone in video record mode. One had helped her onto the bed earlier, while the other was someone new. The third guy—the other helper—lay naked on top of her.

"Stop!" Leah yelled.

No one twitched.

"Stop!" she yelled again.

She ran over and tried to grab the camera from the guy nearest her, but her hands slipped right through him. To the three guys, she wasn't there.

Though she knew it would make no difference, she couldn't keep herself from yelling, "Stop! Stop! Stop! Stop!"

Flash.

The scene the same but different. Now one of the other guys was on the girl, and the first guy, still unclothed, held his partner's camera.

Oh, God!

Flash.

The inevitable. Guy number three in the starring role.

Flash.

A different bedroom. A girl's bedroom. A dorm, maybe? Leah had never been in one, but the layout looked like ones she'd seen on TV. Someone was huddled on the bed under the covers.

Leah approached the bed, and could see a face peeking out from under the blanket. A girl's face. The unconscious girl from the other room. Her eyes were red, her cheeks tear stained.

Leah knew the assault would forever mark the woman.

When the light flashed again, Leah was afraid to open her eyes, afraid she might be presented with a vision of the girl wandering through a destroyed life, or worse, dead at her own hands.

But what she saw instead was the apartment bedroom again, empty and unlit like it had been when she first arrived.

And then she knew the truth. She knew the attack had not happened yet.

For a moment, she felt elated. There was still time to save the girl. But how? How was she supposed to do that?

The thread pulled her forward as the light flashed again, and kept pulling after the white had disappeared.

She was in the living room of a different apartment, this one nicer, cleaner. The TV was on, showing a movie she'd seen before. *Good Will Hunting.*

The thread urged her toward the hallway. As she passed the couch, she noticed a woman slouched on it, asleep. There was something vaguely familiar about the sleeper's face, but Leah's guide didn't allow her time to study it, as it kept her moving into the dark hall and down to the closed door at the end.

She reached for the knob like she had before, and once more all went black for a moment as she transitioned to the other side.

A bedroom, average size, with a desk, bookcases, a bed, and a closet. The only adornment was a photograph tacked to the wall next to the bed. The dim light slipping in through the window was enough for her to see the picture was of three boys, though it was too dark to make out their faces. If the person sleeping in the bed was one of them, then the picture must have been taken long ago. From the shape under the covers, she could see he was a man now. Or perhaps the picture was of his children.

The thread urged her closer to the bed. The man was lying on his side, his profile partially covered by the sheet. The thread's anchor point suddenly switched from her heart to the tips of the index and middle fingers on her right hand, and tugged them toward the man's shoulder.

She couldn't touch him, she thought. She would pass right through him like she had with the guy in the other apartment. But when her fingers reached his shoulder, they tapped against his solid flesh.

The man stirred.

At the insistence of the thread, she touched him again. He rolled onto his back, the sheet falling from his face.

Leah stared at him, sure she was seeing things. But then of course she was. This was a dream, right?

Right?

The face belonged not to a man but to a teenage boy. A boy she had known. A boy her same age. Though he had grown considerably in the three and a half years since she'd last seen him, there was no mistaking the shape of his mouth or that of his nose or his brow.

Joel.

The boy she had almost forgotten.

He was sweating, his forehead creased in worry. She tried to reach out to stroke his hair and calm whatever was troubling him, but before her hand could move, the light flashed again, and she was once more standing in the bedroom of apartment 319.

The girl. The boys. The cameras.

Flash.

Joel's room.

As much as she'd been trying to convince herself otherwise, this was not a dream, not really. It was the world as it was, or as it soon would be.

But was everything she'd seen already written in stone?

No, she thought. The thread was presenting her with an opportunity to change the outcome of what she'd witnessed, the dream-that-wasn't-a-dream showing her that Joel and apartment 319 were not far apart. Nothing else made sense.

With a gasp, Joel's eyes shot open.

Leah started to lean toward him, but jerked back in surprise.

Something was horribly wrong with his shoulder, and there were bruises on his arms and face. His nose also looked broken. She couldn't understand it. A moment before he'd looked fine.

His face clinched in pain, his breaths rapid, almost desperate. She wanted to do something for him but didn't even know where to start. Then right before her eyes, his bruises began to fade and his shoulder eased back into its socket as his breathing slowly returned to normal. Several seconds later, it was as if nothing had happened at all.

Was this another premonition brought on by her dream state? Had it made her see things that weren't there? Clearly that was possible. But his reaction, that had been real.

Joel's gaze swept past her to the digital clock on the nightstand. He hadn't seen her. She reached out to touch him but her hand passed through his arm.

He let out an exhausted breath and fell back on his pillow, looking at the ceiling.

Flash.

The girl, alone and unconscious. The men standing together in one corner, looking at the playback on one of their cameras as they smiled.

Flash.

Joel blinked a few times and started to close his eyes.

Without even thinking, she yelled, "Get up!"

Nothing.

"Get up!"

Still no response.

"Joel! Get up now!"

He sat up in a shot and looked around, but again his gaze swept through her without stopping.

Maybe he couldn't see her, but apparently he could *hear* her.

"Get up! Get up! Get up!"

He froze, his eyes staring almost, but not quite, in her direction.

She tried to grab his arm but of course she passed right through it. Frustrated, she shouted, "On your feet and get dressed! Hurry!"

He jumped from the bed.

It's going to work, Leah thought. *Oh, please, let it work.*

THIRTY

Joel

JOEL! GET UP now!

Joel pushed himself up and looked around. The voice—he couldn't tell if it was male or female—had come from somewhere in the room. But he was alone.

Get up! Get up! Get up!

He had no idea how it was possible, but the voice seemed to be coming from *all* sides of his bed.

On your feet and get dressed! Hurry!

Urgency bloomed in his chest. He had no idea why, but he knew he had to listen to the voice, to trust it, do as it asked. He jumped out of bed, grabbed his Stanford hoodie off the floor, and donned it and his jeans. He didn't bother with socks, just shoved his feet into his shoes and tied them faster than he ever had before.

As he crossed the room, the voice spoke again. *Quiet.*

He eased the door open and crept down the hallway. When he reached the living room, he peeked in. His mother was at one end of the couch, leaning to the side, asleep. On the coffee table sat an empty wineglass and the TV remote, the tableau of her nightly ritual.

He snuck past her with more caution than he knew was necessary. If she stuck to her pattern, it would be another few hours before she woke enough to shuffle off to bed.

Focus! There's no time to waste.

Within seconds, he was downstairs, standing outside his apartment building. "Which way?"

Instead of hearing the voice again, a map appeared in his

head of an area near campus. A red dot glowed on a street about a mile and a half from where Joel stood.

His seventeenth birthday was a few weeks away but he had yet to get his driver's license, so he ran. He covered the distance in less than nine minutes, arriving only slightly winded, and feeling no other strain from the exertion.

The glowing dot on his mental map had led him to another apartment building. Unlike the complex he and his mother lived in, this one appeared to be primarily occupied by students. A banner hung from the roof, wishing someone named Aaron a happy birthday. At least twenty people milled about out front, most holding cups that reeked of beer.

Inside. Apartment 319.

While Joel's Prodigy reputation had abated, his face was still known by a lot of people, so he pulled the hood over his head and weaved through the crowd, his gaze on the ground. No more than a handful of partygoers glanced in his direction.

Inside, he bypassed the elevator and took the stairs. The first floor was empty but the second was packed with more students, drinking and talking and laughing. A portion of the crowd overflowed into the stairwell, and Joel had to push past them to keep heading up. Whoever Aaron was, apparently he had a lot of friends.

On the third-floor landing, a boy and girl were pressed together in the corner making out. For half a second, Joel felt a tinge of jealousy. He'd never come close to kissing a girl before. He'd never even held one's hand.

Or had he?

Joel! Move!

He turned away from the groping couple and hurried into the empty corridor.

Left, the voice said.

He jogged down the hall until he reached the door for apartment 319.

He wasn't sure if he should knock or what. He didn't even know why he was here. Or what he was supposed to be doing.

Open it!

He checked both ways to make sure he was still alone,

then grabbed the knob. It was locked.

Hurry! Hurry!

He added his other hand to the first, then twisted the knob. For a second, it resisted, and then there was a pop and the latch was free.

He rushed into a small living room. The décor was classic student—cheap couch, outdated coffee table, beanbag chair, and a bookcase made from boards and cinder blocks. The only things that looked new were the TV hanging on the wall and the Xbox console beneath it.

Back bedroom.

Joel headed down a dingy hall. As he approached the only closed door, he could hear muffled voices on the other side.

Hurry!

He shoved the door open.

There were four people inside, three guys and a girl. Two of the guys were standing next to a queen-sized bed, one holding a video camera and the other recording on a cell phone. The third was on the mattress with the girl. He had his shirt off and was unzipping his pants. The girl was completely undressed.

She was also unconscious.

For half a second, no one seemed to notice Joel's arrival, then the guy on the bed looked over and said, "What the hell are you doing in here? Get out!"

His friends turned, their cameras swinging with them until they were pointed at Joel. From their delayed reactions, he could tell all three were drunk.

"Get away from her!" Joel growled.

The closest camera guy moved toward him. "This is a private party, asshole."

He reached out, intending to shove Joel toward the door, but his palm never made it that far. With a quick grab, twist, and pull, Joel dislocated the guy's shoulder and pushed him out of the way.

His fellow cameraman rushed at Joel in an attempt to tackle him. Though he was slightly larger, avoiding his outstretched arms was child's play.

Taking advantage of the guy's momentum, Joel shoved him in the back as he passed and sent him flying into a dresser. The guy roared as he unsteadily whipped back around, face bloody, but Joel was ready with a right hook to the creep's jaw. The guy spun back into the dresser, dropped to a knee, and collapsed, eyes closed.

The shirtless one on the bed scuttled off the mattress and backpedaled into the corner. "Hey, man, I don't want any trouble."

Joel tilted his head toward the girl without looking at her. "Her clothes, where are they?"

Shirtless stammered for a moment before pointing at the floor a few feet away.

"Dress her. Carefully."

As the guy did this, Joel glanced at the other two. The big one was still unconscious, and the guy with the dislocated shoulder probably wished he was, too.

Once Shirtless had finished dressing the girl, Joel checked her to make sure she wasn't in need of immediate medical attention. He then pointed at the camera that had been tossed on the bed. "Give that to me."

Shirtless picked it up and lobbed it to Joel.

"Don't move." Joel popped out the memory card and shoved it in his pocket. He then threw the camera into the wall, where it broke with a loud crunch.

The smartphone that had also been recording was on the floor where Dislocated Shoulder had dropped it. Joel stomped on it several times to make sure it was completely destroyed before he put it in his pocket. He then walked around the side of the bed.

Shirtless pressed his back against the wall as if he could squeeze through it. "Come on, man. Just leave me alone."

Joel looked at the girl and then at the son of a bitch who'd almost raped her. "Up."

"Please. I swear, she...she wanted to be here. She—"

Joel grabbed Shirtless by the arm and yanked him to his feet.

"Buddy, please. I didn't do anything. Just—"

Joel slammed his fist into the guy's nose. Now all the wounds Joel had experienced when he'd woken were accounted for.

Groaning, Shirtless slipped down the wall and huddled on the floor.

"If you ever try this again…" Joel said.

"It was just a joke," Shirtless sputtered. "We weren't—"

"Stop."

Shirtless peered up at him through his fingers. "We…we won't."

Joel carried the girl into the living room and laid her on the couch so he could adjust his hood. He realized it wouldn't be enough to hide his face from the attention he was about to receive, so he found a towel in the kitchen and tied it around the lower half of his face, bank robber-style.

With the girl in his arms again, he exited the apartment and descended the stairs to the crowded second floor. When the partygoers on the landing noticed he was holding someone, they backed away a few feet and stared. Within seconds, a ripple of concern rushed through the corridor.

"What's going on?" a guy with long sideburns and a starter mustache asked. "Is she all right?"

"What's with the mask?" the blonde girl with him asked.

In a loud voice, Joel said, "Does anyone know this girl?"

Those nearest now took a good look at her. Though most shook their heads, a brown-haired girl with freckles said, "That's Sandra. Sandra, um, Wilson, I think."

Another murmur moved down the hall as the name was shared from person to person.

Someone near the middle of the pack yelled, "Sandra?" This was followed by the same voice urgently saying, "Let us through!"

Two girls and a guy pushed their way to the front of the crowd. When they saw Sandra, they rushed over.

"What happened?" the boy asked.

"What did you do to her?" one of the girls said.

"*I* didn't do anything."

"Then what the hell happened?" the second girl asked.

MINE

"Take her," Joel said, and transferred the girl to the boy's arms. "If you're really her friends, you'll get her to a doctor right away. I think she may have been drugged. I don't know."

He could feel the crowd tense as someone shouted, "You drugged her?"

Teeth clenched, Joel said, "I found her."

"Where?"

Joel looked at Sandra's friends. "You're wasting time. Get her out of here."

The boy looked at him, unsure, but the first girl said, "He's right. Let's go."

The three headed down the stairs.

Joel turned to follow them, but someone grabbed his arm and twisted him back around. Another guy reached for the towel covering his face, but Joel grabbed his wrist and squeezed hard enough to show he could break it.

The student who'd spun him around said, "If you had something to do with this—"

"I told you. I found her."

"Where?"

An image. Shirtless saying, "It was just a joke."

It had *not* been a joke. And Joel was sure, despite the promise he'd extracted, it would not be the last time the a-hole and his friends tried something like this. Unless someone stopped them.

"Apartment three-nineteen," he said.

"Three-nineteen? That's—"

"That prick!" a woman yelled.

Several members of the crowd surged up the stairs, and in the ensuing chaos, Joel made his way out of the building.

Thirty-one

OVER THE FOLLOWING days, the three students who had been in apartment 319 were arrested and subsequently expelled from the university after a cache of illicit videos were discovered on their computers. Rumors soon spread that the videos were homemade sex tapes of the trio with unsuspecting women, something that was confirmed when charges were filed a week later.

There were other arrests, too. Several people who had confronted the perpetrators were facing assault charges, as the three suspects had been badly beaten when the police arrived. It wouldn't be long, however, before news sources reported that these latter charges had been dropped due to lack of evidence.

THIRTY-TWO

JOEL SAW SANDRA Wilson several times over the remainder of that school year. Once he even bumped into her at the bookstore and said, "Excuse me."

She smiled, said, "No problem," and went about her business.

Outwardly, at least, she seemed unaffected by the events in apartment 319. It probably helped that hers had not been one of the videos the police discovered. Joel had snapped the memory card into small pieces and ripped the phone apart as soon as he returned to his apartment. For good measure, he had thrown the pieces out in separate trash bins around town.

THIRTY-THREE

Leah

THE COLORS AND shapes of Leah's initial enhanced dreams never returned. Now each time she had one, it involved the real world and bad situations that needed correcting.

And, of course, Joel.

That was fine—more than fine. Every moment she was able to spend with Joel was a gift. Knowing he was out there experiencing much of the same things she was made her feel less alone. The missions she led him on were dangerous, yes, but he was never outmatched and he never failed.

The only annoyance was that she couldn't tell him she was his guide. She tried. God, yes, she tried, but the force that connected them turned her mute at each attempt.

She told herself it was for the best, that if he knew she was the voice in his head, she might become a distraction and keep him from completing his task. She mostly believed it.

But *she* didn't have to remain in the dark about *him*, and she set about learning as much as she could about his life.

This was no easy task. The dreams contained little excess time in which she could poke around looking for clues. An online search would have been easier, except she couldn't for the life of her remember his last name. This didn't keep her from trying, of course. And failing.

She did, however, figure out he'd somehow left high school early and was attending Stanford University, which explained why the weather in her dreams seldom matched that of her hometown. She envied him his college life and the educational challenges it presented. Of course, she only had herself to blame for not being in the same position.

Enough was enough.

On May 2, near the end of her junior year and almost three months after she'd reestablished contact with Joel, she took the SATs. Originally, her plan had been to achieve a score consistent with her school performance. Not anymore.

She might not be able to graduate early, but she could do everything in her power from this point forward to up her standing. Though she knew it was a long shot, her goal was to be accepted at Stanford. Joel would be a senior when she started, but that wouldn't matter. She'd find him and together they could figure out what was affecting them.

She finished each section of the test long before any of the other students. During the instructions at the beginning, they had been encouraged to use any extra time to go back over their answers, but Leah didn't need to do that. She knew all her responses were correct and the essay she'd written was excellent.

So when the results arrived that summer and she learned she'd received a perfect score, it was no surprise. Rather, it was no surprise to her. Her parents, on the other hand, were both stunned and excited.

"I am *so* proud of you." Her father beamed. "This is incredible."

"I knew you were smart, sweetheart, but wow," her mother said.

The administration at Verde High School was also surprised, though their reaction was not quite the same as her parents'. On the first day of her senior year, she was called into the counseling office and taken into a room where her counselor, the senior counselor, the vice principal in charge of academics, and the principal all waited. Moments after she sat down, her father was also ushered in.

"Dad? What are you doing here?"

"Good question." He looked at the others. "What's this all about?"

"We just have a few…things that we need to clear up," Leah's counselor, Ms. Mead, said.

"What things?"

Obviously uncomfortable, Ms. Mead glanced at the senior counselor, Mr. Harvey.

He cleared his throat, then smiled and opened the folder in front of him. "First, we'd like to congratulate you, Ms. Bautista, on your perfect SAT score. That's an incredible accomplishment."

"Thank you," Leah said cautiously.

"We've been told that out of the students who took the test on the same day as you, only one other person in the entire country had a perfect score, and for the whole year there have only been five."

"Is that true?" Leah's father asked.

"It is," Principal Munson said. She smiled. "Leah here is actually the first student from Verde High to receive a perfect score."

"Ever?"

"Ever."

Leah's father grinned at his daughter. The reactions of the others were more reserved, however, and when he noticed this, his smile dimmed. "Is there something wrong? You're not going to tell us there's been a mistake, are you?"

"No *mistake*," Mr. Harvey said.

Leah's dad frowned. "Then what's the problem?"

For a moment, it seemed as if no one was going to answer, then Vice Principal Iger leaned forward. "Don't misunderstand us. We are very excited. We just need to make sure the score is, well, legitimate."

Leah's dad narrowed his eyes. "Legitimate? Why wouldn't it—"

Leah put a hand on his arm. "Dad, they want to know if I cheated."

"What? Why would they think that?" he asked her. He looked back at the others. "Why would you think she cheated?"

The principal held up her palm in an attempt to calm him. "We're not saying that she did. But there are enough factors that we need to look into it."

"What *factors*?"

"Well, her performance in school, for one," Iger said.

"What are you talking about? Leah gets great grades."

"*Good* grades," Iger corrected him, adding, "Grades better than the majority of our other students, to be sure. But not grades that we would generally expect would lead to a perfect SAT score."

"So what?"

"We've had some excellent students here over the years," Harvey said. "Many who maintained well over a four-point-oh average, and none of them ever achieved a perfect score."

"That's what you're basing your accusations on?" Leah's dad stood up. "Come on, honey. I'm sure you have a class you should be in."

"No one's accusing her, Mr. Bautista," the principal said. "But we wouldn't be doing our job if we didn't investigate, that's all."

"It sounds like an accusation to me! Leah, let's go."

Leah remained where she was and said matter-of-factly, "I didn't cheat."

"Of course you didn't, sweetheart. Now come on."

"No. I didn't cheat, Dad. Let them ask whatever they want."

Her father hesitated a moment before sitting back down. "All right. But if I think their minds are already made up, I'm shutting this down."

"No one has their mind made up," Principal Munson said.

From the smile on Vice Principal Iger's face, Leah knew that wasn't true. She was also pretty sure he was the one behind this.

"Perhaps you can tell us why you did so well," Iger said.

Leah locked eyes with him. "I read the questions and put down the correct answer."

"We all understand. Getting into a good school is not easy, and you want to do everything you can to get yourself noticed. So it's understandable that you might try…unconventional methods to pass."

Leah's father leaned forward. "That's totally out of—"

"The only thing I did, Mr. Iger, is study," Leah said. "I'm

pretty sure that's not unconventional."

"So you took one of those cram courses, then?"

"No. I studied like I always do. At home. Alone. There was nothing on the test I didn't already know."

"Hold on," Iger said. He glanced through his file and then looked at Harvey. "Where's her class history?"

Harvey went through his papers and handed a couple of sheets to the vice principal.

Iger studied them and said, "I happen to know there were math questions on the test that your class will only start covering this term."

"My *class* will only start covering them," Leah said. "That doesn't mean I didn't study them already."

"Are you saying you taught yourself?"

"That's exactly what I'm saying."

He leaned back. "Leah, it's important we be truthful here. So I'm going to give you another chance. How did you—"

"That's enough!" Leah's dad said, standing again. "Honey, we are leaving *now*." He looked at the others. "I'm officially excusing my daughter from school today. She and I are going to stop in and have a talk with my lawyer and then pay a visit to the district office."

Leah, still seated, stared at Vice Principal Iger. "I can prove it."

Iger furrowed his brow. "How do you plan on doing that?"

"Leah!" her dad said.

"Simple. Give me a test. Any test you want. I don't even care what subject. If I get even one answer wrong, you can tell the SAT people that I admitted to cheating and they can throw out my score."

"Oh, no," her dad said. "That is *not* going to happen. You earned that score and you're going to keep it."

Eyes still on Iger, Leah said, "You're right, Dad. I am going to keep it."

She could feel him looking at her. After a moment, he leaned down and whispered in her ear, "Sweetheart, you don't have to prove anything to these people."

"I know," she said. "Just trust me, okay?"

He remained standing for a few seconds longer before he retook his seat. "Well?" he said. "Are you going to give her a test or what?"

There was some disagreement at first among the administrators about whether or not they should do it. Harvey and especially Iger were against it, both saying they should take more time to look into the matter.

It was Principal Munson who had the final say. "If she wants to take a test, then give her a test."

Leah ended up taking not one test, but two. The first was a practice SAT that hadn't been in use for a few years. When she aced it in record time, Iger argued she must have used a copy of it when she'd been preparing. And while her father pointed out there was nothing wrong with that, Leah came up with another solution by suggesting they give her an AP Calculus test. Since she was only about to start Pre-Calculus that term, the subject should be beyond her scope of knowledge. Her father was even more against this, but she was adamant.

Iger himself retrieved the test from the math department and dropped it on the desk in front of her. "It's the end-of-the-year test, and don't forget, in the free response section you need to show your work."

Leah shrugged, picked up a pencil, and began.

AP Calculus finals were allotted just over three hours, and even then few students ever finished the entire test. Leah completed it after one hour and thirty-four minutes. She handed the test to Mr. Harvey, who was acting proctor. The head counselor called the others back in.

Iger flipped through the pages and then looked at her. "We'll get this graded and get back to you."

"No," Leah's dad said. "You'll grade it now, in front of us."

"It's not my subject."

"Then get someone whose subject it is. We'll wait."

Iger looked like he was going to say something again, but Principal Munson stopped him. "It seems only fair. I believe Mrs. Jans is free this period."

Looking less than pleased, Iger headed for the door, test in hand.

"No," Leah's dad said. "Leave that here."

Principal Munson stifled an amused smile as Iger tossed the test down on the table.

He returned five minutes later with Mrs. Jans, one of the math teachers. She went over the test question by question. When she was done, there wasn't a red mark anywhere.

"Perfect," she said, then looked at Leah. "Well done. I'm very impressed."

"Thanks," Leah said.

"Are you sure?" Iger asked. "Did you check her work?"

"This isn't the first time I've ever graded a test. It's perfect." Mrs. Jans handed the test to Iger. "If you don't mind, I need to finish prepping for my class now."

With that, she left.

"It's obvious this meeting was completely unnecessary," Principal Munson said. "Ms. Bautista, Mr. Bautista, you have my sincerest apologies. If you wish to file a formal complaint, I will completely understand."

"Damn right, we do," Leah's dad said.

"No," Leah said, "we don't."

She stared at her dad until his anger ebbed.

"Fine," he said. "But if there are any future problems because of this…"

"There won't be," Munson told him. "Will there, Mr. Iger?"

Though Iger mumbled, "No," Leah was sure he still thought she had conned them.

"Leah," the principal said, "I think it might be a good idea for you to get together with Ms. Mead when you have a few moments, and see if we can get you into some more appropriate classes."

In the back of her mind, Leah could hear her old above-average-but-not-too-above-average self say, "No, thank you. I'd like to stay in the classes I have." But that persona no longer held sway.

She smiled. "I have time right now."

THIRTY-FOUR

ONE OF THE predictable results of Leah upping her academic game was what she had always feared.

One by one her friends began distancing themselves from her. They'd been okay with her gradually increasing intelligence, and had even accepted the little quirky things she could do faster than anyone else. But when she made the leap from acceptable smart to unexpected genius, they didn't know how to handle it. Maybe if she had only switched to a few harder classes, they could have made the adjustment. Or if her perfect SAT score had been the only issue—a fluke, Leah could have called it. But together the changes made even the smartest kids in school look at her as if she weren't entirely human.

It was for the best, however. She could still handle her new classes with ease, but they did require additional time. And then there were the dreams that seemed to be coming more often.

Soon the time to apply for college arrived. At the top of her list was, of course, Stanford. To hedge her bets, she also applied to Berkeley, San Jose State, and San Francisco State. After thinking about it, she included a fifth school, UC Santa Cruz. This last was a bit farther away from Stanford than she would have liked, but it would still put her in the general area.

Her parents were less than enthusiastic about her desire to go to school in California. There was the expense, they argued, and the distance from home. They insisted she apply to some closer universities. Dutifully, she filled out applications for Colorado State and the University of Colorado Boulder, and had her mom and dad sign them, but she never sent them in.

Her first response came right before Christmas break—

San Jose State. The school was happy to inform her she had been accepted into the incoming fall class, and told her to look for the financial-aid letter that would arrive within a month. Said letter showed up on January 21, the same day she received responses from UC Santa Cruz and San Francisco State. The San Jose State scholarship money was better than she'd hoped for and severely undercut her parents' argument regarding the cost. As for the other two colleges, San Francisco State accepted her, while Santa Cruz declined due to her less than stellar grades in her first three years of high school.

One week later, the letter from Berkeley arrived. Since the school was her second choice, she decided not to open the letter until she'd heard from Stanford. On February 7, she came home from school and finally found the letter she'd been waiting for.

For over an hour and a half, she sat on her bed, the envelopes from Stanford and Berkeley side by side in front of her. She kept going back and forth about which she should open first, and finally decided it made more sense to start with Berkeley. But as she reached for it, she changed her mind and snatched up the one from Stanford.

She sliced it open with a pair of scissors and let the contents fall onto the bed. Only a single piece of paper was inside. She told herself the number of pages meant nothing, but from previous experience she knew that wasn't true.

Within two lines, she knew her plan of going to school with Joel was not going to happen. It felt as if the floor had opened up beneath her, dropping her into a chasm that stretched all the way through the center of the earth and out the other side. For months now, she'd been daydreaming about a future that included walking across campus with Joel as he helped ease her into college life.

She fell onto her side and curled up crying.

As smart as she was, she'd been such an idiot. If she hadn't played down her intelligence from the beginning, she would have been accepted. She might have even been able to leave high school early like Joel had, and would have already been in California with him for a year or two. She had screwed things up for herself merely to fit in.

At least two Bay Area universities still wanted her.

She blinked and sat up.

In her disappointment, she'd forgotten about the Berkeley letter. She snatched it up and opened it.

> Dear Miss Bautista,
> It is my pleasure to offer you admission to the University of California, Berkeley, for the fall semester.

Leah had to read the letter four times before she believed it. It wasn't Stanford, but it was a great alternative. Most of the rest of the letter was the same kind of general information that had been in her other two yes responses. The exception was the paragraph near the end.

> You should know that one of the determining factors in our decision was the recommendation of Berkeley alumni Kari Munson. She made it very clear that your grades prior to your senior year didn't reflect your true story, and that you are potentially the smartest student to have ever passed through her school. We look forward to you being one of the smartest we've had here, too.

Principal Munson? But Leah never asked her for a recommendation. She didn't even know the principal was a Berkeley alum. It must have been Ms. Mead who told her Leah was applying there. Leah's counselor was the only one in administration who knew. Whatever the case, a huge thank you was in order.

As excited as she was, she decided it was best to wait until she heard about financial aid before letting her parents know.

In bed that night, she reread the Berkeley letter over and over. It was her ticket to finding Joel and her future, two things she was beginning to think might actually be the same.

As her eyes finally grew heavy, she felt a tingling across her back.

Dream night. Why didn't I feel it earlier?

Or did she?

She'd been on such an emotional roller coaster since coming home, maybe she'd blocked it out. Whatever the reason, it didn't matter. To visit Joel in her dreams on the very day she'd learned their physical separation wouldn't last much longer seemed perfect.

Too bad she was wrong.

THIRTY-FIVE

Joel

TWO QUESTIONS DOGGED Joel during his last year of undergraduate study: which graduate school was he hoping to attend? What subject would be his focus?

His mother wanted him to go to medical school and become a doctor. His professors were split into several camps, including theoretical physics, particle physics, astrophysics, and chemistry. One suggested he consider architecture, while another was sure he'd be a natural at economics.

The truth was, he'd already studied most of those subjects enough that if he composed a dissertation for each right then, they would all pass critical review.

But there were expectations to fulfill and paths to follow, even for prodigies. So he applied to all the right schools and decided he'd make his decision once he knew who wanted him.

He received his first response on a Tuesday only three and a half weeks after he sent in his applications. Two more came the following day, and the fourth the day after that.

Much to his mother's chagrin, he refused to open any of them until he received answers to all his inquiries.

"What if some of them are time sensitive?" she argued. "You might miss an opportunity."

"Then I miss an opportunity. This is the way I want to do it."

A year or two earlier, she might have been able to pressure him into changing his mind. But he was nearly eighteen now and had sloughed off most of his obedient adolescence.

Between Friday and Saturday, six additional letters came,

bringing the total to ten. That left five outstanding, including the ones from the three schools in Europe.

On Sunday, his mother could barely contain herself. She was all energy, flittering around the apartment, cleaning things she'd already cleaned and cooking enough food to last them at least a week.

Even with the door to his room closed that evening, he could *feel* her. Finally, unable to take it anymore, he grabbed his laptop, shoved it in his backpack, and left without saying a word.

His intention was to go to the library to finish a paper that was due in a few weeks. He was only a block from campus when—

Go right.

The voice.

He stopped dead in his tracks.

He hadn't woken with any breaks or bruises or cuts that morning. Never before had he heard the voice without those coming first.

Go right, the voice repeated.

As he turned right, the mental map appeared and showed him where to go. He was used to this now. Since the Sandra Wilson incident, he'd been visited by the voice at least once a month. Few of the assignments—as he came to think of them—had been as bad as that first night, but they hadn't exactly been easy, either. A convenience store robbery quickly thwarted, a teenage fight halted, and multiple nonsexual assaults stopped.

The one that had probably reached the same disturbing level as Sandra's involved the kid. A boy eight years old lured into the car of a man claiming to be a friend of the kid's parents. Joel hadn't been able to stop the abduction, but the voice had guided him to the man's house, where Joel was waiting when the guy pulled his car into the garage. The kid was seen safely home, while the man was found by the police tied up, broken, and unconscious on the floor of his kitchen.

Currently the map was guiding him through a residential area and onto a street where several shops were located. The glowing red dot corresponded to a yogurt place across the street, but as Joel dodged between cars to get there, the dot moved.

Now it was in the alley behind the store.

Hurry.

He could circle around the block and enter the alley from either end or run through the yogurt store. Though he might meet some resistance from the staff, the latter was the most direct route.

He adjusted his hoodie, pulled over his face the scarf he now always kept with him, and ran into the store. Yogurt machines lined one wall and tables the other. At the back was a cash register, a scale for weighing the product, and a bored-looking red-headed girl talking to an equally bored-looking black-haired boy. To the left of the counter was an opening to the back with a placard overhead reading RESTROOMS.

Hurry.

As Joel passed beneath the sign, the girl said, "Hey, those are for customers only."

"Was he wearing a mask?" her coworker asked.

Joel ran past the restrooms and straight out the back door. As he stepped into the alley, the dot in his head began moving again. To the left and fast.

Turning, he spotted one of those big cars from the last century—a Cadillac or Pontiac or something like that—turning out of the alley and speeding away.

Hurry.

The dot in his head was traveling so fast now that even as he ran toward the alley exit, the distance between him and the dot kept increasing. He rounded the corner and stopped. The car was out of sight.

Hurry.

"How?" he pleaded.

A new dot appeared on his map. Blue and blinking and stationary, it hovered over a residential street in San Jose, twenty miles to the southeast. It was similar to the dot that had helped him save the abducted boy, but it was so much farther away.

"How am I going to get there?" he whispered.

Hurry.

His only chance was a taxi, but there were none on this street, so he raced to the next corner and looked both ways. Parked at the curb half a block down sat a Prius taxi, its service light off and its driver behind the wheel looking at his phone.

Joel rushed over and tapped on the window.

Without looking up, the driver shook his head and said, "Off duty."

"Please. I need a ride."

"I said off duty."

Joel pulled out his wallet and counted his cash. "Seventy-eight dollars and forty-two cents if you take me to San Jose right now." He could hit an ATM later to get home.

The guy looked at him, his face tired. "Off duty means I'm not working."

Taking a cue from countless movies and TV shows, Joel said, "You can leave the meter off. It's all yours." When the driver said nothing, he added, "Please. It's important."

The man stared at him for a moment longer, and then rolled his eyes and nodded toward the backseat. "Get in."

Hurry.

Joel gave the cabbie the address and off they went.

Closing his eyes, he checked his mental map. Three dots were on it now. One for the San Jose location, one for the big car, and a yellow one for the cab Joel was in. At its current pace, the other vehicle would reach the blue dot a good five minutes before Joel arrived.

"Can we go any faster?" he asked the driver.

"Not for seventy-eight bucks."

"Come on, please. I'm begging you."

Another frown was followed by the Prius increasing its speed by three miles per hour.

Seriously? Joel thought, but refrained from pushing again in case the guy decided Joel wasn't worth the trouble and dropped him off at the bottom of the next exit.

They took the 101 past Mountain View, Sunnyvale, and Santa Clara, and exited near the San Jose airport. That's when the blue dot winked out. A second later, a new one appeared, also in San Jose, but in a different area.

Hurry.

"I, uh, I just realized I gave you the wrong address," Joel said.

The cabbie looked at him in the rearview mirror. "What?"

Joel told him the new location. "It's about the same distance, so shouldn't make a difference, right?"

"Kid, if you're trying to pull something…"

Joel leaned forward and dropped his money on the front passenger seat. "I'm not trying to pull anything. I'm just—" He took a breath. "It's an emergency."

The cabbie started to pull to the curb.

"What are you doing?" Joel asked.

"I don't know where this is. I got to input it into my nav."

"I'll direct you."

The man gave him another look, and then sped back up. "All right. Where are we going?"

Joel guided him through the city into an area of business parks and workshops and distribution centers.

"There," Joel said, pointing at a group of metal buildings ahead.

After the cab pulled over, the driver looked around and said, "You sure this is where you want to go?"

At this time of night, most of the buildings were dark, the only light coming from street lamps and a few security floodlights.

"Yeah," Joel said as he hopped out of the car. "Thanks."

Joel's destination was not the place he'd told the cabbie it was, but rather a windowless building across the street and half a block down.

Hurry!

There was more urgency in the voice than Joel had ever heard before. He crossed the street and raced over to the building. Attached to the front above a large garage-type door was a sign that read PHILLIPS MACHINE WORKS.

Joel looked down one side. It was a solid wall, no entrances or windows and no big car parked nearby.

"What do I do?" he asked.

Hurry!

The garage door?

He ran over and spotted a pair of damp tire tracks running into the building. The big car was *inside*.

He scanned the door but found no way to open it, so he hustled to the far corner and searched the other side.

Joel, there's no time. Hurry!

A quarter of the way down was a set of double doors nearly as tall as the wall. He raced over and tried them, but they were locked. At a loss, he stepped back. That's when he noticed the beam jutting out of the building at the very top of the doors. A hoist of some sort.

Joel!

The hole the beam stuck out of was wider than the beam itself. Remnants of a rubber seal meant to cover the gap filled some of the opening, but much of the seal had rotted away. If he could get up there, he should be able to slip inside.

Hurry, Joel! Please!

A ladder would have been great, but none was around. There were, however, some pipes attached to the wall near the door that, if he was creative, he could use to climb up.

He slipped once but caught himself before he fell, and then continued on. The frame at the top of the doors was just wide enough for him to get half the sole of his shoe on. He inched his way across it to the beam by keeping one hand on the roofline and the other above his head to maintain his center of gravity.

Now! Now! Now!

The moment he reached the hole around the beam, he shoved his head through the gap. Immediately he heard the sound of someone crying in pain. He worked his shoulders inside, and then shoved against the interior wall to pull the rest of his body through.

The room was a maze of machinery, much of it old and covered with dust and cobwebs. Though dozens of work lamps hung from the ceiling, only three were on, creating an undulating vista of deep shadows and weak light.

More sounds—mechanical, an electric motor and pistons;

and human, slapping and punching—all coming from the back of the facility.

The area directly below Joel was empty, but even with his superior abilities, he knew he'd break a leg or more if he jumped. Near the center, however, were several machines he could drop onto.

He made his way quickly along the beam in a crouch, slowing only to work his way around the occasional support anchors hanging from the ceiling. As he lowered himself onto an industrial cutter, an electric motor at the back of the room began to whine.

Oh, God. Too late, Joel. You're too late.

He scrambled across the machine and dropped the final few feet to the concrete floor. As suddenly as it came on, the motor went silent and a hush fell over the shop.

In all of Joel's outings since the voice had first come to him, he had never failed to accomplish the task it gave him, so he refused to believe he would do so now.

He wove around the machines until he heard someone humming a string of random notes, as though unaware he was making any noise at all.

It's over. Get out.

Joel had always obeyed the voice before, but not this time. He homed in on the sound, creeping forward until it was only a dozen feet away. Light hit the area at an angle that created long shadows, giving him plenty of darkness to hide in, and allowing him to peek unnoticed around the machine he was crouched beside.

A man, maybe five foot eight if he was lucky, was cleaning off a large flat metal table—with a cloth that sounded wet. He appeared to be in decent shape, the arms sticking out of his black T-shirt having seen some weight training. His hair, either dark brown or black, was cut high and tight. His face was unremarkable.

Joel crept backward and circled to the other side for a better view.

Don't, Joel. Please. Just go!

As he moved forward again, he saw why the voice wanted

him to stop. On the floor next to the table lay the body of a woman, but not just any woman.

No. Turn back.

Though she was bloodied and damaged in ways that made his stomach churn, he still recognized her. Sandra Wilson. The girl from apartment 319. There was no question she was dead. Her head was turned farther than anyone could survive.

He stared at her, unable to move, unable to understand why or how this could have happened. Had she been fated to die no matter what he did? Or had she just been in the wrong place twice? His guilt at his failure leaned toward the former, while his gut leaned toward the latter. The only way to know for sure was for it to happen again.

Get out. There's nothing here for you to do.

That was where the voice was wrong.

Joel eased into position behind the man and purposely scraped his foot across the floor.

Sandra's killer whirled around, a bloody rag in his hand. For a moment, their eyes locked, and then the man threw the rag at Joel and ran.

Joel easily moved out of the cloth's path and chased the man around the machines.

The dust on the floor did the man in. As he tried to take a sharp turn around one of the giant devices, his foot slipped out from under him. He threw out a hand to stop his fall. It glanced against a power button, turning a machine on, and then landed on a flat surface. He tried to jerk his hand back, but was unable to clear it out of the way before a metal plate slammed down on it.

Joel arrived a second later and hit the off button so that the plates didn't separate. The man, his pancaked arm caught inside, dangled against the machine, barely conscious.

Now Joel knew why he hadn't woken with any injuries. The man had done this to himself. Joel was tempted to finish the job, but unlike the monster before him, he was no killer.

Though Joel knew it was unnecessary, he confirmed Sandra was dead. Then, using wires he found on one of the worktables, he tied the man to the machine just in case he somehow managed to free himself, and then used the man's own phone to call the police.

When he heard the sirens, he quietly made his way to the Caltrain station.

THIRTY-SIX

ACQUIESCING TO HIS mother's wishes, Joel accepted a position in the medical program at Johns Hopkins University. She was too happy to notice he didn't share her joy.

Though his grades during his final months at Stanford didn't fall, a few of his professors did notice a curtailing of his involvement in class discussions. Joel was just doing time.

At graduation, he went through the ceremony for his parents' sake. Afterward he and his mother and father, who had flown in for the event, had a nice dinner at a seafood restaurant in San Francisco, overlooking the bay. They discussed Joel's cross-country move to Maryland, and his mother's reluctance to let him go alone.

"He's only eighteen," she argued. "And he's going to be busier now than ever. He's going to need someone around."

His father insisted it was time for their son to "spread his wings" and "embrace his independence."

Joel nodded when he needed to nod and smiled when he needed to smile, and politely agreed that maybe it was time for him to be on his own.

Back at the apartment, they opened champagne. Joel took a few sips to make it look good. His parents, on the other hand, finished off the first bottle and made a pretty good dent in a second.

When Joel rose the next morning, he was not surprised to find them still asleep. He showered and dressed and picked up the backpack that held the few things important to him.

Then he walked out the front door and never returned.

THIRTY-SEVEN

Leah

LEAH STAYED HOME "sick" for three days after the death of Sandra Wilson.

She knew Joel's inability to get to the girl on time was her fault. She had guided him to the alley behind the yogurt shop to stop the kidnapping, when what she really should have done was send him directly to San Jose, so he would have been there when the killer arrived.

Leah wasn't sure what Joel had done to the man. She had kept yelling at him to get out of there. But she could feel he was no longer listening, and then, as he closed in on the man, her connection to Joel simply stopped.

The answer was only a few clicks away on her computer, but she couldn't bring herself to check. Reading a news story about Sandra would only add to Leah's devastation.

She returned to school numb to nearly everything but her personal torment, and had to focus harder than ever to keep her grades from slipping. She couldn't jeopardize her move to California. She knew Joel would be as distraught as she was, and would need her as much as she needed him. So she labored through the final months of her senior year, aced all her finals, and graduated with honors.

June and July were spent cleaning out her room, figuring out what she was going to take to college, and earning a little extra money at her summer library job. Not once during this time did she have a single enhanced dream. She tried not to let that bother her, told herself it was a normal lull, but in her quiet moments the lack of the dreams terrified her.

On August 18, exactly four days before she was allowed to move into her dorm room, Leah and her father set out in her used and jam-packed Honda Civic on the thirteen-hundred-mile drive to Berkeley.

When the big day came, her dad helped her transfer all her things to her room. She met her roommate, Naomi Dinh, and Naomi's parents. Like most of the other students moving in, Naomi was all smiles and excitement. Leah shared some of that feeling, but mainly she was anxious to drive down to Stanford.

From the missions she'd undertaken with Joel, she'd been able to finally piece together where he lived, so she planned on going straight to his apartment at her first opportunity. But that trip should wait until after her father had left for home. She went out to dinner with him and made plans to meet for breakfast the next morning, after which she would take him to the airport.

The urge to head to Stanford took hold of her moments after she dropped off her dad at the hotel. She fought it for a few blocks, but soon found herself on the I-80, driving across the Bay Bridge.

It was just past 8:30 p.m. when she reached the street where Joel lived. After spending a few minutes finding a parking spot, she walked to his building. If she'd had any lingering doubt about her dreams being real, they were gone now. She recognized everything. Even many of the cars parked along the road were ones she'd seen before.

Her plan, what little she'd come up with during the drive, was not to visit him tonight. If she did, they might end up talking until morning and then she'd be a wreck when she met up with her father. She wanted to just *be* on his street, and *see* his place, hoping that would ease some of her impatience.

But hasty plans were easy to break, and it didn't take much to convince herself she could at least check out the lobby of his building. As she knew it would be, the front door was unlocked. The lobby was exactly as she'd seen it, large with a locked door opposite the entrance that led to the rest of the building. She was actually here. *Inside.*

Beside the locked door hung a directory of residents, with

call buttons by each name. As she ran her finger down this list, the names seemed to come alive—BAUDLER, BROUGHAN, DOLPHUS, GORMAN, HILDRETH, KURDLE, GABOURY, MAJOR, STUFFLEBEAM, UTTERBACK.

Wait.

She stared at the list, her eyes momentarily unfocused. Though she still couldn't remember Joel's last name, she was positive none of the ones here belonged to him.

Panic started to set in.

Hold on, hold on. Apartment number. She closed her eyes and pictured the door outside Joel's apartment: *203.*

She looked for the corresponding number on the list. STUFFLEBEAM. That was definitely not his last name. Did his mother have a different one than he did? Leah had never seen his father around so maybe his parents were divorced and his mother had gone back to her maiden name.

Go home, Leah. Send your dad off, then settle in and come back when you have some time.

It was a good thought, maybe even the right one, but her feet wouldn't budge.

She checked the time—8:43. Bordering on late for a visitor, but not too late, right?

Before she could talk herself out of it, she pushed the button next to STUFFLEBEAM 203.

A ring blared from a tinny speaker, then a click. "Yes?"

The voice was female, adult but young sounding.

"Hi, yes, um, I'm looking for Joel," Leah said.

"Sorry, you got the wrong place."

"Hold on, is this apartment two-oh-three?"

"Yeah."

"May I ask how long you've lived there?"

A pause, but then instead of an answer, the line went dead.

Leah pushed the button again, but this time it only rang and rang.

She took another look at the list, searching for a building manager, but found nothing.

As she walked back to her car, a thought hit her. Joel was eighteen now like she was. He would have likely not wanted to live with his mother anymore, which meant he'd probably moved into his own place, something smaller, maybe closer to the other students.

Of course.

It would take a little more work to find him, but she headed back to Berkeley feeling that everything would be fine.

LEAH'S FEAR OF spending most of that night awake came true, but instead of missing out on sleep because she was catching up with Joel, the time was spent getting to know Naomi and a few of the girls from nearby rooms. In the morning, once she'd had breakfast with her dad and taken him to the airport, she dragged herself back to her dorm and fell fast asleep, wasting a whole day she could have used to find Joel.

It turned out not to matter, though. Joel wasn't living in another Stanford-area apartment or a dorm room. He had *graduated* the spring before, finishing school in near record time.

It had taken Leah two and a half weeks to dig up that fact. The only helpful bit of information she learned was his last name: Madsen.

She didn't give up. She was sure someone at Stanford knew where he'd gone. But another month filled with back-and-forth trips between Berkeley and Stanford proved her wrong. Joel had been accepted into several graduate programs, including one right there at Stanford, but he had apparently not joined any of them and no one had a clue as to where he was now.

Desperate, she turned to the only resource she had left—her dreams. Up to this point, she had never tried to force herself into one of them. They'd come to her at will, and she'd always assumed she had no control over them. But it had been nearly nine months since her last one. Nine months since she'd had any contact with Joel.

Starting that night, she tried to bring one on. If she could reestablish contact with him, she could hopefully figure out where he was. But night after night her attempts ended with her falling into an exhausted, dreamless sleep.

After a while a thought began creeping into her mind. What if the failure to save Sandra had been too much for Joel? What if it had crushed his will to go on?

What if he, too, were dead?

No! He can't be!

But what if?

On the twenty-second consecutive day of trying, a Tuesday, Leah closed her eyes, concentrated her thoughts, and focused on rekindling the dream. This time something was different about the darkness that encompassed her. It had always been empty before. Tonight, something was there. Something as black as the void, but solid.

A wall, she realized, that seemed to run forever in both directions.

She rubbed a hand against it. It felt miles thick and as solid as anything ever made, like nothing real or imagined could ever dent it. She pounded on it anyway. It didn't even make a sound. Moving along the surface, she kept knocking on it, knowing she had to get to the other side.

A crunch, so slight she was already moving on before she registered it. She looked back and stared at the black mass where she'd last hit it and saw a crack, no thicker or longer than an eyelash.

She hit it again. And again. And again.

The crack spread and divided until it filled the shape of an arched doorway.

One more hit and the wall within the arched space crumbled, revealing a tunnel.

Without hesitation, she stepped inside.

She seemed to walk for hours, before she finally emerged on the other side and entered what turned out to be a small room lit only by the glow of a laptop computer. The device sat on a desk, the chair in front of it empty. Tucked in the corner of the room was a narrow bed, unmade and unoccupied. Spiderwebs hung from the walls, and the only window looked out at a dark night through grimy panes.

"Go away."

Leah twisted around.

Joel stood near the room's only door. Like the first time she'd come to him through her dreams, he was looking toward her but not quite at her.

"Joel?"

"Go away."

"Joel. It's me…" She tried to say her name, but as in the past, her voice went silent.

"I don't care who you are. Go!"

With a sudden roar, he threw his arms up and ran in the direction he'd been looking. Reflexively, Leah jerked to the side.

He stopped a few feet past her and yelled without turning back. "Go away! Get out of my head!"

A flash of light, the most intense ever. She threw an arm over her eyes as her whole body clenched.

"Leah? Leah? Are you okay?"

Leah lifted her arm and found Naomi kneeling beside her bed.

"You scared the crap out of me," Naomi said.

"I did?"

"You started mumbling, then all of a sudden you screamed."

Someone knocked on their door. "Is everything all right in there?" It was Lucy, their resident advisor.

Naomi looked at Leah, raising an eyebrow to silently ask the same thing.

"I'm okay," Leah said. "Just, um, just a bad dream."

"Hey," Lucy called. "What's going on in there?"

Naomi looked at Leah for a second longer, and then went over to the door. She and Lucy talked for a moment, the RA glancing at Leah a couple times before giving Naomi a nod and leaving.

When Naomi returned, she said, "You *are* okay, aren't you?"

"Yeah, I'm sorry. I didn't mean to wake you."

"Please tell me that's not something that happens a lot."

"I've never had a dream like that before," Leah said.

"Good." Naomi sat on her own bed. "My heart's still

pounding."

"I'm really sorry."

"It's okay. I'm glad you're all right."

"Thanks."

After Leah was sure Naomi had fallen back to sleep, she climbed out of bed, pulled on her robe, and went down the hall to the communal bathroom. At this hour, it was mercifully empty. She took the stall at the very end, sat on the toilet, and wept.

She'd been so focused on finding Joel that his rejection gutted her.

"Get out of my head!" he'd screamed.

He doesn't know who you are, she told herself.

"Get out of my head!"

He doesn't know.

"Get out of my head!"

When she could cry no more, she returned to her room, telling herself, *Give him time.*

What other choice did she have?

THIRTY-EIGHT

LEAH GRADUATED FROM Berkeley after four years, with a double major in Psychology and Molecular & Cell Biology.

Her choices of study were purely selfish. She wanted to find answers to what was going on with both her and Joel, and thought the two majors would give her the best tools to do so. She realized fairly early on, though, that to get to the real meat of things, she would have to go to grad school. Luckily for her, Berkeley had programs in both fields. After much contemplation, she decided to focus on molecular & cell biology, as she could more easily continue learning about psychology on her own.

Throughout her undergrad years and at the beginning of grad school, she continued trying to contact Joel, several times each month. She always encountered the wall, though, and not once was she able to crack it again. She realized now she'd been able to pass through it that one time only because Joel let her in so he could tell her to leave him alone.

As much as it hurt, she understood why he felt that way. But ultimately it didn't matter what he wanted. They were linked, and she had to keep trying to find a way back to him.

As a grad student, she shared an apartment off campus with Naomi, who'd become her best friend. It had two bedrooms, with a comfortable living room and a too-small galley kitchen.

Returning home from the library on a cold wet April night, Leah sighed with relief when the warm air of the apartment enveloped her.

"Hey," Naomi called from the couch where she was curled up, watching TV. "I picked up some of that lentil soup you like.

It's in the fridge."

"You are my hero."

Leah shed her jacket and hung it on the rack by the door. She heated up the soup, carried it into the living room, and sat on the sofa next to her friend. As was often the case these days, a show about a real-life criminal investigation was playing. Naomi, who would be starting law school in the fall, couldn't get enough of them.

During commercial breaks, they filled each other in on their mundane days, and laughed again about the awkward date Naomi had gone on the previous weekend. About an hour after she sat down, Leah washed her dishes and went to her room.

While her days were given over to her school studies, her nights—when those studies didn't bleed into them—were filled with non-academic research. Since Joel wouldn't let her back in his head, she'd resorted to looking for him using more traditional methods.

After firing up her laptop, she started as she always did, with a Google search of his name, hoping something new had popped up. But like most nights, the search revealed no new entries, so she moved on, employing targeted data mining programs at various social media sites.

When the screen began to blur, she turned off the computer and pulled out her logbook. Each line on a page represented a different day. She added that day's date at the end of the list, noting what she had checked and how far she had gone. Under the column labeled POTENTIALS, she wrote 0. There were a lot of zeros.

As she closed the book, she repeated her nightly mantra, "I *will* find you," and returned the log to the drawer. Donning her nightshirt, she felt an odd sensation on her shoulders. She tugged at the fabric, thinking maybe a loose thread was rubbing against her, and stepped into the bathroom to brush her teeth.

Her mind already half asleep, she went through her routine—upper molars, bottom, outside, in—and then spit into the sink. When she turned on the water to wash off the toothbrush, the sensation returned, only now it was working its way down her back.

Not just any sensation. A tingling.

It can't be, she thought. It had been so long since she last had the feeling, she'd almost forgotten it.

The sensation spread until it reached her waist. She pulled up her shirt and turned so she could see her back in the mirror. No red blotches, no spreading rash. Everything looked fine.

She told herself the dream couldn't be coming. When she used to get the sensation, it had taken hours for it to spread from her shoulders to her back. What she was feeling now had happened in minutes.

And yet, despite the speed, the feeling was the same.

She walked back into her bedroom, apprehensive. If the wall between her and Joel had come down, that would be a great thing, a cause for celebration. But given the way he had banished her, she'd been sure he would never voluntarily let her back in.

Images began slamming into her mind. Joel sprawled at the bottom of a cliff. Joel crumpled in the wreck of a vehicle. Joel lying in a hospital bed, pale and weak. And Joel in a thousand similar near-death scenarios.

What if he's contacting me to say good-bye?

The tingling intensified, begging her to sleep. She crawled into bed but hesitated before closing her eyes, as if the longer she stayed awake, the longer Joel would stay alive. She was no match for the dream's pull, however. One moment she was staring at the ceiling, the next she was out.

When the dream world materialized around her, however, she didn't find herself at the base of a cliff or beside a flipped car or in an antiseptic room filled with beeping machines. Rather, she was standing in the middle of a violent lightning storm, where white-hot electric arcs struck all around her, blinding her.

Flash.

Flash.

Flash.

Flash.

She tried closing her eyes but her lids wouldn't budge, nor could she move her hands to cover them.

Flash.
Flash.
Flash.
"Stop!" she yelled.
Flash.
"Stop!"
Flash.
"For God's sake, please stop!"

THIRTY-NINE

The Translator

THERE WERE TIMES when the Translator was mostly present and in the solid world. He liked those times. The solid world was where he came from, and where—when he was allowed to dream his own dreams—he wanted to return.

Other times, floating times, he was the box all things flowed through. Information entered his mind, then would be reformed and recalibrated before flying out on its way to the Reclaimer.

::MORE, the Reclaimer would say. It was her second favorite word, and one of the few he'd heard her speak in his native language.

And more he would give.

The information came from many places, much via those the Translator came in contact with day after day. These sources were the easiest to tap into. They never knew they were being used. The Translator would record their lives, and those of the people they came in contact with, and of the people *they* came in contact with, and so on, and so on, the network growing vast and wide. Before the Translator sent the data to the Reclaimer, he converted it into a form she could more readily understand.

He was her conduit.

It was his sole purpose.

The most prolific source of information was not one of those near the Translator. This person was…somewhere else…and set to report in…automatically. The Translator had been instructed to refer to her as Satellite One. There'd been a second Satellite for a while, but that one had stopped reporting long ago. How long? The Translator wasn't sure. Time was…hard for him.

The Satellites had different names, real-people names. The Translator knew what they were, but he kept that knowledge locked so deeply in his mind—to prevent the Reclaimer from realizing he remembered—he actually forgot them most of the time.

The Reclaimer used the Translator as her pathway to instruct the Satellites to LEARN and REPORT. And, like always, she would end each contact with her favorite word, MINE, and leave the Translator to deal with the collection of data.

The Translator's connection to the Satellites, however, went beyond merely acting as their link to the Reclaimer.

They were his…friends.

His *good* friends.

His *only* friends.

And he didn't like how the Reclaimer was using them.

To her they were only funnels for the information she craved as she learned about…everyone and…everything. Though he could not stop the process, he found over time that he could edit the information that passed through him. This allowed him to protect his friends by preventing the Reclaimer from knowing how her augmentations had changed them.

He had taken things a step further. From the safety of the [*secret place*] he'd created for himself out of sight of the Reclaimer, he showed his friends what they could do with their skills, and, when he could, provided guidance on their journeys.

These [*missions*]—as Satellite One called them—and [*assignments*]—as Satellite Two referred to them—he also kept from the Reclaimer. He knew it was a huge risk, but the altered information packets he did forward from the Satellites never seemed to raise any concerns from the Reclaimer. Of course, it was the [*assignments*] that had resulted in Satellite Two's disappearance. The Translator had seen what happened on the last one, seen everything.

Horrible. Horrible.

The Translator was glad that Satellite One, whom he now thought of as only the Satellite, was still connected. She and his [secret place] were the only things that made life bearable. If he could, he would choose to accept data only from her. But the Reclaimer had made it clear from the beginning that the Translator's job was to send whatever the Reclaimer wanted whenever the Reclaimer required it.

And as for his [secret place], it provided the sanctuary he needed to remember the [was] and not think about the [is].

Unfortunately, it had become harder for him to go there as of late. The Reclaimer wanted more and more, eating up much of the little time the Translator had previously used for himself. This meant he had to carefully plan his sneakaways to coincide with times when he was sure she wouldn't suddenly pop into his mind looking for him.

He'd almost been caught once, returning from his hideaway just moments before she came calling. Knowing he could have lost his [secret place] forever was enough to make him avoid it for months before he'd felt safe enough to go again.

::I HAVE MATTERS TO ATTEND, the Reclaimer told him that morning—or was it afternoon? TRANSLATE ANY PACKETS YOU RECEIVE AND PLACE THEM HERE.

In his head he was presented with the familiar image of a large room filled with empty shelves. All he would have to do is think about the room and he could move the packets there. It was a technique the Reclaimer only used when she would be gone for a while.

Yes, Reclaimer, he said.

A pause, and then the questions she always asked before she left.

::ARE YOUR CHANNELS OPEN?

Yes.

::ARE YOUR RECEPTORS WORKING?

Yes.

::ARE ALL LINKS INTACT?

Yes.

There were no other words to mark her departure, just a

sense of empty space in his mind, letting him know he was alone.

He waited for a minute or an hour, he wasn't sure which, and then entered his [*secret place*].

FORTY

Leah

EITHER LEAH'S PLEA had been heard or she had the best timing in the world—which, given her reaction skills, could very well have been the case—because the lightning suddenly stopped, leaving behind a soft glow bright enough for her to see her surroundings.

Though she knew she was in an enhanced dream, it was different from all the others. She was not in the real world where she had visited Joel, nor was she in the land of ribbons and color that she'd found herself in during her first dreams. She was in…

The Secret Place.

The words, though not spoken, infused the space.

She turned in a circle, taking everything in.

A room no larger than her own living room, and yet gigantic. Regardless of which direction she looked in, no more than fifteen feet separated her from the wall in front of her. Yet out of the corners of her eyes, the room appeared to go on and on and on.

Finite and infinite.

Shelves were everywhere, stuffed to overflowing with items familiar and strange, some moving as if alive. There were no doors or windows, only a wall always in front of her and the forever space to the sides.

A tingle, not like the one preceding a dream but deep in her stomach and chest. Someone was here.

"Hello?" she said.

A shuffle.

"Hello?" she repeated.

Movement in the endless space to her left, at the very edge of her sight. She twisted toward it, but the forever hall turned with her, staying out of direct view. She took a calming breath and focused back on her side vision. More movement. Someone was there for sure, small like a toddler.

She stood very still, hoping whoever it was would come closer. For a moment nothing happened, and then the shape began creeping in her direction from one set of shelves to another. The person grew taller and taller with each step, until his head nearly touched the ceiling.

A man, older than the oldest who had ever lived, stared at her.

"Hi," she said softly.

He took a step backward, mumbling under his breath.

"I'm not going to hurt you," she said.

His volume increased, his words coming out in a rush. "Four, three, one, one, one, zero, three, two, zero, four. Seven, one, eight, eight, three, four, one, six, two, zero. Nine, nine, three—"

"Do you have a name?" she asked. "Mine's—"

Clamping a hand over his mouth, he staggered backward and began to shrink and grow younger again.

"No, please, don't go," she said.

"You-you-you should not be," he told her, each word a struggle. "You should not, should not be here."

Except for Joel, she had never communicated with anyone in her dreams. And with him it had been different, not as direct.

"My name's Leah," she said, as calmly as she could. She could feel his fear, and knew one wrong word would send him running. She desperately didn't want that to happen. Whoever this man was, she thought he'd have at least some of the answers as to what had happened to her and Joel.

"You...should not...be...here."

"Where should I be?"

He pointed beyond her. "Apartment."

FORTY-ONE

The Translator

THE TRANSLATOR RIPPED himself from his [*secret place*] and curled up on his bed, hyperventilating.

What had happened?

She was there. The Satellite was in his [*secret place*].

He had not wanted that, but somehow he must have summoned her.

Numbers passed over his lips in an unending loop—more information for the Reclaimer—the sound, as it always did, calming him. "One, four, four, three, four, eight, one, two, three, six, four, three, two. Three, two, three, nine, seven, seven, seven—"

"Shut up!"

The Translator twisted around and saw the Beast glaring at him from the other bed.

"Shut up, or I'll do it for you!"

It was an empty threat. Like every night, the Beast was restrained to keep him from doing bad things.

The Translator snarled at him, showing he wasn't scared.

"In the morning I will kill you," the Beast told him.

But he wouldn't do that, either. In the daylight, the Beast was not a beast, but a docile, repentant man-child. It was the darkness that brought on the Beast's demon. The Translator knew all about him and had long ago sent his story to the Reclaimer.

He flipped over so his back was to the Beast, putting the monster out of his mind and concentrating once again on important things.

On the Satellite.

Not only had she been in his [*secret place*], but she had *seen* him and even tried to *talk* to him.

You should have let her. A boy's voice, one of the first the Translator could ever remember hearing.

Are you crazy? another said, this one more familiar, his everyday protector. *Dangerous! Much too dangerous!*

You should have spoken with her, the boy said.

Impossible. Impossible!

You should have.

The Translator began rocking.

You should have. You should have. You should have.

"One, four, four, eight, four, two—"

"Shut up!"

"—zero, nine, three, nine, four, three, two. Three, two…"

FORTY-TWO

Leah

LEAH SAT UP, gasping. She was on her own bed, in her own apartment, the forever room of the dream gone.

The...Secret Place.

"No," she whispered. "No, no, no. Not yet."

She lay back down, closed her eyes, and tried to force herself back to sleep. While the Secret Place had initially confused her, she knew now she needed to get back there and talk to the changing man. She needed to make him understand there was no reason to be frightened. She was convinced he was a key to unlocking what had happened to her and Joel.

Try as she might, though, her mind refused to fall back to sleep, and instead whirled with thoughts of what she'd seen and what it could mean. Finally acknowledging it would be a while before she drifted off again, she focused on the details of the dream.

She started with the items displayed on the shelves. She had no idea what many of them were, but others she recognized right away: popular action figures, games, toys, all from at least a decade ago. Even an old computer with a big heavy monitor and a wide keyboard. Other things, too. Stuffed animals and competition ribbons and pictures and DVDs.

She then thought again about the man's shy approach as he grew taller and older, and then the reverse when he retreated. He had changed from old man to newly minted senior to nondescript middle-ager to starter adult to growing teen. He was changing again when she was pulled from the room, his new form younger still.

This last glimpse felt…familiar. Like she knew him.

Annoyed, she climbed out of bed and opened her closet. Along with her clothes and shoes were two stacks of boxes filled with personal items she'd slowly been bringing to California from her parents' place in Denver. She'd told herself that someday she'd unpack everything, but someday had yet to come.

The box she wanted was in the back row, second from the bottom. Under an old sweater and several *Wired* magazines she'd kept for some unknown reason, she found her high school yearbooks. One by one she went through them, searching for the face of the boy in the Secret Place. Though there were a few guys who, if she squinted just right, might have been him, none was an exact match.

Not high school, then, and since most of the kids she went to middle school with had also attended Verde High, she could rule them out, too.

So where did she know him from?

Camp Cedar Woods? Now there was a possibility. She'd seen plenty of teen boys passing through camp. She thought for a moment, her near perfect memory of that time allowing her to clearly see each camper's face. But none belonged to the changing man.

Camp Red Hawk?

If that were the case, she was out of luck. Camp Red Hawk was like a black hole from where few memories escaped.

She had to give it a try, though, so she lay back on her bed and attempted to recall that summer. She was surprised when a few things actually filtered through: a fire in the pit, a cookie she shared with one of the other girls, and the cannonball competition again.

And the Hershey's bar.

She smiled at that. She still had the wrapper, protected by a plastic bag and hidden at the bottom of her jewelry box.

"You had a, um, pretty good jump. I-I'd say you came in second."

"It wasn't that good."

"You were in the water. You couldn't see it."

"True."

"Um, would, um, you like some?"

"Uh, sure. Thanks."

The Hershey's bar in his hand, then hers.

With this image, she finally crossed the line between awake and asleep, but the dream of the Secret Place did not return.

FORTY-THREE

The Translator

THE TRANSLATOR WAS terrified that the Reclaimer would find out about the visit from the Satellite, that somehow someway the meeting would be revealed. If that happened, the Reclaimer's punishment would be fierce.

Perhaps she would even cut him off and wall him inside his own head, unable to touch the minds of others, to hear their voices. That would be the end of him for sure. He would go mad. Not that he wasn't mad already. He knew that. He knew he wasn't like the others, and yet he was one of them. But he would rather the Reclaimer kill him than sentence him to forever without the connections that had become his everything.

And what would happen to the Satellite?

Oh, God, no.

He couldn't allow her to be hurt. No, no. He could never let that happen.

He steeled himself, ready for the inevitable.

But time and again, the Reclaimer made no indication that she knew what had happened.

::ARE YOUR CHANNELS OPEN? she would ask.

Yes.

::ARE YOUR RECEPTORS WORKING?

Yes.

::ARE ALL LINKS INTACT?

Yes.

And that was it.

He suspected for a while that she was stringing him along until the mood to punish him hit her. So he concentrated on his translations, sending each packet off to her as soon as it was ready, all the while staying away from his [*secret place*].

But the anticipated trap never sprang.

::ARE YOUR CHANNELS OPEN?

Yes.

::ARE YOUR RECEPTORS WORKING?

Yes.

::ARE ALL LINKS INTACT?

Yes.

FORTY-FOUR

Leah

WHILE LEAH CONTINUED attending classes and doing the associated work, she had come to the realization she was spinning her wheels. She was never going to find the answers she sought within the confines of a university.

Every night when she went to sleep, she attempted to reestablish a connection to the changing man and his Secret Place. The first few nights, her efforts worked no better than they did when she tried breaking through the wall to Joel. But then one night, as she was drifting off, she saw a spark. Though it vanished almost as fast as it appeared and did not return that night, she knew it was the way back.

The following evening, the spark lasted longer, and the next longer still. Night after night it added to the crooked path it was tracing through the darkness. After two weeks she realized it wasn't a path at all, but more like a slit in a piece of fabric. She focused on it, picturing the two sides pulling wide enough apart for her to slip through.

Sure enough, the hole opened and she moved once more into the Secret Place. Unlike her first visit, however, she could sense the changing man was not there.

"Hello?" she called, but the room remained still. "Hello? Are you there?"

Nothing.

She felt strange being in the room without him, like she was trespassing in his home. Tentatively, she approached the nearest shelf. On it was a stack of books, a deflated football, a square stone, and a dozen other equally commonplace items.

"Hello?" she called again.

When she didn't receive a response, she decided it was time to go.

She turned to the spot where she'd appeared, assuming the exit would still be there, but it was gone. She had a moment of panic before remembering what had happened on her last visit. The changing man had sent her away. Could she do it herself?

"Home," she said.

The slit opened in the wall, and after she stepped through, she woke in her bed.

She'd done it. She'd forced herself into an enhanced dream, to the exact place she wanted to go. *And* she had left on her own terms.

If I can get into the Secret Place, I should be able to break through to Joel, shouldn't I?

Eager to test this, she closed her eyes and gave it a try. She didn't reach Joel, but it wasn't a complete waste of time. She found his wall, could actually *see* it, the darkest of gray against the blackest of black. She'd never been able to do that before.

For the next several weeks, she would visit Joel's wall first, and when she couldn't find a way through, she'd go to the Secret Place, hoping to see the changing man again.

FORTY-FIVE

AS SOON AS he was sure the Reclaimer had no knowledge of his meeting with the Satellite, the Translator wanted to return to his [secret place]. But he knew he couldn't just rush right off, so he bided his time until a suitable opportunity arose.

When it did, he jumped on it.

The [secret place] held everything important to him. It was his link to [life before].

Upon arriving, he stopped in the middle of the room and breathed in the air of freedom.

Yes, yes. That's it, he thought as his worries melted away.

He shuffled along the shelves, heading toward the item with which he always started. [*The most important picture ever taken*] lay on a shelf between a Slurpee cup and a stack of Playstation games. He picked it up and smiled as his finger caressed the faces of the two people standing behind the child-him in the photo.

"Are those your parents?"

He nearly dropped the picture as he whipped around.

The Satellite was standing behind him. She was here in his room *again*!

How? He had done nothing to bring her this time. He had purposely not thought about her for days.

"Go!" he yelled. He wanted to back away from her but she had him pinned against the shelves.

"Not yet."

"Go! Apartment!"

His command should have sent her away, but she didn't

disappear.

"You know me, don't you?" she asked.

"Please, you must, must, must leave."

"I told you my name. Do you remember it?"

"Please!"

"Just tell me."

"Y-y-you are the Satellite," he said.

Her brow furrowed. "The *satellite*?"

"Yes. You are the Satellite."

For a moment she said nothing, her eyes uncertain. "What was the name *I* told you last time? I'm sure you remember it. Just say it."

He didn't need to remember. He already knew. "I cannot."

"You can."

He had to get out of there. Now. He closed his eyes to summon his exit, but the Satellite touched his hand, sending a jolt of electricity through his whole body.

"Who am I?" she asked, her hand still on his.

"L-Leah."

She grinned. "That's right. I know who you are, too."

"Please," he whispered. "Don't."

FORTY-SIX

Leah

LEAH WAS JUST thinking it was time to go when the changing man appeared. If his eyes hadn't been closed upon arrival, he would have seen her. But this had given her the moment she needed to hide among the cabinets.

From there, she had watched him walk with purpose to a specific shelf, his form shifting from an old man to young adult. When he arrived at his destination, he picked up a picture, one she'd examined on a previous visit. It was of a boy standing in front of a man and woman who were obviously his mother and father.

After she surprised him, it had taken some prodding to get him to say her name. But she knew he remembered it, not from when she'd said it before, but from years ago, when they were kids together. On another shelf on another night, she had found a brochure for Camp Red Hawk, and in the margins had been written her name and Joel's, and several other names she had forgotten but apparently he had not.

"I know who you are, too," she said.

In his panic, his form changed again, this time into the teen she had once known. "Please. Don't."

"Your name is Mike." That was the name scrawled across the top of the brochure in big letters.

He was the do-good boy. The rule follower.

One of the Three Who Returned.

"You're Mike, and I'm Leah. We met at Camp Red Hawk. There were others, too. Joel Madsen and George Dooley and Antonio Ca—"

"—navo and Courtney Reed and Kayla Witten," he finished.

"You do remember."

"Always remember. Always, always, always."

"What about your last name, Mike? Can you tell me what that is?" His surname had not been on the brochure, or on anything else she'd come across, and for the life of her she couldn't recall it.

"I-I-I…uh, no, don't have one. Don't have one."

"Everyone has one. Just think for a moment. What's yours?"

"Don't have one, don't have one," he said.

She decided to try something different. "Do you remember when we were at camp?"

He bit his lip and nodded.

"Something happened to us there, didn't it?" she asked.

"I can't talk about that." He tried to pull his hand away from her but she wouldn't let go. "Can't. Can't. No, no, no. Can't talk about that."

"The thing is, I remember almost nothing from then. I really need you to help me."

He shook his head over and over as he shouted, "Can't! Can't!"

She'd pushed too far, she realized. She should have waited, maybe made another visit or two and let him get used to her first. Now she was sure that wouldn't be an option. He would never let her get this close to him again.

"Tell me where you are."

He looked at her, confused. "My hideaway. My *secret place*."

"No, where are you physically? Not in the dream."

"Not a dream. My *secret place*."

"Your physical body, Mike, where is it?"

He started shaking his head again. "No, no, no. No."

As he tried to yank free from her again, she gripped harder.

Suddenly images began flashing in her head: Mike on a bed in a dimly lit room; another bed with a small man restrained to it; a different room, a big room, with lots of people moving around, some shouting, some rocking, a few talking with one another or to themselves; a window with bars on the outside and a view of a parking lot.

"No!" Mike yelled as he finally pushed her away. The moment he was free, he disappeared.

But he gave her one last gift right before he broke contact—an image of a metal door with a small placard beside it reading:

> 307
> Lowell, J.
> Hurst, M.

Mike Hurst.

"Thank you," she whispered.

She still didn't know where this room 307 was, but she was confident she could figure it out. And when she did, she would help him like she was going to help Joel. Whether or not they wanted her to.

And then together they would find out the truth about that night long ago.

The
End
of
Hide
&
Seek

FORTY-SEVEN

JOEL WISHED HE'D seen the punch coming, but that's not how things worked.

A nice solid hit to his cheek, something he knew he'd be feeling for a few days.

His opponent sneered, fists balled, ready to punch again.

"Don't get cocky," Joel said in flawless Spanish. "That's the best shot you're going to get."

Growling with anger, the creep threw a wild right hook even a child would have seen coming. Joel juked to the side, letting the guy's fist fly by. Momentum twisted his opponent to the side, exposing the man's lower back, just the invitation Joel had been waiting for. He smashed his fist into the guy's kidney, and mentally placed a checkmark next to the corresponding item on his imaginary to-do list.

Enraged, the man whipped around and tried to grab Joel's arm, but Joel's other fist, already on the move, slammed into the guy's jaw before the a-hole's fingers touched Joel.

Another checkmark.

The guy stumbled out of range, glaring at Joel and breathing heavily as he rubbed his chin.

"Enough?" Joel asked. "We can stop anytime."

The creep should have given up right then, but he wasn't a smart man. With a huff, he came at Joel again, his arms throwing punches as if he had a surplus. Most either glanced off Joel's arms or missed entirely. Joel, on the other hand, landed hits to the creep's face (check), stomach (check), shoulder (check), and, using a knee, a painful blow to the guy's groin (check).

The creep doubled over, sucking in air.

"Come on, you want to stop, you know you do," Joel said. "Just say it. Please. Surprise me."

But as much as he wished the guy would walk away, Joel knew the fight wasn't over yet. There was still one item left to mark off his list.

The yell started low in the a-hole's throat. When it reached a crescendo, the guy shot toward Joel. Right before he reached him, though, Joel slipped below the creep's outstretched arms and smacked his shoulder up into the guy's chest. Something snapped, and the creep instantly dropped to the ground and rolled onto his back, screaming.

Broken rib, heart high.

Checkmark and done, Joel thought.

Gently, he placed his foot at the base of the injured man's rib cage. The guy tried to push it away, but his body was not cooperating.

"That hurts a lot," Joel said. "Trust me, I know. But I did give you a chance to stop. Twice."

Joel looked over at the small group of people gathered in the alley. They had all come at his request. He picked out the woman, Liliana. As far as he knew, she was the only English speaker in the group.

"Everybody knows what he did?" he asked in his native tongue.

"*Si*," she said.

"And will they let him do it again?"

"No. Not again."

Joel wished he had some way of knowing for sure they'd be able to prevent the guy from abusing his own kids anymore, but that wasn't how Joel's "gift" worked.

Liliana trailed him back to the roadhouse where he'd been staying, and watched him gather his things and put them in the back of his beat-up car.

"You can stay," she said. "The others are thankful for what you did and would never tell anyone."

"I appreciate that. But I have places to go."

He climbed into the car, coaxed the engine to life, and headed down the road.

The truth was, staying had never been an option. He'd tried that a few times, but at some point either the person he'd taught the lesson to or the person's friends always found their way to him. He'd known they were coming, of course. His waking injuries never lied. But he could avoid these fights, so now he did.

He had no idea where he was going next. He'd been in the small town near Tampico for over two weeks, part of the grand tour that had taken him south along the west coast of Mexico and through Central America, all the way to the canal before heading back north to come up the Gulf side.

There wasn't a lot of territory left between him and the US border, though, so he would have to figure out someplace new soon. Maybe Asia again. He'd done that for a while a couple of years ago. He could still go to plenty of places there where no one would recognize him. All of India, for instance. He should be able to get lost there for a few years at least.

The first main road he came upon gave him the choice of southeast or northwest. He picked the latter only because the southeast route would end at the Gulf Coast an hour away.

He settled back in his seat and tried not to think about what mess he would get into next. Because there would be a next. There was always a next.

He seldom thought about his nomad existence anymore in terms of *have I made the right decision?* or *should I be doing something else?* He'd come to accept it for the escape it was.

After finishing college, he had run from his old life, from the pressures of his parents and his teachers and a society that wanted him to use his intelligence in ways *they* saw fit. Maybe if their expectations had been the only things weighing on him, he could have found a way to make that kind of life work and would've already been on the path of becoming the researcher his professors encouraged him to be, or the doctor of his mother's dreams.

But other things were crushing him, too. The death of the girl he couldn't save had been a big blow, but as far has he'd been able to tell, the pattern of repeated tragedy had not occurred to any of the others he'd helped Perhaps the biggest reason for leaving was his need to escape the Voice.

Two months after he walked out of his Palo Alto apartment, he'd left the country and had yet to return. The reason was simple. He wanted to put as much distance as possible between himself and the last place he'd been when the Voice came to him. For a little while it worked, but it wasn't long before he could feel the Voice reaching out to him again. He did everything he could to keep it away, but it was relentless, so he had let it back in once for the sole purpose of telling it to never come back. Much to his surprise, it had worked.

Without the Voice in his head, he thought he'd be free from his assignments. But what he ended up being free from was someone telling him what he needed to do. Because the curse continued to wake him, bruised and battered, with the knowledge that at some point before he slept again, he would inflict the same injuries on someone else.

He'd begun to think of himself as a fight magnet. He didn't ask for confrontations but they came looking for him anyway. He kept hoping they would stop, but the violence followed him wherever he went.

He realized he had a choice to make. He could continue stumbling into events haphazardly, or he could keep his eyes open and look for opportunities to channel his curse into something useful. In other words, revive the assignments he'd been so determined to put behind him.

It took him a while to get the rhythm of things. Without the Voice, he was initially operating blind. But over time his unique abilities adapted to his new situation. It was harder than it had been with the Voice, but it worked, and the incidents of random violent encounters decreased until they hardly happened anymore.

Money was never a problem. With the Internet, he was

able to get work whenever he wanted, doing things like programming and freelance writing and even some scientific analysis.

About an hour into the drive, he felt a slight tingle on his right cheek. Less than a minute later, he came upon a sign indicating an upcoming turnoff for the town of San Ernesto.

Apparently he'd found his next stop.

FORTY-EIGHT

JOEL WAS BEWILDERED.

This was the fourth morning in a row he'd woken without any cuts or breaks or pain of any kind. He usually experienced something by this point at one of his stops, but there hadn't been even a scratch.

He'd already identified three people in San Ernesto as potential targets for his unique form of justice—a farmer Joel suspected was stealing from his neighbors, a thirty-year-old mechanic Joel had heard was fond of forcing himself on women, and the chief of the local four-person police department who seemed to be the richest man in town.

While he'd been waiting for the inevitable confrontation with one of them, he found out as much as he could about the men without raising any suspicions, and came up with plans on how to deal with each. The cop would be the trickiest. Joel had experienced only one run-in with a law enforcement official over the four-plus years of his self-imposed exile. That had nearly ended with him in prison for life. Not wanting to repeat that experience, he hoped this cop was on the up-and-up.

After showering and dressing, he left his hotel and headed down the street to grab breakfast at one of the town's five restaurants. As was the case on the previous two mornings, potential target number three was already sitting at his usual table with one of his officers. The chief looked up as Joel walked in, and tracked him all the way to an empty table before moving his gaze away.

Joel ordered *chilaquiles* and a coffee, and then opened the newspaper he'd picked up as he left the hotel. He'd barely started skimming the headlines when he had the feeling someone was watching him. Assuming it was the chief again, he casually glanced toward the cop's table, but the man was engaged in conversation with his officer and seemed to have forgotten Joel was there. Joel scanned the room, but neither of the two other customers was facing him.

I'm just keyed up from the wait.

Focusing on the paper again, he listened in on the cops' conversation, hoping it might prove useful. But all they talked about was a TV show they'd watched the night before. Not long after Joel's meal was served, the two cops left.

Joel took his time eating, and then leisurely strolled across town to the auto shop where potential target number two was servicing his car. Joel had brought the vehicle by the day before, knowing it would be a good way to get close to the mechanic. Roberto—that was the guy's name—had told Joel to leave it there and come back in the morning.

When the mechanic saw Joel approach the shop, he set down the alternator he was working on and met him at the garage doorway.

"So?" Joel asked. "How's it look?"

"I'm surprised you were able to make it here." He rattled off a list of things that needed fixing.

"What's the least amount of work I can get away with?"

"The least? A full tune-up, I guess. Though you're going to have problems soon if you don't take care of these other things."

"How much for the tune-up?"

"It's not cheap, *señor*."

"How much?"

The man quoted him a number that was indeed not cheap. If Roberto did turn out to be innocent of the rumors about him, Joel thought he might still have to beat a little sense into the guy for price gouging. For the moment, though, he didn't argue about the cost and only asked how long it would take.

"Should be done by tomorrow morning, ten, maybe eleven o'clock."

"Okay, let's do it." Joel looked out the garage door at the

sun-drenched road. "Can I use your phone? The hotel said they'd pick me up if I wanted a ride back, and it's getting damn hot out there."

"No problem. It's in my office."

Joel entered the small room, pulled the door shut, and put his phone away. As quickly and quietly as possible, he searched the desk drawers and the cabinet by the wall. All contained what they should have contained—invoices and work orders and parts catalogs. He did, however, find a suspicious envelope secured to the underside of one of the cabinet drawers. He was pretty sure it contained nothing work related.

He opened it and found it full of pictures of women, clothed and unclothed, all in candid poses with Roberto, and clearly not knowing they were being photographed. Joel recognized several of the women from around town.

With the envelope hidden under his shirt, he exited the room, thanked Roberto, and left.

Perhaps this was why he hadn't woken with any signs of an oncoming fight. All he had to do to take Roberto down was put the evidence into the right hands. Not the police chief's, though. Perhaps the man wasn't worthy of Joel's attention, but there was something corrupt about him. If the police were going to get the package, it would have to come from someone who would make sure the chief followed through with appropriate punishment.

Rosa, the owner of the hotel where Joel was staying, would do. He would pick up his car in the morning, go back and get his things from his room, and leave the envelope and a note explaining where it had been found.

As he entered his hotel, sweaty from his walk, he gave the kid behind the desk a nod and headed toward his room.

"*Señor,*" the kid called, and held out a folded piece of paper that had Joel's room number on it. "Message for you."

The hair on the back of Joel's neck rose. It must have been a mistake. No one knew he was here.

"Who's it from?"

"I don't know. It was here before I started work."

Joel reluctantly took it from him. The paper had been

folded in half then half again, and had a piece of tape holding it closed.

"Is this *Señora* Rosa's handwriting?" Joel held up the side with the room number on it for the kid to see.

The boy studied it for a few seconds. "It doesn't look like it."

Joel said, "Thank you," and went to his room.

When he was inside and the door was closed, he opened the note.

One line:

Joel, come down to Casa Carmen's when you get a minute.

The words appeared to be written in the same hand as his room number had been. No signature. The note was written in English, not Spanish, and by someone who knew the language well. The most disturbing aspect, though, was the use of his name. No one in town knew it, not even the people at the hotel. He'd checked in with a fake ID.

The desire to grab his bag and get the hell out of there was almost overwhelming. But San Ernesto was at least fifty miles from the nearest town, and until he picked up his car, he would be going nowhere fast. He could catch a bus, but the only one he'd seen came in the evening.

His choices, then, were either to hide out somewhere until he could get his car, or see who this person was.

Actually, he thought, he could do both. Casa Carmen's was a bar on the same block as the hotel. He'd spent a couple of hours there his second night in town, and knew he could probably sneak in the back door without being noticed.

He packed his bag and left the hotel through the room's window in case someone was waiting for him in the hall. Sticking to the alley, he made his way to Carmen's and hid his bag under a car parked in a space marked CASA CARMEN ONLY in Spanish. He then slipped through the back door, eased past a storage room, and stopped just shy of the bar area.

For a small place early on a midweek afternoon, Carmen's was doing a decent amount of business. He scanned the customers, trying to guess who'd left him the note, but no one stood out.

He didn't like this. Not at all. It felt like a trap. Like if he stepped into the room, a swarm of men would storm the place.

Screw this.

He left the way he'd come and reached under the car to retrieve his bag. When he stood back up, he found a young, tall Hispanic woman standing nearby.

"Do you always store your luggage that way?" she said in perfect, unaccented English.

He looked around, but she was alone. "You're the one who sent me the note?"

"Yeah."

"I don't know who you think I am, but I'm not who you're looking for."

"You're Joel Madsen. Age twenty-four. Left high school early to attend Stanford University. Received a double major in physics and pre-med six years ago, and though you were accepted to grad school, you never went. You have a knack for helping those who can't, or won't, help themselves. Am I close?"

His eyes narrowed. "Who *are* you?"

Something passed through her eyes. Hurt? Disappointment? It happened so fast he couldn't be sure.

"You don't recognize me?"

"Should I?" he asked.

"What about the way I sound? You couldn't have forgotten that."

"The way you—" He stopped.

No, he thought. *It's not possible.*

"I believe you thought of me as the Voice," she said.

He stared at her, unable to move. How could this woman be the Voice?

"We knew each other before that, though," she said. "We held hands once. Please tell me you haven't forgotten that." She reached into her pocket and pulled out a plastic bag. From inside she removed a piece of paper and unfolded it. "You gave this to me when we were kids." She held it out.

A Hershey's chocolate bar wrapper.

"You do remember, don't you?"

FORTY-NINE

Leah

THE EXPERIENCE LEAH had gained from finding her own way to Mike's Secret Place helped her finally defeat Joel's wall.

Worried he'd banish her again and build a barrier ten times as thick and a million times as high, she'd nibbled away at the darkness for months, digging a spy hole through which she could look but not disturb him. It took her another several weeks to figure out where he was. As soon as she did, she'd flown to Mexico City and driven east toward the gulf. She'd planned on approaching him in the town of Ramona near Tampico, but by the time she got there he was gone.

Tracking him, she'd arrived in San Ernesto less than twenty-four hours after he did, taking a room in the same hotel.

She had wanted to go to him right away but was afraid of how he might react. What finally prompted her into action was a sense he would be moving on again soon. She had left the note for him on the front desk when no one was there, and then returned to her room where she watched from her window as he climbed out of his.

And now here they were, standing in front of each other for the first time in over ten years.

"The camp," he said, low, almost to himself.

"Red Hawk."

"We were the ones who came back."

She nodded. "Two of them."

"The ones who didn't…"

"Dooley and Courtney and Kayla and Antonio."

He was silent for a moment, the names doubtlessly hitting

him in much the same way they had hit her when she's read them on Mike's brochure—names neither of them should have ever forgotten.

"Mike," he said. "He came back like us, too."

Though she said, "Yes," she knew Mike had not come back quite like them.

Another pause, then, "*You* were the Voice?"

A gust of wind blew down the alley, giving flight to an old plastic bag.

"Yes."

"How?" he asked.

"How did I get in your head? Or how is it that we are both smarter and stronger than we should be? Maybe how am I able to see things a fraction of a second sooner than the rest of the world? Or how is it you can wake up some mornings with the wounds of someone you'll hurt later in the day?" She paused. "*How* is a complicated question, and I don't know the answer. Not yet. I was hoping you could maybe help me find it."

FIFTY

Joel

"OR HOW IS it that we are both smarter and stronger than we should be?"

Joel's head pounded so loudly it was a wonder he could hear anything else she said. How could she be experiencing the same things he was?

And then came the question that revealed she knew about his darkest secret—his phantom wounds.

He opened his mouth but didn't know what to say. He'd been isolated by his differences since he was thirteen.

His mind seized, unable to process anything. All he felt was a deep desire to flee.

So he ran.

"Joel!" she yelled. "Joel, please. Can't we just talk?"

He weaved through the streets of San Ernesto and into the desert, not stopping until he came across a shack somewhere north of the village.

The building was long abandoned and would be as good a place as any to hide out. He could wait there until dark, and then make for the main road where he could hitch a ride to wherever.

He fashioned a place to lie down out of discarded cardboard boxes, and stretched out. Suddenly exhausted, he closed his eyes. His sleep was bombarded by short bits of memories: his first day at Stanford, playing Ultimate Mortal Kombat 3 at the arcade with Justin, the shirtless guy in apartment 319 saying "I didn't do anything" right before Joel punched him in the face, Joel's mother passed out on the couch as the TV played on and on.

And a forest trail in the dark of night, a hand slipping into his and making him feel—for a moment, anyway—like the luckiest boy in the world.

Leah.

He had forgotten her name. Had forgotten that moment. Had forgotten everything about Camp Red Hawk.

When Joel woke, the dying embers of the setting sun filtered through the hut's only window. He sat up, wanting to get moving as soon as possible. But as he started to stand, he saw Leah sitting quietly in the corner.

"Jesus!" His heart jumped in his chest.

"Sorry," she said softly. "Would it have been better if I woke you?"

"It would have been better if you just left me alone." He picked up his bag and headed for the doorway.

"Even if I wanted to, I couldn't," she said, still sitting.

"What's that supposed to mean?"

"The connection between us is stronger now than it's ever been. I think seeing each other in person triggered something inside us. Don't tell me you can't feel it, too."

He scowled. "I don't know what the hell you're talking about. All I want is for you to stay out of my head."

He walked quickly into the desert, but made it no more than half a dozen yards when she called to him from the doorway. "You can try to build up the wall between us again, but it won't keep me out. I'm always going to know where you are, Joel."

He stared down at the dirt for a moment before looking back. "Just because you know where I am doesn't mean you have to follow me."

She stepped outside. "You're right. And I won't if that's what you really want. But Mike needs our help in a bad way, and I know you can't turn your back on him."

"Watch me," he said and started walking again.

"If helping him doesn't mean anything to you, then come with me for yourself," she called. "Help me find out why we are the way we are."

He didn't stop.

FIFTY-ONE

Leah

LEAH REMAINED IN the doorway of the hut for an hour, staring out at the desert before she allowed herself to accept that Joel wasn't coming back.

She had failed.

Wrapped in despair, she returned to the hotel. It felt like she was both there and not, the world becoming a blur that could easily have been a dream—the normal kind, not her special brand.

In her room, she sat on the bed, lights off, staring at the wall. How long she stayed like that before crawling under the covers and falling asleep, she didn't know. When the sun woke her in the morning, she was still fully clothed and stinging from Joel's rejection. It would have been easy to stay in bed all day, but she couldn't let herself fall into that trap.

Thirty minutes later, she was on the road again. If Joel wasn't going to join her, she would have to move forward on her own.

LEAH FLEW FROM Monterrey to Dallas, Texas, where she transferred to a flight to Colorado.

Since moving to California, she'd traveled back to her home state once or twice a year to see her folks in Denver. She wouldn't be stopping by on this trip, however.

At the airport, she rented a sedan and drove an hour and a half south to Colorado Springs. Though she had been able to get into Mike's Secret Place, she still hadn't figured out where he physically lived. From the items that filled his infinite room, she did discover several things that, when taken together, pointed her to where he'd grown up, hence her current destination.

An Internet search had provided her with the phone numbers of several area families with the last name of Hurst. She had called as many of them as she had time for during a layover in Dallas, saying she was an old friend looking for Mike. All but one had no idea whom she was talking about. That one had hung up the second she'd mentioned Mike's name.

The number belonged to Franklin and Marnie Hurst, address unlisted. But by the time she arrived in Colorado Springs, she'd formulated a plan.

Worship was a huge part of daily life in this part of the country. With the next day being Sunday, she began calling churches, using the story of a person who'd just moved to town looking for a church to join, preferably the one where her mother's dear old friend Marnie Hurst went. If pressed on why she hadn't received Marnie's number from her mother, Leah would say her mother had passed away the year before.

There were a lot of churches in the city, and she went through thirty-two of them before she got lucky.

"Marnie Hurst?" the woman on the other end of the line said. "Sure. She's on the committee that runs our women's group."

"Oh, that's wonderful. I hope I see her when I come tomorrow."

"Marnie and Frank never miss a Sunday. They usually come to the nine a.m. service. I'm sure they'll be glad to see you."

LEAH SPENT A restless night in a cheap motel, full of dreams of chasing Joel through deserts.

When morning finally came, she put on her nicest outfit, checked out of the motel, and waited in her car in the church lot until 8:30. After taking a seat in the back of the church, she watched the parishioners arrive.

The Hursts walked in at ten minutes before the hour. She

recognized them immediately from Mike's photograph. They were older now, both gray-haired, and Mr. Hurst had packed on more than a few pounds. Mrs. Hurst must have picked up on Leah's stare because she looked over at Leah and smiled before moving down the aisle.

Leah barely heard the service as she anxiously waited for it to be over. After the last prayer had been uttered and the closing song played, the parishioners slowly made their way out, stopping here and there to greet others.

Leah could have easily approached the Hursts right then and there, but she thought it better if the setting was more private. So she followed them home to their upper middle-class neighborhood of big yards and nice cars, gave them ten minutes inside, and then walked up to the front door and rang the bell.

Footsteps tapped across a tiled floor before the door opened and revealed Mrs. Hurst.

"Can I help you?"

"Hi, Mrs. Hurst. My name is Leah. I was wondering—"

Recognition twinkled in the woman's eyes. "Didn't I see you at church earlier?"

"Um, uh, yes, ma'am. I'm, um—"

"You must be the young lady who talked to Ava yesterday. Your mother and I are friends?"

Leah was saved from having to answer by Mr. Hurst shouting from inside, "Who is it, dear?"

His wife glanced over her shoulder. "It's that girl Ava told us about."

A moment later, Mr. Hurst was at her side, holding out his hand. "How you doing? I'm Franklin Hurst."

Leah took it. "Leah. Um, Leah Bautista."

Mrs. Hurst's brow furrowed as she tried to place the name.

"Don't just stand there. Come on inside," Mr. Hurst said.

"Thank you." Leah stepped over the threshold, relieved the coming conversation wouldn't have to start on the front porch.

She was led into a large living room that looked like it could have been featured in a magazine. The furniture, the accessories, even the art on the cream-colored walls were all just right.

"You have a beautiful home," Leah said as she sat on the sofa.

"Thank you so much," Mrs. Hurst said. "That's very kind."

"Just renovated the place last year," Mr. Hurst said.

"Well, you did an excellent job."

"I'm curious," Mrs. Hurst said. "You said Bautista, correct?"

"Yes, ma'am."

"I don't recognize your last name. Did I know your mother by her maiden name?"

"I'm, um…I'm afraid I misled your friend at the church."

"How so?"

"You have met my mother, but you don't really know her. I'm here because I needed to talk to you about your son."

Mr. Hurst's face hardened, all the kindness gone. "You're the one who called yesterday."

"Called?" Mrs. Hurst said. Apparently her husband hadn't told her about his and Leah's short conversation.

"Yeah, that was me," Leah admitted.

"You need to leave now," he said.

"Please, you are Mike's parents, right? Mike Hurst? He'd be about twenty-three or twenty-four now. Went to Camp Red Hawk in—"

"Get out!" Mr. Hurst yelled, pointing at the door.

Mrs. Hurst's face had gone white, her hand covering her mouth.

"I just need to talk to him, that's all. Do you know where—"

Mr. Hurst grabbed her arm and yanked her to her feet. "If you don't leave now, I'll call the police. We don't need to see this plastered all over the Internet. Leave it alone!"

"What? No! You misunderstand me."

Mr. Hurst started pulling her toward the door.

"I'm not with the press," Leah said. "I was there! I was at Camp Red Hawk with your son. I was one of the three who returned!"

At the mention of the three, Mr. Hurst tightened his grip and glared at her. "That is just sick. I am calling the police."

"I'm not lying. It was me and Mike and Joel. Joel Madsen. A sheriff's deputy found us walking along the highway. He took us back to camp where you were all waiting for us. You, my parents, Joel's."

Mr. Hurst looked less than convinced. His wife, however, stared at Leah in growing astonishment.

"Bautista," she whispered. "Oh my God, I do remember you,"

"That girl was barely a teen," her husband said. "This woman could be anyone."

Mrs. Hurst, her gaze still on Leah, said, "It is you, isn't it?"

"Yes," Leah said.

"And your parents…" Mrs. Hurst paused, unable to remember their names.

"Leon and Helena."

"Right." Mrs. Hurst smiled. "Leon and Helena. They were so worried about you. We were all so worried about all of you."

She walked over and took hold of Leah's hand, then started leading her back into the living room.

"What are you doing?" her husband said. "She's lying. She's just trying to get a story. She's not who she says she is."

Undeterred, Mrs. Hurst guided Leah back to the couch and gestured for her to sit. "Can I get you something to drink? Have you had lunch?"

"I'm fine, thank you."

Behind them came a pair of soft beeps from a phone being dialed.

"Frank, put that down," Mrs. Hurst ordered.

Leah looked back and saw Mr. Hurst holding a phone, a finger hovering over the screen.

"I'm calling the police. They can deal with her."

"You are not calling anyone. Now put that away."

"We don't know what she wants. She could be—"

"It doesn't matter what she wants."

"Of course it does," he said.

"It's okay," Leah said. "If you want to call them, go ahead. We can talk while we wait for them to get here. I promise, I won't cause any problems."

After a few quiet seconds, Mrs. Hurst said, "Put it down, Frank, and come over here and join us."

Her husband hesitated a moment longer, and then set the phone down and took the easy chair farthest from Leah.

Mrs. Hurst, who had yet to take a seat, said, "I'll be right back." She glanced quickly at her husband. "Manners." With that, she disappeared up the stairs to the second floor.

An awkward silence ensued, Mr. Hurst eyeing Leah suspiciously and Leah trying to look as non-threatening as possible. Finally, she said, "I'm not here to cause you any problems."

"Too late for that."

"I just have a few questions."

"About Mike."

"Yes."

He shook his head and looked off to the side. "Do you know how many years it's taken my wife to get to the point where she doesn't think about that summer every moment of every day? Sending him to that camp was her idea. It doesn't matter how much therapy she gets or how many times I tell her what happened wasn't her fault, she blames herself."

Leah couldn't stop herself from asking, "What *did* happen?"

His eyes narrowed again. "If you were really there, you should know."

But I don't, she wanted to say. *I don't remember what happened.* Instead, she said, "I mean after we came back."

They heard a creak and Mr. Hurst's gaze flicked toward the stairs. A moment later, Mrs. Hurst reentered the living room, carrying an envelope a half-inch thick.

"Sorry," she said as she joined Leah on the couch. "It took me a minute to find this. I…" She seemed to lose her train of thought.

"What is it?" Leah asked.

Mrs. Hurst glanced at the envelope as if she was unsure.

"Pictures. From Camp Red Hawk."

"From when we came back?"

"No, of course not. From when we dropped off...our son."

She pulled a stack of photos out of the envelope and began going through them, handing Leah each one as she finished looking at it.

The pictures weren't actually from the camp itself, but from the bus departure lot in Boulder. The photos featured a chaotic mess of children hugging parents and goofing off, in front of a background of luggage that sat next to buses that would be taking them into the mountains.

Leah couldn't help but run her finger over images of kids she recognized—Molly, the one who couldn't swim; Derrick, the clown; Jonah, the boy who won the pie-eating contest; Wendy, the one with the streak of purple in her hair; and—

Leah gripped the photo she'd just been given. "Joel," she whispered.

He was far from the lens and in profile, but it was him.

"I'm sorry?" Mrs. Hurst said.

Water gathering in her eyes, Leah showed the woman the picture. "It's the other boy who was with us. Joel."

Mrs. Hurst looked at the photo and nodded. "I remember him. He was very concerned about you. He kept asking if you were okay."

A tear escaped Leah's eye and ran down her cheek. She'd never heard that before. She wiped her face and took the next photo.

Several pictures later, Mrs. Hurst said, "Here we are."

She held out a photo of Mike looking off to the side, anxious. Standing no more than a dozen feet behind him were Leah and her parents.

"That's you, isn't it?" Mrs. Hurst said.

"Yes."

The shot had caught Leah looking directly at the camera.

Mrs. Hurst leaned toward her husband and held the photo out for him to see. "Now tell me this isn't her."

Mr. Hurst glanced at the picture, but from the look in his eyes, Leah knew he'd already decided she was who she said she was.

After they finished the photos, Mrs. Hurst made them some coffee. "It's decaf, I'm afraid," she said. "We can't abide the hard stuff anymore."

There were cookies, too, but Leah avoided them for fear she'd eat them all. The emotional journey the pictures had taken her on had made her famished. What she really needed was a steak followed by a heaping bowl of pasta and topped off with an entire gallon of ice cream.

She took a polite sip of her coffee and then set the cup down. "I was hoping you could tell me where I could find Mike."

"Why?" Mr. Hurst asked, some of his suspicion returning.

"There's something I need to talk to him about."

His eyes narrowed. "But you haven't seen him since you were thirteen."

"You're right. I haven't."

"Then what could you possibly have to talk to him about?"

"Frank," Mrs. Hurst said.

"No, I think we deserve an answer," he said.

Instead of providing one, Leah said, "Something happened to him, didn't it? Something was different when he came back."

Mr. Hurst pushed up from his chair. "It's getting late and I don't see how continuing to talk about this is going to accomplish anything."

Leah thought Mrs. Hurst would calm him down again, but the woman said nothing, the fight apparently drained out of her.

Mr. Hurst walked over to Leah and held out a hand to help her up. "It was...*kind* of you to stop by."

Leah looked at his hand and saw his fingertips move, urging her to take them. She couldn't let the meeting end like this, though. She still didn't have what she needed.

"Something changed me while we were missing, too. I don't remember what caused it. I don't remember anything about our time in the woods. But I was never the same." She held her still-full cup of coffee out to Mr. Hurst. "Take this."

His fingers reflexively curled around the handle.

"Now let go," she said, angling her gaze so that while she was looking him in the eye, she could still see the cup.

"What?"

She barked, "Drop it!"

In surprise, he let go of the cup. Without moving her head, she snatched it out of the air, only a dribble of coffee jumping over the rim onto her finger.

He stared at the cup and shook his head, as if snapping himself out of a trance. "What's that supposed to prove? You've got good timing?"

"I don't have *good* timing. I have the best timing anyone has ever had. We could do this all night and I'd never miss." She glanced over at Mrs. Hurst and saw both dread and recognition on her face. Maybe they hadn't seen this kind of talent before, but they had seen something. "I can run faster and farther than anyone you know. I am immensely stronger than I look. And there are few people in the world as smart as I am." She nodded at the photo of Joel. "He's one of them. And I'm willing to bet your son is another."

"Dear God," Mrs. Hurst whispered. "What did they do to you?"

"I don't know. I don't even know who *they* are." Leah turned back to the woman's husband. "That's why I need to talk to your son."

Mr. Hurst looked at her for several seconds before his resolve broke. He walked over to a cabinet along the wall, removed a piece of paper, and wrote something on it. "This is his address," he said, holding out the paper. "We'll let them know you're coming, but I'm afraid he won't be much help."

She read what he'd written, and while she had never heard of the name, she wasn't surprised by the kind of place it was.

GENESEE MENTAL CARE FACILITY

"How long?" Leah asked.

Lips trembling, Mrs. Hurst said, "Our boy has been there for nine and a half years."

FIFTY-TWO

THE GENESEE MENTAL Care Facility was located outside
Flagstaff in northern Arizona. If Leah were to leave right then,
she could be there by midnight. But with what little sleep she'd
gotten the night before, she'd likely doze off behind the wheel.
So she opted to pick up some food and take a room at the
Holiday Inn.

By three p.m., she'd fallen asleep on the bed, a half-eaten
burger in her hand and the TV on. Spurred by the Hurst's
pictures, she dreamed of the day she and the other kids had
headed to Camp Red Hawk. She found herself searching for
Joel, though in reality she hadn't met him yet. Each time she
caught a glimpse of him, other kids would move in her way,
and when she looked again, he'd be gone.

"I'm here," she heard him call, his soft voice floating over
the cacophony of shouts and laughs and screams of excitement.

She again saw him for a second and again he disappeared.

"I'm here," he said.

She whirled around and headed the other way, spotting
him by bus number three.

"I'm here," he said after he vanished again.

"I'm here."

"I'm here."

"I'm here."

As she drifted toward consciousness, the dream faded but
her frustration at not reaching him stayed with her.

Light from the TV flickered through the room while
outside it was dark. Feeling something wet and sticky on her
arm, she raised it and saw it was streaked with mustard and

ketchup from the burger.

She groaned in disgust, balled up the remains of her meal in the wrapper, and swung her legs off the bed.

That's when she saw Joel sitting in a chair by the wall.

FIFTY-THREE

Joel

LEAH'S WORDS ECHOED in Joel's head as he ran through the desert.

"Help me find out why we are the way we are."

The idea was crazy. Whatever caused them to turn into the freaks they'd become was in their past and long gone. Even if it wasn't, what would it matter if they could find the source? It wasn't like they'd change back to who they'd been and get to live the lives they were supposed to have lived.

"Mike needs our help."

Shut up.

"You can't turn your back on him."

Shut up.

"Help me find out why. Help me find out why. Help me find out why."

Shut up!

He increased his pace, running faster than he'd ever run, the dirt flying beneath his feet. He must have gone two or three miles before he stopped. Hands on his thighs, he sucked in the cool air.

Why couldn't Leah have left him alone? He'd created a path for his life that was working just fine without her interference.

Okay, maybe not fine, but it *was* working. He wasn't dead or rotting in jail. He'd call that a win.

He took another breath and straightened up. Ahead, car

lights lit the night here and there, a connect-the-dots map of a nearby highway. He started moving toward them.

No, it's not a win, a voice in his head chided. *What you're doing is barely surviving.*

Though the voice was right, he wasn't sure he knew anymore how to live another way.

When he reached the road, he stuck out a thumb. It took nearly twenty minutes, but finally a three-axle moving van swung onto the shoulder. Joel jogged over and jumped onto the running board outside the passenger door.

"*Gracias,*" he said through the partially open window.

Two men were inside, one maybe in his twenties, and the driver closer to forty.

"Where are you going, my friend?" the driver asked.

"Nearest big city."

"We're heading to Monterrey. Big enough for you?"

North was not the direction Joel preferred, but he wasn't going to be choosy. "Plenty big enough."

"Climb in."

The young guy scooted into the middle and Joel hopped inside.

"I'm Arturo," the driver said as he pulled the truck back onto the highway, and then nodded at his companion. "This is Jorge."

"Joel. I really appreciate the ride."

"You Mexican?" Jorge asked, eyeing him as if he already knew the answer.

"No."

"Your Spanish is really good," Arturo said. "Where you from?"

"California." It was true enough.

"I thought maybe Texas," the driver said. "But a lot of Mexicans in California, too, I know."

"Yeah."

"I have a cousin in Los Angeles," Jorge said. "You from Los Angeles?"

"Closer to San Francisco."

"Oh, San Francisco." The young guy smiled and then said

in strained English, "Golden Gate Bridge."

"That's right," Joel told him.

They had a few more question about the States, but none asking the obvious—what was Joel doing out on the highway at that time of night alone? But Joel was tired and mentally drained, so he was just glad it didn't come up. Eventually, the conversation stalled, and the ensuing silence was filled by the rhythm of the tires humming against the road.

Joel leaned against the door and stared out into the darkness. It was a quiet night, no one within a couple of miles of them on their side of the highway and few cars passing them on the other, so it wasn't surprising that he was lulled to sleep.

It was the missing bounce of road and rumble of engine that woke him.

After opening his eyes, he had a split second to notice he was alone in the cab before painful stings screamed at him from the knuckles of his right hand. Glancing down, he saw each was scraped and bleeding. As he raised his hand to get a closer look, the wounds disappeared.

His head drooped. "Great," he muttered.

He checked his body for any other injuries, but found none. That was confusing. These days it wasn't often that he'd have such a mild premonition.

Outside the night was as dark as it had been when he'd climbed into the truck. He looked out the side window, thinking maybe they'd stopped for food or fuel or to take a leak, but there was just the endless dark.

He reached down to grab his bag, intending to climb out and stretch his legs, but his bag was gone. He felt around to see if it had moved under the seat, but the space wasn't big enough. Angry now, he almost threw his door open, but caution took hold before he could, and he released the latch silently.

He snuck around the front of the truck and saw his bag wasn't the only thing missing. The highway was gone, too, the road he was on now made of dirt.

The glow of a flashlight at the back of the truck caught his attention. He crept to the rear corner and took a peek.

Jorge stood a dozen feet away, his flashlight trained on a

pile of stuff on the ground.

Joel's stuff.

Joel took a step into the open. "What's going on?"

"Where do you keep your money?" the young guy asked as if it were an everyday question.

"What?"

Behind him, Arturo said, "Your money, where is it?"

As Joel spun around, a fist slammed into his face.

He staggered against the truck. Before he could regain his balance, Jorge swung the business end of a shovel into his gut.

Down Joel went, his head bouncing off the ground, dazing him enough that he couldn't react in time to block Jorge's foot from slamming into his ribs.

Hands moved over his body, patting down his clothes.

No, he thought as one neared the concealed pouch at the bottom of his pant leg where he kept his passport, bank cards, and money.

Yelling in fury, he lunged to his feet and tried to grab Arturo by the shirt, but the son of a bitch scrambled out of reach and ran around the back of the vehicle. Joel whirled the other way, ready to take on Jorge, but the guy was already running toward the truck's cab. Apparently they didn't mind a little fight if they were in control, but otherwise they weren't interested.

He could have chased them down but he let them go, and was soon watching the truck's taillights bouncing away. Eventually the lights flared, and the truck made a ninety-degree turn onto what Joel guessed was the highway. At least they'd done him the courtesy of showing him where to go.

It was well after midnight when he reached the paved road. His head had mostly cleared, but his ribs still ached, and the cheek that Arturo had cut his own knuckles on hurt when touched. Nothing felt broken, though.

At that late hour, he assumed it would be impossible to find a ride. So he walked along the shoulder and made only halfhearted attempts to flag down the few cars that drove by.

He'd been walking for nearly two hours when an old rattling sedan stopped. In the front was an elderly couple, shrunken by time so that the man, who was driving, could barely see over the wheel. In the back, a sleeping child took up half the seat.

"Our great-granddaughter," the woman said with pride as Joel climbed in.

"We will pass through Monterrey so we can drop you wherever you want," the man said.

"Thank you."

They pulled back onto the road.

"You're hurt," the woman said. "Your face."

"I fell. I'll be fine."

She fumbled around and then handed him a cloth and a bottle of water. "We don't have any ice but this should help. Wet it and keep it on your cheek."

"Thank you."

When he'd been riding in the truck, he'd been thinking he would catch a bus back to Mexico City from Monterrey, and then fly south to Brazil or Argentina or perhaps Chile.

But who was he kidding?

Help me find out why we are the way we are.

His nomad life had only been a placeholder. All this time he'd been waiting for Leah and he hadn't even known it.

The sun was starting to rise as they pulled to the curb at the airport.

"Thank you," Joel said. He started to get out, but then stopped. "Could you do me another favor?"

"If we can," the woman said.

Joel pulled the envelope he'd found at the mechanic's office out of his bag, sealed it, and then handed it and a business card for the hotel in San Ernesto to the woman. "If you could mail this to the address on the card, I'd appreciate it." He pulled out some money and gave it to her.

"This is too much," she said.

"For your kindness," he told her, and climbed out.

FIFTY-FOUR

Now

Leah

LEAH SAID, "HOW did you find me?"

Joel said, "How did you find *me*?"

She moved to him as he moved to her, and they fell into each other's arms.

THE
THREE
WHO
RETURNED

FIFTY-FIVE

THE TRANSLATER WOKE, dizzy and frightened.

Something was…different.

Worried that the Beast had somehow freed itself, the Translator turned in his bed but kept his eyelids closed enough to look like he was still asleep. His roommate, however, was strapped to its own bed like normal, mouth slack.

Cautiously, the Translator sat up and scanned the room. No one was there, and yet he felt another's presence.

Maybe under the beds. Maybe. Maybe.

He leaned down and searched the netherworld beneath his mattress. Nothing. He twisted around and scanned under the Beast's bed. Nothing there either.

He sat back up, confused. There was no clock in the room, but he always knew the precise hour and minute and second. He could feel the information packets processing in the back of his mind, each marked with a time notation to better serve the Reclaimer. Though the time designations were different from those he'd been taught growing up, he'd long before learned how to equate the two.

Why am I up? Why? Why? Do I have to pee?

He pressed a hand over his bladder.

No. No pee. Not for several hours yet. Then what is it? What is it?

He climbed out of bed, shuffled to the door, and peered out the rectangular window. As always, half the hallway lights had been turned off for the night. He looked left and right, squishing his cheek against the glass so he could see as far as possible. Not a soul in sight.

Turning back to the room, his gaze landed on the window. *There. Yes, yes. There.*

He crept over to it and peered down at the parking area behind the building.

One, two, three, four, five, six, seven, eight. Eight cars.

Some nights there were as few as six while others had as many as ten. Never more, never less. Eight was good. Eight was right. Eight was in the middle.

So not the cars, then. No, no, not the cars. The trees?

Behind the parking lot was a grove of pines, the closest trees partially illuminated by the lot's security lamps. He looked around, not sure what he was searching for.

Something moved. Not in the trees but back in the parking area, in his peripheral vision. He had *excellent* peripheral vision. Whatever it had been, though, had stopped. Everything looked the same as before.

It was there. I know it. I know it. I'm not seeing things. It was there.

The longer he couldn't spot the culprit, the more frustrated he became.

"Where?" he spat under his breath.

Behind him, the Beast stirred.

The Translator jerked around and slapped a hand over his own mouth. *Stay asleep. Stay asleep.*

The Beast's lips moved as if it were talking to someone. *Stay asleep.*

Finally the Beast settled down again, and the Translator was able to return his attention to the outside world.

All was still. All was the sa—

Not the same.

Something had changed.

One, two, three, four, five, six...seven.

Before he counted eight cars. It was eight, wasn't it? He remembered eight.

He counted again.

One, two, three, four, five, six, seven.

He counted a third time. And a fourth. And a fifth.

But the missing car never reappeared.

FIFTY-SIX

Joel

THE GENESEE MENTAL Care Facility looked only a bit less dreary in the daylight than it had the night before, when Leah and Joel stopped by for a look around after they'd arrived in town. It was a four-story off-white block of concrete, punctured by metal-framed, barred windows and a double-wide glass entrance. Even if Joel hadn't known what it was, he would have guessed hospital.

During their night excursion, they had taken a walk around to get a sense of the place. The only area they hadn't been able to scope out was a fenced-in section on the north side. Leah was the one who had detected Mike's presence at the third-floor window, right before she and Joel drove off. The only person Joel had ever been able to detect until that point was her, but as they pulled out of the parking area, he sensed a voice repeating "stay asleep," and knew it was his old cabin mate.

Leah was right. The connection between the three of them was growing stronger.

Joel and Leah took adjoining rooms at an old roadside motel not far away, but neither slept very well, and they were up and ready to go by seven a.m. Unfortunately, the facility didn't open to visitors until nine. They extended breakfast for as long as they could, and then drove around for a while before finally entering Genesee's lobby at 9:05.

A male attendant sat behind a sliding glass window. "May I help you?" he asked.

"Yes," Leah said. "We're here to see one of your patients.

Michael Hurst."

"Do you have an appointment?"

"Appointment? No, no appointment."

"Then I'm sorry. Visits require a twenty-four-hour notification. If you're not already on the calendar, then you're not getting in today."

"We have his guardians' permission," she said.

"Doesn't matter. Our procedures are in place for a reason."

"Of course, but this is an unusual—"

"Is there someone else we can talk to?" Joel cut in.

The receptionist stared at him, blank faced, and then rolled his eyes. "Who was it you were trying to see again?"

"Mike Hurst," Leah said.

"Have a seat."

Ten minutes later, a pale, thin-lipped woman entered the lobby.

"Good morning," she said. "I understand you want to see Michael?"

"Yes," Leah said. "That's correct."

"May I ask your relationship to him?"

"We're friends," Joel replied.

A raised eyebrow. "Friends?"

"When we were younger," Leah said quickly.

"Who are *you*?" Joel asked.

"I'm Dr. Renner, Michael's psychiatrist."

"I saw his parents two days ago," Leah said. "They told me it would be okay to visit him. You can call them. They'll tell you the same."

The woman said, "And your name?"

"Leah Bautista. And this is Joel Madsen."

"I did receive a call from Mrs. Hurst yesterday. They mentioned you would be coming by, Ms. Bautista, but they never mentioned your friend here."

"We...didn't think he would be able to make it."

The main entrance opened and a tired-looking woman walked up to the reception counter.

"Perhaps there's someplace more private we can talk

about this," Joel suggested.

"There is," the doctor replied, "but it won't be necessary. Unfortunately, I can't get you in right now. The only visitors Michael has ever had are his parents. I'm concerned about what his reaction to you might be, so I need a little time to prepare him. Tomorrow is the best I can do. In the afternoon, say, four o'clock."

"He's not going to hurt us, if that's what you're thinking," Leah said.

"And how would you know that?" the doctor asked.

"He'll want to see us."

The doctor frowned. "I'm not sure how much his parents told you, but Michael is not well. Most of the time he is barely aware of the world around him. There's a good chance he won't even know you're here."

"He will," Joel said.

Dr. Renner looked at him, her expression unchanged.

"Please," Leah said. "Seeing us will be good for him. I'm sure of it."

The doctor considered them for a moment, and then sighed. "Call me this afternoon around two. I'll let you know if he's in any condition to have visitors."

FIFTY-SEVEN

Leah

LEAH GUIDED THE rental car into the half-empty parking area of a shopping plaza and took a spot far from the other vehicles.

"You need me to do anything?" Joel asked.

"Just make sure no one bothers us."

While Leah moved to the back and lay down, Joel climbed out and leaned against the car, pretending to use his phone.

Closing her eyes, Leah concentrated on slowing her breathing and calming her body. Soon she felt her mind start to numb with coming sleep. As she'd done many times now, she focused on Mike's Secret Place—the shelves, the picture of him with his parents, the stacks of comic books, all the mementos that tied him to his past. She felt the slit in the blackness separate before she actually saw it. As soon as it was wide enough, she hurried inside.

Mike wasn't there, but she hadn't expected him to be. What she hoped was that he would come soon.

I'm here, she said. *I'm waiting for you.*

A stillness greater than any possible in the real world.

I need to talk to you. Just for a moment.

Was that a ripple in the air, or her imagination?

Mike, please, come.

FIFTY-EIGHT

THE TRANSLATOR SAT quietly in the corner of the busy room, ignoring the others as he rocked back and forth while the information packets processed in his head.

I'm here. I'm waiting for you. I need to talk to you. Just for a moment.

He stopped mid-rock.

Without thinking, he started to reach out for his [*secret place*] and then pulled back. What was he doing? He couldn't talk to the Satellite. No, no. The Reclaimer might find out.

Mike, please, come.

Mike.

Her use of his [*before name*] soothed him and beckoned him to come, as if it had a power all its own. He wanted to hear it again. He wanted her to say it one more time.

I'm your friend. I'm not going to hurt you. I'm waiting, Mike. I'm waiting for you.

There it was. He breathed in the beauty of it. A word like no other. His word.

Mike.

He checked his pathways to make sure the packets were still flowing, and that the Reclaimer was not connected to him.

A moment or two won't hurt, he thought. *Just a moment or two.*

Carefully and quietly, he slipped sideways into his [*secret place*].

There she was, near the shelf where he kept [*the most important picture ever taken*], her back to him. Maybe he could just watch her and she would never know he was there. Maybe he could—

"Hello, Mike," she said, turning to him.

He lurched backward, very nearly leaving the room altogether, but he held on.

"H-h-h-hello, L-L-Leah."

She smiled. "Thank you for coming."

"What-what-what do you want?"

"You remember Joel, don't you?"

The missing Satellite. "I-I-I remember Joel. Yes. I remember."

"Mike, Joel is with me now."

The Translator spun around, thinking Joel was somewhere in his [secret place].

"Not here," she said. "In the real world."

"Real world," he whispered.

"We've come to help you."

He took another step backward.

"Don't be afraid, Mike."

Hearing his [before name] calmed him again.

"You and Joel and I are special," she said. "There is no one else like us. We only have each other. Do you want us to help you?"

"I'm fine. I'm fine, fine, fine. Don't need help."

She picked up [the most important picture ever taken] and turned it so the Translator could see it. "Your parents said it was okay if we came to see you. If they say it's okay, don't you think you should see us?"

"My parents?" he whispered. The word felt foreign and yet so meaningful.

"They told me where you are, and now Joel and I are nearby."

"You-you are close?"

"We are, and we're going to help you. You do want our help. I know you do."

"Help...me?"

"Yes."

That small voice that lived in the back of his mind grasped

this and said, "Help me." Only the words didn't stay in his head, but passed across the Translator's lips. "Help me." And again, more urgently. "Help me. Help me!"

She stepped toward him but he backed away again, so she stopped. "We will. We'll help you. But it's up to you how soon that can happen. Listen carefully. This is very important. Dr. Renner is going to tell you someone is here to visit you. She's talking about Joel and me. You need to say it's okay. You need to make her believe you want to see us. Do you understand?"

It was as if his mind had split in two, the small voice in the back suddenly grabbing territory in leaps and bounds. "I understand," he heard himself say. "I understand."

FIFTY-NINE

Leah

CONTRARY TO DR. Renner's instructions, Leah and Joel showed up in the lobby at two p.m. instead of calling.

A new person sat behind the reception window, a woman approaching retirement age with the disinterested expression to prove it.

"We're here to see Dr. Renner," Leah said. "She's expecting us."

"Names?"

"Leah Bautista and Joel Madsen."

The woman grunted and picked up her phone.

Leah and Joel moved near the interior door to wait. Not a minute later, it swung open and Dr. Renner strode out.

"I believe you were supposed to *call*, not show up," she admonished them.

"We were feeling optimistic," Joel said.

The doctor looked annoyed but said nothing.

"So? Can we see him?" Leah asked.

Dr. Renner took a deep breath and turned back toward the door. "Follow me."

They walked down sanitized corridors of off-white walls and off-white tiled floors, the only splash of color the red metal box containing a fire extinguisher. Even the doors of the elevator the doctor led them to were the same neutral tone.

When the car started moving up, she said, "You're lucky. You've caught him on a good day. He, um, even says he remembers you."

"Why wouldn't he?" Joel asked.

"Let's just say it's unusual."

A ding signaled their arrival on the third floor.

The only difference between the corridor they entered and the one at ground level was this one had windows along the outside wall. They were large, with safety wire running through them and bars on the outside.

"You don't have criminals living here, do you?" Leah asked.

The doctor frowned. "I'm sorry?" Then she noticed Leah looking at the bars. "Those are there for our patients' protection. The last thing we want is for someone to hurt themselves jumping out the window."

A few moments later, they passed a long interior window that looked in on a large room filled with chairs, most facing a wall-mounted TV. There were at least two dozen patients inside, and several uniformed orderlies.

After they rounded another corner, the doctor stopped in front of a door marked with a plaque reading: FR 03. She opened it and ushered them inside.

To Leah's surprise, the space looked very much like a living room—a couch and chairs and even a TV. Framed paintings hung on the walls that were not off-white but a soothing light blue.

"This is our family visitation room," the doctor explained. "Please have a seat and I'll go get Michael."

When she was gone, Joel whispered, "This is kind of creepy. I mean, who is this fooling?"

Leah sat on the couch. "I think it's more to make everyone feel comfortable."

"Well, it's not working for me." He walked over to the windows and looked out. "What I'm feeling is claustrophobic."

She couldn't deny she was feeling a bit of the same, but she knew it was the hospital and not the room itself that was causing it.

Soon, the door opened again, and Dr. Renner ushered Mike into the room. He stopped just inside, his eyes dancing around, taking in the walls and the furniture and the windows and everything except Leah and Joel.

He was skinnier than Leah had expected, but otherwise looked like an early twenties version of the ever-changing man she'd seen in his Secret Place. She rose from the couch and started toward him, Joel right behind her.

"These are the people who have come to see you," Dr. Renner said. "They're friends of yours from when you were all younger."

Still Mike didn't look at them or move.

"You said you knew who they were, remember?"

Sixty

THE TRANSLATOR HAD been preparing for this moment since the Satellite told him they were coming, and yet when Dr. Renner came for him, he couldn't help feeling like his mind was about to explode.

He and the Satellites should not be together. The three were *never* supposed to be together. The Satellites were to experience and learn and report, and he to translate.

If the Reclaimer suddenly checked in and saw them in the same room…

No, no. Cannot let that happen.

As he and Dr. Renner walked down the hall, he rapidly built a wall in his mind. He pulled together images of the busy room where everyone watched TV and put himself in it. Hopefully, if the Reclaimer did return, it would fool her.

They reached the meeting room far too fast. While his ruse for the Reclaimer was ready, he still wasn't. He almost told Dr. Renner to stop when she reached for the handle, but the small voice that had usurped control of his mind squeezed his vocal cords so that no sound could escape.

Inside he could sense the Satellites hovering nearby, but he could not look at them. Dr. Renner spoke some words he didn't hear. It was hard enough to breathe, let alone listen to anything.

He'd been in this room before. It's where he sometimes met the two other people in [*the most important picture ever taken*]. He concentrated on that, hoping it would give him the strength he needed to face the Satellites.

What it did instead was prevent him from realizing what was about to happen.

SIXTY-ONE

Joel

JOEL PACED IN front of the window, concerned.

Leah was sure Mike was the key to figuring out what had happened to them. Joel still hoped she was right, but being here, seeing where Mike had spent most of his life since they were last together, he thought the chances of finding answers were slight, and was pretty sure they would have to forge ahead with just the two of them.

And then the door opened.

And Mike shuffled in.

The goofy kid in the next bunk. The goody two-shoes with the kind heart. Joel's friend.

Joel stopped pacing and joined Leah as she headed across the room.

As they neared, the doctor looked at them and said, "Please give him a little distance."

But they ignored her, unable to stop themselves until they were directly in front of Mike.

"Hey, a-hole," Joel said. "How you doing?"

SIXTY-TWO

Mike/The Translator

THE TRANSLATOR JUMPED at the sound of Satellite Two's voice. The alarms in his head were screaming at him to run from the room, but then the words the Satellite had said cut through his panic.

"Hey, a-hole. How you doing?"

The Translator looked at the long missing Satellite for the first time in years. He felt the small voice ease up on his throat as it sent a message to his lips.

"You're...the a-hole...Joel," he said.

The Satellite smiled and wrapped his arms around him. For a moment the Translator froze, but then his own arms moved around the Satellite—around *Joel*—and hugged his old friend tight.

SIXTY-THREE

Joel

LEAH FOUGHT THE urge to join in the embrace, thinking it best to let her two friends reconnect on their own first. She couldn't keep the grin from her face, however.

Dr. Renner tried to appear neutral, but Leah could see the surprise in the woman's eyes.

When Joel finally released Mike, Leah could hold back no longer. She threw her arms around Mike. "Hi," she whispered in his ear. "This is so much better than seeing you in your Secret Place."

He stiffened a bit and whispered back, "Shhhh. Don't say that."

"Sorry. Just between you and me."

"Between you and me," he repeated.

When they separated, Dr. Renner said, "Michael, are you okay? If this is too much for you, you need to let me know."

"Not too much. No, no. Not too much. My friends. They are my friends."

Leah put a hand on Mike's back and led him toward the couch. "Why don't we sit down?"

"We're okay now," Joel said to the doctor. "You can go."

"Oh, no, that's not how this works," Dr. Renner said. "Only family members are allowed to be alone with patients, and that's only with patients who are not at risk."

"Do you really think something's going to happen?" Leah asked. "Mike, are you going to hurt us?"

"No, no. I would never hurt you," Mike said. "Never."

"It's not hurting anyone I'm worried about," the doctor

said to Leah and Joel. "He's fragile."

"We just want to have a private conversation," Joel said.

"Yes, private," Mike said. "Alone is better."

The doctor looked at her patient, surprised. Leah had a feeling this was not the Mike with whom the woman was used to dealing.

"Please, I'll be good. I will. I will," Mike said. "I won't be...fragile."

"I'm not about to break the rules," Dr. Renner said, but then she relaxed a little. "What I can do is leave the door open and wait in the hallway. It's either that or I stay here."

"That's more than generous," Leah told her. "Thank you. We'd appreciate that."

The doctor hesitated, but after a moment she stepped out of the room.

Leah and Mike sat on the couch while Joel pulled up a chair and leaned in so they could talk without being overheard.

"We have to hurry, hurry before she comes," Mike whispered. "Maybe she won't believe my trick. Maybe, maybe."

"I'm sure Dr. Renner will give us plenty of time," Joel said, his voice also low.

Leah sensed something else was troubling Mike. Something not *here*. "I don't think that's who he's talking about." She looked at Mike. "Who is it you're worried about?"

"Can't say. Can't say." His gaze darted around as if he expected someone to appear out of thin air.

"If someone's bothering you here, we can take care of that," Joel said.

"No one here. No. No."

Joel started to say something again, but Leah gave him a subtle shake of the head.

She smiled at Mike. "You were saying we don't have much time."

"Not much time, no. Maybe. I don't know. Better if we're quick, I think. Better, better."

"Then quick it is," she said. "Something happened to the three of us when we were at camp. Something that changed us."

"Yes, yes. Made you the Satellites, and me the Translator."

Leah's brow furrowed. "What does that mean?"

"Nothing, nothing," Mike said, looking as if he'd said something he shouldn't have.

She wanted to pursue it, but it could wait until they had more time. "We're trying to find out what happened to us. What do you remember?"

"Not remember. Not want to remember."

"But you do know."

He shook his head, but the look in his eyes said differently.

"Mike, please. If you do know something, then maybe it will help us figure out how to make you better."

"Better?"

"Yes."

He was silent for a moment, but then shook his head again. "Cannot say. Can never say."

"Why can't you say?"

He continued to shake his head, his lips pressed together.

She knew if he did know something, he wasn't going to give it up. Maybe if they gave him some time, came back in a few weeks. Then again, maybe not.

She put her arm around his shoulder. "That's okay. You don't have to say anything."

He relaxed.

"We can go there, you and I," Joel said. "We'll figure it out."

They truly were getting more in sync, as she'd been having the same thought.

"Go?" Mike said. "Go where?"

"Camp Red Hawk," Leah said.

"Oh, no, no, no, no. Can't go back. Not you," he said, pointing at Leah. He then pointed at Joel. "Not you." And finally at himself. "Not me."

"Why not?"

"She will not let us."

"We're still not talking about Dr. Renner, are we?" Joel asked.

"Not Dr. Renner. The-the-the..." Mike pressed his lips together again, frustrated. "She will not let us."

"No one said anything about you going, Mike. But Joel and I are."

"No, no, can't go." Mike was becoming agitated, his voice rising.

Leah shot a look toward the door, worried that Dr. Renner would hear, but the woman remained outside.

"Tell us why not," Joel said.

"Because, because you are supposed to experience and report."

The words triggered something deep inside Leah's chest. It appeared to have done the same to Joel. And then another word appeared in her mind.

Joel said it first. "Mine."

Mike gasped, his nervousness turning into outright terror. "You cannot say that word. That's *her* word. Hers!"

"Is everything all right?" Dr. Renner was leaning in the doorway.

"Everything's fine," Leah said. "We were, um, just remembering something we did together. Sorry."

"Michael?" the doctor said.

"Fine, fine. I'm fine."

"I think it's best if we wrap this up in a few minutes," Dr. Renner said.

"No problem," Leah replied.

The doctor hesitated a moment longer before disappearing again.

"You can't go," Mike whispered. "You can't go."

"We have no choice," Joel said.

Mike began rocking on the couch. "Nine, six, six, three, two, three, seven, one, six, three, seven. Eight, four, five—"

Leah touched his arm. "We'll be careful. I promise. If we sense any trouble we'll turn back, all right?"

"—three, two, three, seven, one, six, three, seven. One, zero, six, zero, eight—"

Leah looked at Joel as Mike continued to count. They'd had him for a while but now he was gone. Joel made a motion asking her if she wanted to leave. She didn't, but knew it might be for the best so she reluctantly nodded.

She stood, leaned down, and kissed Mike on the head. "We'll come back to visit you again. I promise."

Joel put a hand on Mike's back. "I promise, too."

They started for the door.

"Wait," Mike said.

They turned back, surprised.

"You're going."

"The doctor won't let us stay all day," Joel said.

"No, no. I-I-I mean you're *going* going. To camp."

"Yes," Leah said.

"Then I, then I, then I will go, too."

"Whoa!" Joel said. "They're not going to let you out of here, Mike."

Mike motioned for them to come back. When they were huddled together, he whispered, "Tonight. Twelve fifteen. Wait-wait-wait by the road. Near the, the big sign. Genesee sign. I'll be there."

"Not a good idea," Leah said. "We'll come back as soon as we leave there and tell you what happened. But you're not—"

"I have to go. You need me. You will not, will not, will not make it without me. Remember, twelve fifteen. Near the big sign."

He shot out of his chair in an unexpected burst of speed and hurried past them out the door.

"Michael!" Dr. Renner called. "Stop." A pause. "Stay right there." She looked into the room. "What happened?"

"Nothing," Joel said. "We were talking and then he said he had somewhere to go."

The doctor looked less than pleased. "I'll be right back." She vanished again.

"Should we tell her?" Joel asked.

Though Leah had no idea if Mike could really get out, telling Dr. Renner would ensure it wouldn't happen. She shook her head and said, "I think he's right. I think we do need him."

"Why?"

How could she explain the feelings of anticipation and dread in her gut?

"Because we came out of there together once before, so it might be the only way we can make it out again."

SIXTY-FOUR

Mike/The Translator

THE TRANSLATOR LAY on his bed, staring at the ceiling. The markers on the data packets told him it was a quarter until midnight. A few more minutes and it would be time to set things in motion.

No! Cannot! Cannot! the big voice, the scared voice, screamed. *The Reclaimer. If you leave she'll know and you'll be dead!*

He started rocking, his bed creaking with each back and forth movement.

"Cannot, cannot, cannot," he silently mouthed.

"Stop it!" the Beast ordered. "Unless you want me to tear you apart."

The Translator stopped rocking.

11:49.

One minute. One minute and you do it.

No! Cannot!

You must. Joel and Leah are waiting.

He turned on his side and wrapped his pillow around his head to cut off the sound of the small voice. But it didn't work.

Thirty seconds.

"No," he whispered.

"Shut up," the Beast said.

Twenty.

The Translator clenched the pillow tighter.

Fifteen.

And tighter.

Ten.

"No, no, no, no."

"Shut up!"

Five, four, three, two.... Get up.

The Translator let go of the pillow and swung his legs off his bed, the big voice no longer in control.

"What are you doing?" the Beast asked, staring at him. "Lie down and be quiet!"

The Translator walked over to the Beast's bed. He knew what he had to do, but he didn't like it.

"I'm sorry," the Translator whispered.

The Beast pulled at the restraints, the muscles in its neck and shoulders straining. "I swear to God I will rip your head off if you don't get away from me!"

After all these years of sharing a room, the Translator knew everything there was to know about the Beast, like how the Beast absolutely could not stand anyone touching its head. The Translator moved around to the end of the bed, rubbed his hands over the Beast's skull, and backed away.

The Beast began to flail on the mattress, roaring in anger.

The Translator hurried to the door and listened. No footsteps yet.

Back at the Beast's bed, the Translator did it again, this time adding a tap-tap-tap against the Beast's ear.

If the Beast's yells had been loud before, they were deafening now.

The Translator checked the door again.

Yes, yes, yes, he thought, hearing running steps.

He climbed back into his bed, pulled the cover over his body, and shut his eyes.

This only enraged the Beast further, its movements causing its bed frame to bounce off the floor.

A moment later, the door swung open and the light flicked on.

"What's going on in here?" The voice belonged to the Night Supervisor. A big man who didn't like problems. The Translator couldn't have asked for a better responder.

The Beast continued to scream, most of it unintelligible, but with the occasional *kill him* and *weasel* and *rip apart* coming through clearly.

The Night Supervisor radioed for help. While the man waited for his Orderlies to arrive, the Translator thought it was a good time to "wake up."

Blinking, he groaned and said in a sleepy voice, "Too loud, too loud. Why so loud?"

"I'm sorry, Michael," the Night Supervisor said. "Try to go back to sleep."

"Why so loud? Why?"

"Mr. Lowell's having a little problem at the moment, and it would be a big help to me if you would just try to rest."

"Okay, okay. Rest. Okay."

"Thank you, Michael."

"Okay. Rest."

He rolled onto his side, facing the Beast's bed, and squinted through his mostly closed eyelids. It was difficult at first to keep the grin off his face. He was pleased with how well he had played the part of himself, saying things the way he would have said them if he had indeed woken to find the Beast yelling and the Night Supervisor in the room.

The Night Supervisor tried to calm the Beast, saying it needed to quiet down so "Michael can sleep." The Beast's bed bounced so high at that, it made the Night Supervisor jump back.

Less than a minute later, two Orderlies rushed in. One was carrying a package with a syringe. The Night Supervisor took this and had the orderlies hold the Beast down as he stuck the needle into its arm. He told one of the men to fetch a gurney so they could transfer the Beast to one of the isolation rooms near the nurses' station.

The Translator waited anxiously for the gurney to arrive, and then watched as the Beast was transferred to it.

Now came the tricky part, the most important part, the part that if the Translator got wrong, he would fail before he could even leave his room.

After the two orderlies wheeled the bed out, the Night Supervisor flicked off the light and turned for the door. The moment his back was to the room, the Translator silently slipped out of bed.

The door had an automatic closer attached to the top that, with a simple tug on the knob, would ensure the door shut. The bonus for the Translator was that it also slowed the door down so that it didn't crash into the frame, giving him more than enough time to catch it before the latch clicked into place. He slipped over the latch hole the piece of Scotch tape he'd taken from the art supplies that afternoon, and then let the door close the rest of the way. He waited, rock still, listening to hear if the Night Supervisor would come back to double-check the door. But he didn't.

The Translator had to fight the urge to pull the door open right then, but he knew the Night Supervisor might still be in the hallway.

Wait. Wait. Wait.

He counted to thirty, the numbers soothing him much in the same way those identifying the packets did. When he reached zero, he eased the door open and peeked into the corridor. Not a person in sight.

There were stairs at the end of the hall in the opposite direction from the one the Beast had been taken in. Stairs with a door that would sound an alarm if opened.

That was okay. The Translator knew a way around that. He'd been at the facility for so long, there was little about the place he didn't know. Like how Ronald, one of the other residents, had gone through a phase when he'd pushed the door open whenever he had a chance because he liked the sound of the alarm. And how Nurse Sanders had hidden a key in the monitor's desk in the busy room that would turn off the alarm.

Smart, very smart. Not Nurse Sanders, but the Translator.

He snuck into the now dark busy room, retrieved the key, and made his way to the stairwell door. He slipped the key into the slot on the arm and turned it.

So far so good. He put a hand on the bar, took a breath, and pushed.

SIXTY-FIVE

Joel

THE SEDAN SAT at the side of the main road, a dozen yards shy of the sign that marked the entrance to the Genesee Mental Care Facility. The building itself was hidden from Joel's and Leah's sight by a grove of pines.

Joel glanced at the car's clock again—12:17. "Where is he?"

"We need to give him time," Leah said, her gaze focused on the woods.

The clock ticked over to 12:18.

"He probably got caught," Joel said. Genesee was a locked facility, after all. What were the chances Mike would be able to escape?

Two minutes later, the rear driver's side door opened, and Mike, wearing only a pair of flannel pajamas and no shoes, smiled at them from outside.

"Get in or you'll freeze to death," Leah said.

As Mike climbed into the back, he said, "Not freezing. Not that cold."

The moment the door was shut, Joel pulled the sedan from the curb, his eyes darting back and forth between the road ahead and the rearview mirror. "Did anyone see you leave?"

"No one, no one. Very quiet. I'm smart. No one saw me."

Leah reached into the back and squeezed Mike's knee. "I'm glad you're here."

"I'm glad, too. Glad." His smile faltered a little. "Do you think maybe, maybe…"

Joel looked at him in the mirror. "Maybe what?"

"Maybe we can stop for a cheeseburger?"

"I think we can make that happen."

SIXTY-SIX

Leah

THEY DROVE THROUGH the night to put as much distance between themselves and Flagstaff as possible, finally stopping after seven a.m. at a roadside motel near Grand Junction, Colorado, on the western edge of the Rocky Mountains.

Once in her room, Leah checked the Internet for any news about a missing Genesee mental patient. Nothing so far, but she knew that wouldn't last. She thought she should call Mike's parents to let them know he was okay, but that would bring questions she wasn't ready to answer. Maybe after she woke up she'd feel differently.

She took a quick shower, climbed into bed, and was out within a minute. But she didn't stay asleep long. Less than an hour after closing her eyes, a fist pounded against her door and jerked her awake.

"Leah!" Joel called.

"Huh?" she said, not loudly enough for him to hear.

"Leah! Wake up!"

She crawled out of bed, still half asleep, and opened the door just enough to see out. "What is it?"

"Mike. He's…"

"What? Gone?" she asked, suddenly alert.

He grimaced. "Um…kind of."

"What does that mean?

"He's in, I don't know, some kind of trance, I guess."

"I'll be right there."

She pulled on jeans with the T-shirt she'd slept in, and hurried to Joel and Mike's room.

Mike was lying on the bed closest to the window. His eyes were half open but unfocused, and his lips were moving rapidly as if reciting something.

"What's he saying?" she asked.

"Numbers," Joel replied.

She leaned in close and heard ones and sevens and twos and fives. It was like what he'd started doing at Genesee.

"You tried waking him?" she asked.

"Yeah."

"And?"

"Obviously it didn't work," he said, annoyed. "Sorry. I didn't mean that. Do you think you can reach him? You know, like before?"

"I can try."

She stretched out on Joel's bed and focused on slowing her heart rate. From there it was a fairly easy slope back into the half-sleep that would allow her to navigate her way to Mike's Special Place.

"Mike, where are you?" she said when she reached the forever room. She turned in a circle, hoping he'd materialize, but she remained alone. "Are you all right?" No movement anywhere. "Can you even hear me?"

A gust of wind blew through the room, whipping her hair into her eyes, and then it was gone.

He could hear her.

"Are you hurt?" she asked.

Nothing.

"Do you need our help?"

Nothing again.

"Mike, please. We're worried about you. We don't know what to do."

The wind returned, this time carrying a whisper. "You can only wait. Wait, wait."

SIXTY-SEVEN

Mike/The Translator

THE RECLAIMER CAME to the Translator as he slept.

::YOUR OUTPUT IS DOWN. WHY?

The answer was easy. Since fleeing the room he shared with the Beast, his mind had been occupied by real-world things. Naturally, his input had dropped. He'd been smart, though—very smart—and had begun limiting his dispatches so he could stretch out the finished packets he still had. Of course she would notice; he'd known she would. But he'd hoped it would have taken her more time.

I am-I am-I am not operating at my optimal level, he said.

::EXPLAIN.

The...flu, he said. *I-I vomited most of the night.* It was a good cover, yes, a good cover. Every time the Translator was sick, his output always decreased.

The Reclaimer was silent for a moment. He worried she would push him to show her his memories of this. He did have some from past incidents, but it would take time to recall them.

::HOW MUCH LONGER WILL THE INTERRUPTION LAST?

He had to clamp down hard on his thoughts to hide his relief that she hadn't pushed. *Medicine they gave me makes me very...tired. Very tired. A day. Maybe two.*

::YOU WILL INCREASE OUTPUT THE MOMENT YOU ARE ABLE.

Of course, of course. Yes, of course.

::I WILL MONITOR YOUR PACKETS FOR A WHILE IN CASE OF TRANSLATION ERRORS.

I understand. I think everything, everything is okay. But good to check. Very good.

He concentrated on the packets, retranslating those that had already been translated as slow as possible to extend the process. Any thoughts of his friends and their journey he kept boxed away so the Reclaimer would not sense them. It was only the information that filled his mind, until...

Mike, where are you?

Leah. She was in his [*special place*]. The Translator glanced at the Reclaimer—figuratively, of course, because he could never see her, but he always had a sense of where she was concentrated. She made no indication she'd heard his friend.

It's your secret place, his small voice said. *Only you can hear things from your secret place.*

While that was logical, he couldn't help worrying the Reclaimer would somehow sense something was up if Leah continued to talk. He needed to stop her.

When Leah asked if he could hear her, he willed the breeze that ruffled her hair, hoping she would understand he didn't have time for her right now. But she kept asking questions, and when she said she and the Joel didn't know what to do, the Translator took a huge risk and sent a message with the breeze, hoping that would ease her concern.

The moment it left him, the Reclaimer's attention whipped back on him. ::WHAT WAS THAT?

What was what?

::YOU THOUGHT A WORD: WAIT. EXPLAIN.

The Translator hesitated before saying, *Wait. Yes, yes. I did.*

:: EXPLAIN.

"The translations. The translations are...difficult. In my current condition, I mean. I-I-I discovered one that was harder, harder than others, and-and I decided I should wait until my mind, my mind was clearer."

The Reclaimer fell silent.

I can show you, the Translator said, *but it will interrupt my translation schedule, and-and you will, you will also not fully understand it in its-its current state.*

Silence again.

Then,
::ARE YOUR CHANNELS OPEN?
Yes.
::ARE YOUR RECEPTORS WORKING?
Yes.
::ARE ALL LINKS INTACT?
Yes.
The Reclaimer left.

SIXTY-EIGHT

Joel

NOT LONG AFTER Leah went under, the numbers began flying off Mike's lips nearly too fast for Joel to understand. And then Mike just stopped. The silence that followed was almost more disturbing than the counting had been.

Feeling helpless, Joel paced in front of the beds, his mind spinning. What if neither of his friends woke up? Would he have to try to reach them himself? Could he even do that?

These thoughts were consuming him when Leah's back suddenly arched and her eyes shot open.

He hurried to her side. "Are you all right?"

She took a moment and then nodded.

"Did you get through to him?"

"Sort of," she said, and told him what had happened.

"So he's okay."

"I think so...maybe. Honestly, though, I'm not sure."

Once Joel was positive she was fine, he went out to pick up some food. When he returned, Mike was sitting up, Leah's arm around him.

Joel mouthed, "How is he?"

Leah tilted her head side to side—so-so.

Joel put on a smile and raised the bags. "I've got more cheeseburgers. Are you hungry?"

There was a slight delay before Mike looked up. "Hungry. Yes, I'm hungry."

Joel set the bags down, pulled out a burger, and handed it to Mike.

Mike looked at it for a moment. "I don't-don't have to eat

cheeseburgers every time." He glanced at Joel. "I like pizza, too."

Joel smiled. "Got it. Next time, pizza."

"And Chinese food."

"They serve Chinese food where you live?"

"My…" Mike hesitated, searching for the right word. "P-p-parents. My parents bring it with them when they visit."

"When we see a Chinese place, we'll hit that, too."

"Good." Mike took a large bite of the burger. "Thank you."

After Mike finished chewing, Joel asked, "So, um, what was that all about?"

"What do you mean?"

"The numbers? While you were, I guess, sleeping?"

Mike looked down at his burger. "Not sleeping. I was hiding us."

"Who were you hiding us from?"

Another pause. "Her."

Leah put a hand on Mike's back. "You mean the person you were talking about yesterday?"

"Yes. Her."

"Who is she?" Joel asked.

Mike seemed to be struggling with how to answer.

"It's okay," Leah said. "You don't have to tell us if you don't want to."

"Don't want to, but need to," Mike said. "You need to know." He stared at the floor for a moment before looking at them. "She is the one who…made us."

A shiver ran down Joel's spine. "You mean changed us?"

"Yes," Mike said.

"You're in communication with her?" Leah asked.

"I am…I am her translator."

"We don't know what that means," Joel said.

Several seconds passed before Mike whispered, "I help her understand our world."

"And how do you do that?"

"I send her your information." He frowned. "Well, not yours. Not for a long time." He looked at Leah. "But yours. I still send her yours."

Leah appeared confused for a moment, but then looked away, lost in thought.

"What information?" Joel asked.

Instead of Mike responding, it was Leah who said, "Everything."

SIXTY-NINE

Leah

LEAH SLEPT IN fits and starts the rest of the day. In the years since she'd started changing, a part of her had hoped that whatever had intervened in her, Joel's, and Mike's lives was benevolent. The changes, at least with her and Joel, were improvements after all. And what about the missions she and Joel had undertaken? The people they had—with one notable exception—helped?

But now she knew better. Whatever it was had been using them all along. Mike most of all.

Her desire to return to Camp Red Hawk was now stronger than ever. She needed to confront this thing. She needed to know why it had done what it had to them. Most of all, she needed to make it release its hold on them.

They were on the road again by five that afternoon.

As they ascended into the mountains, a tingle started at the base of Leah's neck. It was similar to but not quite the same as the ones that preceded her dreams. The farther they went, the more the sensation spread, and by the time they reached Boulder, she could feel it everywhere.

Since the camp was another two and a half hours back into the mountains and it was already dark, they found another motel and made plans to start out again before sunrise.

Leah was wary of going to sleep, worried that the sensation might mean she'd be spending her night in the augmented reality of her dreams, so she lay there for a while, thinking about what might be waiting for them in the woods. These thoughts led her back to Joel's and her missions. There was something about them she had barely questioned, but suddenly it was all she could focus on. And by the time she drifted off, she was pretty sure she knew the answer.

Upon waking, the tingling still clung to her, though not as intensely as it had the night before. She quickly dressed and headed outside, where she found the boys waiting at the car.

"I'll drive," she told Joel as she approached.

"I can do it," he said.

"I was the last one up there. I know the area a little better than you."

He snorted. "That was like seven years ago."

She held her hand out for the keys. "I'm driving."

With a shrug, he gave them to her, and then climbed into the front passenger seat.

"How you doing?" she asked Mike as she got in. He'd already settled into the back.

His lips curled up in what was supposed to be a smile before they dipped again, his face tense.

"It was you, wasn't it?" she asked.

"Me what?"

"When Joel and I were helping people. You were the one who guided me. Showed me what I needed to see."

His gaze darted away.

"It was, right?" she asked.

Another quick not-smile. "Yes."

"So the three of us have been back together longer than we thought."

"Than *you* thought."

She laughed. "Good point."

"Can we go now? We need to go. Go, go."

"Does she know we're coming?" Joel asked.

"Doesn't know. Not yet. But I'm not sure, not sure how long I can keep the secret. Go, go."

Leah started the car.

THE SUN HAD barely risen over the horizon when they reached the county road into the mountains. The last time the three of them had been on that road together was on the buses to camp.

The higher they went, the more patches of snow they saw. Small clumps at first, but soon a layer a few inches thick covered everything—old snow, mixed with dirt and pine needles.

Leah's tingling staged a roaring comeback as the elevation increased, making it hard for her to sit still in her seat. Joel seemed to be just as fidgety. She wondered if he was suffering the same infliction but she didn't ask.

When they neared the two-hour mark into their journey, the road crested a pass and turned down into the shallow valley where Camp Red Hawk, Camp Cedar Woods, and at least half a dozen other camps were located.

She had never been here in the winter—well, technically spring now, she corrected herself. The off-white vista was broken only by the trees and the blue lakes that dotted the valley. If anything, the area looked even more peaceful than it did in the summer.

"There," Joel said, pointing out the window ahead and to the left. "That boomerang-shaped lake. That's it, isn't it?"

Leah nodded. "Yeah. That's it."

Given the unexpected tangents their lives had taken since that fateful summer, the lake and the area around it should have looked like Mordor or the gates of hell, but it appeared no less serene than the rest of the valley.

Five minutes farther on, they reached an intersection Leah remembered well. On one corner was the café Monty's Eats, and on the other the combination gas station and mini-market where she and Todd had bought slushies. Neither place seemed to have changed at all in the years since.

A turn to the left sent them toward Camp Red Hawk. Beside her, she could hear Joel taking shorter and shorter breaths. She touched his thigh, hoping it might calm him. He gave her a forced smile, but his breathing slowed only a little.

"It's going to be fine," she said.

Without taking his eyes off the road, he said, "I didn't wake up all that great."

For a moment, she didn't know what he meant, and then it dawned on her. "What was it?"

"My shoulder," he said, touching the one on his right. "A nice big bruise."

Remembering when she'd seen his phantom injuries, she said, "Dislocated?"

He shook his head. "Just strained, I think." A pause. "I guess I'm telling you because, you know, in case I do it to you. I'm sorry."

She squeezed his leg. "Potential apology accepted."

She looked in the mirror to check on Mike. He was rocking in his seat, his eyes darting from window to window while his lips silently moved with the recitation of his numbers.

Several minutes later, she almost missed seeing the turnoff. She'd been looking for the painted-over sign that had still been standing on her last visit. Now only one of its posts remained. She didn't realize what it was until they were almost parallel to it.

She slammed on the brakes, ramming the boys against their seatbelts, and then threw the car into reverse.

"What the hell?" Joel asked.

She turned onto the dirt road. "We're here."

It turned out the missing sign wasn't the only change about the entrance. Someone had erected a barrier across.

"I'll check it." Joel hopped out of the car and ran over to the obstruction. When he came back, he said, "It's not a gate. It's a fence. We're going to have to walk in."

Leah pulled the sedan as far forward as possible so that it would be hidden by the woods, and then she and Mike climbed out. Dressed in the T-shirt and jeans they'd picked up for him before leaving Grand Junction, Mike shivered in the cold air.

"Where's your jacket?" Leah asked, then noticed his feet. "And your shoes?" They'd purchased those for him, too.

He looked down.

"You need to put them on," she told him. "You'll freeze otherwise."

"Right, right. It's cold. Okay."

He grabbed the items from inside and pulled them on. When he stood again, Leah stepped over to him.

"Oh, Mike," she said as she zipped up his jacket. The only

outside time he'd probably had since he'd been hospitalized was in the fenced-off area behind the Genesee facility. At the very least, whatever it was that had changed them needed to pay for the life it had taken from him. She put her hand on his back. "Come on."

They walked to the fence.

"We can squeeze through here," Joel said from the trees just off the road.

He pushed down on one of the wires with his foot and pulled up on the wire strung above it, creating a gap wide enough to maneuver through.

As soon as they were on the other side, he said, "Do you feel it?"

She nodded. A pull, like the one that had led her home from the Valentine's Day dance back in high school, only this thread wasn't simply anchored to her chest. It was tugging at her whole body.

Mike rocked back and forth as he stared into the forest. "I feel it, I feel it."

"Is it her?" Leah asked. "Does she know we're here?"

Mike was silent for a moment. "No, no. She doesn't know. It's like, like…" He held out his hands and mimed them being pulled together.

"Like a magnet."

"Yes. Like a magnet. Yes, yes."

"If anyone has any doubts, now's the time to turn back," Joel said.

Mike whipped his head around and looked at Joel. "No, no. Cannot. No turning back. She won't let us."

"I thought you just said she doesn't know we're here."

"She doesn't. Not yet. But if we try to leave, she will…sense us. Yes, yes. Too much fear. She will know, and she will not let us go."

"Well, I guess that answers that," Joel said, and started walking.

They hiked down the middle of the old road, learning quickly to place their steps with care to avoid ruts hidden by the snow. Even then, it took almost fifteen minutes before they reached the camp.

They passed the posts where the chain had once been strung, entered the parking area, and had their first good look at the camp.

"My God," Joel said. "Why would anyone have let the place get like this?"

When Leah had come with Todd and the others, Red Hawk had already looked worn down. Now it was truly decrepit. The roof of the administration building had completely collapsed, and limbs of trees growing inside could be seen peeking over the wall. The cafeteria was still covered, but the entire building was leaning to the side and would likely not last another winter.

"I thought someone would have bought it and fixed it up by now," Joel said. "It's a prime location."

Leah shook her head. "It's cursed. They could rename it whatever they like, but word would get out that this was where 'those kids' disappeared. No parent would ever send their children here."

"Cursed, not cursed," Mike said. "It doesn't matter. *She* wouldn't let anyone have it."

Joel looked at him. "Does this *she* have a name?"

Mike glanced nervously at him and then returned his gaze to the camp. For a few moments his face clouded. Finally he said, "Yes. She is, she is...." He went silent again, and it seemed as if he wasn't going to say anything at all.

"Mike?" Leah said. "Are you all right?"

He chewed on his lower lip for several more seconds before whispering, "She is the Reclaimer."

"The *Reclaimer*?" Leah said.

Mike barely nodded, looking as if he'd said too much.

"Who is she?" Joel asked.

Mike began rocking side to side. "She is the end and the beginning."

Joel was going to say something else, but Leah touched his arm and shook her head. As much as she wanted to know more about this Reclaimer, she thought it unwise to chance scaring Mike so much that he retreated back into his mind.

"That way, right?" Leah said to Mike, pointing toward the pathway to the cabins.

"Yes, yes. That way."

SEVENTY

The Reclaimer

THE RECLAIMER FELT a stir via one of her sensors. A creature was close.

This was not the first time she'd received such a warning. They happened now and then when a creature wandered into the vicinity of the land above. The primitive beings would usually linger for a while before wandering back to wherever their creature lives took them. On a few occasions, however, one or two did venture close enough that the Reclaimer needed to deploy measures to urge them away.

She set up a sub-routine to alert her if the current situation deemed further action. She then returned her attention to analyzing the Translator's data and fine-tuning plans for implementation of her next stage.

SEVENTY-ONE

Joel

WHEN THE BOYS' cabins came into view, it almost felt to Joel like the intervening years had never happened, and at any second his old camp mates would emerge from the bungalows on their way to the lake. Then a cold breeze brushed across his face, and the sturdy cabins of his youth became rundown huts that would never shelter anyone again.

A hand touched his shoulder.

"We should keep moving," Leah said.

"Moving. Yes, yes. Moving," Mike echoed beside her.

Soon they passed the shower and restroom facility—the large building in near total collapse—and hiked by the girls' cabins, which mirrored the condition of the boys'.

The stables were now only a pile of rotted boards coated by a thin layer of snow. The only things that remained of the fence meant to keep the horses in were a few scattered posts and a rail here and there angled toward the ground.

When they reached the last of the posts, the official boundary of Camp Red Hawk, they all paused. They had been told by the camp director never to pass that point without a camp counselor. Though he was an adult now, Joel felt a lingering hesitancy to break the rule.

Of course, this wouldn't be the first time. He now remembered the night hike they'd taken, or at least much of it. Waiting for Dooley in their cabin, joining the girls at the showers, passing the stables and entering the woods.

Leah so close he wanted to reach out to her, to hold her.

Then and now.

As if they were sharing the same memory, she slipped her hand into his, just like she had before. She glanced at him, a hesitant look in her eyes, as if she wasn't sure if he'd object.

He squeezed her palm and didn't let go.

With every turn the path took, Joel remembered more details of that night. There was plenty of new growth but the old trees were familiar. They'd come this way then, this exact way.

Ahead, a shaft of sunlight glinted off something metal. As they drew near, they saw it was a fence, tall and topped by broken strands of barbed wire. Following it, they came to a nearly unreadable sign.

"I remember this," he whispered.

"Yeah," Leah said. "Me, too."

Mike jammed a finger against his lips. "Shhhh. You don't want her to—" He suddenly froze, his eyes losing focus. Then, "Eight-one-two-one-six-six-nine-seven-three-two-two-five-four-one."

SEVENTY-TWO

THE DATA STREAM paused the instant the alarm went off.

The Reclaimer reached out via her sensors, and found that the creatures—information now indicated there was more than one—had ventured closer to the land above. Closer than any had in three years and forty-one days.

She tried to reach directly into their minds to turn them away, but for some reason couldn't get in. Per the protocols she had written but had never had the need to implement, she made two additional attempts. When these also failed, she performed a targeted self-diagnostic but found no faults in her communication system or any degradation of her programming.

Venturing into unplanned-for territory, she tried a fourth time but was rebuffed again.

Analysis of the situation provided her with several scenarios that could account for the problem. At the top of the list was the 48.732% probability that the creatures were wearing some kind of protective shield that interfered with her signal. Though her decades of research indicated the development of such a shield was beyond the technical abilities of these vermin, she was well aware that her knowledge was not comprehensive.

The next closest probability, at 28.629%, was that her sensors had a malfunction her self-diagnosis hadn't picked up, and that there were no creatures present at all.

Beyond this, at greatly decreasing percentages, the other probabilities were: undetected problems with her internal programming; undetected problems with her internal physical systems; faulty categorization of the creatures as those that dominated the planet instead of one of the myriad of other, lesser biologicals; and at the bottom, at 0.154%, the ability of the creatures to shield their own minds without the aid of technology.

The program presented her with the additional recommendation that she run a full, top-to-bottom diagnostic to eliminate any possibilities connected to internal errors. Deciding this was the logical course, she redirected the data stream to a buffer where packets arriving from the Translator could be stored until she could return her attention to them. She then put her essential systems on automatic, and prepared to enter low-power mode while the diagnostic ran. Before she activated the program, however, an idea was brought to her attention by her planning node.

While her systems were being checked, one of her servants could be sent to the land above to collect data while she was indisposed. Two units were still in good enough working condition to be sent up. She chose the better of them, encoded her instructions, and sent it on its way.

She then commenced the diagnostic.

SEVENTY-THREE

Leah

MIKE KEPT RECITING sets of numbers, each time faster and faster. His volume, though, remained at a whisper, as if he were afraid that speaking any louder would bring the sky down on them.

And perhaps it would, Leah thought. This Reclaimer had obviously triggered him somehow. Leah could only hope he was trying to keep them hidden like he said he'd been doing.

She reached out with her mind, wanting to help soothe her friend. She'd never done it while awake, but as she concentrated she could feel him and sense his desperation.

It's all right, she told him. *I'm here. Let me—*

The slap came out of nowhere, stinging her cheek and sending her staggering backward. But Mike hadn't budged from his stationary pose.

"What happened?" Joel asked.

She touched her cheek and looked at Mike. It had come from him, only it had been all in her head, the mental slap registering on the nerves in her cheek.

"Leah?" Joel said.

"I'm okay."

"What happened?"

"I tried to help, but…" She removed her hand from her face. The sting was gone.

"If you want to try again, we could do it together," Joel said.

Before she could answer, Mike's rapid-fire recitation slowed. When the numbers stopped altogether, Mike shook with a brief, powerful spasm.

The moment it passed, his eyes snapped open. "Hurry, hurry! She's sleeping…but-but-but not for long."

He jogged ahead, parallel to the fence.

"What happens when she wakes?" Leah asked as she and Joel kept pace behind him.

"Maybe she finds us…maybe she destroys us."

"That sounds…awesome," Joel said.

"Hurry, hurry."

They circled around the large pile of dead trees and caked dirt and rocks pressing against the fence. When they reached the other side, Mike stopped.

"No hole. No hole." He looked back at them. "No hole to the other side."

"It's been gone a long time," Leah said. "I tried to get over by myself when I was here last time." She studied the debris. "If we work together, I think we can make it."

It wasn't easy, but they were able to reach the other side without being jammed in the ribs and legs by too many branches. Once they were safe on the ground, they scanned the woods.

"I remember…a meadow," Joel said.

"Yes," Leah said. "A meadow and a hill."

"Right, a hill."

"We go to the hill," Mike said. "We go, we go."

They entered the forest single file—Joel first, then Leah, then Mike. They had hiked maybe a hundred yards when Leah touched Joel's shirt and stopped him with a look.

"There's something out there," she whispered. "Do you feel it?"

This wasn't the pull, or even suggestion of one. This was the sense of a thing quietly moving through the trees somewhere ahead of them.

Joel fell silent for a moment, and then shook his head.

Leah glanced back to ask Mike but there was no need. He was slowly turning his head as if he were homing in on something. When he stopped moving, he pointed in front of them to the right.

"What is it?" Joel asked.

"Something she made."

"Something like what?"

"I-I-I don't know what she calls them. They do tasks for her." He paused. "Doer? Is that a word? We can call them that."

"You mean like a robot?" Leah asked.

"Yes…no…both."

"Does it know we're here?"

Mike closed his eyes for a moment. When he looked at them again, he said, "Not yet. The Reclaimer must know something is out here so she probably sent it to check."

"Hunter might be a better name for it, then," Joel suggested.

Mike frowned. "I like Doer."

"Okay. Sure. Doer."

"How do we keep it from knowing we're here?" Leah asked.

"It's…damaged," Mike said. "I can block it from sensing us, but we must, must keep moving. You'll have to guide me."

He held out both hands and closed his eyes. Leah took one hand and Joel the other. They started walking again. The eerie quiet was broken only by the crush of snow beneath their feet. Every few seconds, Leah looked back at Mike to make sure he was okay. His lips moved with his numeric mantra but he made no sound.

Finally the trees began thinning ahead, and they had their first glimpse of the meadow.

"The hill's off that way," Leah said, nodding to the right.

Joel steered them on a course that would take them closer while keeping them under the cover of the trees, and thus avoiding the openness of the meadow.

Leah could still sense the Doer. It was behind them now, moving in a very systematic pattern that hopefully meant it hadn't detected Leah and her friends.

Another few minutes later, Joel veered them toward the edge of the woods and stopped ten feet shy of the field. After they helped Mike sit on the ground, they crouched beside him.

The hill was no more than fifty yards away, and tucked

within, under a ledge, was a building.

Leah didn't need to glance at Joel to know he was feeling the same sense of recognition she was. They had a straight-on angle of the hole in the side of the building where Antonio had been standing. She could almost see him again, beckoning them over. She tried to recall what was inside, but those were memories that had yet to resurface.

"Shall we?"

Joel's voice was determined, but Leah knew he was as wary as she was of what the building hid. She couldn't help but wonder that if they entered, would they ever exit again?

She took a breath and nodded, but when she and Joel tried to move, Mike clamped down on their hands and didn't budge. Leah looked back but Mike's eyes were still closed and his face still in its trancelike state.

"I guess we're supposed to wait," she said.

They settled back on the forest floor.

A few moments later, she heard the rhythmic crunch of snow. She looked toward the noise and saw, backlit by the sun, a vaguely humanoid shape crossing the field toward the building. Its movements were slow and mechanical, like parts of it were no longer functioning properly. Forward-pause-drag, forward-pause-drag, forward-pause-drag.

"What *is* that?" Joel asked.

The shadowy form stopped and turned toward them. A second later it began walking in their direction.

Leah could hear Mike's numbers now, whispered even faster than before.

The Doer—for that must be what it was—kept coming for another dozen feet before stopping again. It held this position for over a minute. It was still too far away for them to discern any details about it other than its grayish hue. Perhaps it was made of plastic or rubber, she thought. It didn't appear to be metal.

The numbers were spewing out of Mike's mouth so fast now, it was as if they were a single word.

The Doer began to move again, but instead of continuing toward them, it made a machine-like forty-five-degree turn and resumed its journey toward the building.

Neither Leah nor Joel said a word as they watched the Doer limp to the hole in the wall, and then, with considerable difficulty, climb inside.

When it was finally out of sight, Joel let out a long breath. "That was close."

Leah checked Mike. The numbers had not stopped, but they had slowed to what she had come to think of as their normal speed.

"Let's give that thing a few minutes' head start," Joel said. "I mean, if you're still up for going in."

"You say that like we have a choice."

SEVENTY-FOUR

The Reclaimer

SENSORS PICKED UP the return of the servant and sent a notification to the Reclaimer. Even though she was still in low-power mode, she registered the information. Once the diagnostic had been completed (she had 19.86% remaining), she would download the servant's report. For now, it could wait.

SEVENTY-FIVE

Joel

WHEN LEAH SAID she could no longer sense the Doer, they decided it was time to go. Joel wondered if Mike would once more try to keep them from leaving, but when they pulled on his hands, he stood and followed without resistance.

The moment they stepped into the meadow, Joel felt intensely vulnerable. If the Doer had stopped just inside the building, all it would have to do was look through the hole to see them. With every forward step, Joel was sure that was exactly what would happen. So he was both surprised and relieved when they made it all the way to the broken wall without incident.

I remember this, he thought as he and Leah looked through the jagged rip at the dim, moldy walled room.

Leah went inside first, and then helped Joel maneuver Mike through the break. Upon joining them, Joel was hit with a foul musty odor that couldn't be explained by the mold alone.

Leah held a hand over her nose and mouth. "It didn't smell like this last time."

Joel scanned the room. The only other thing besides three rusting metal desks and some rotted chairs was a deteriorating mess of plastic and wires pushed against one wall. A phone, he recalled. Leah had picked it up back then. So had someone else. Dooley? Maybe. Though Joel's memories were coming back, there were still holes.

Leah, with Mike in tow, crossed to the door at the back wall. It was partially open but the space beyond was dark. As Joel headed over to join them, Leah pulled out her phone, turned on the flashlight, and shined it inside.

"Yeah, we went in here, too," she said.

When they entered the new space, Joel spotted tables and chairs he was pretty sure had been there last time, though now they were in much worse shape.

Another door was on the opposite wall, half open.

"Dooley," Joel said, staring at it.

"Bloody nose," Leah said, nodding.

Dooley had tried to get through that door and had slammed his face into it. It had taken Joel and Antonio working together to get it open. This time, no extra effort would be necessary.

"So, who goes first?" he asked.

Leah, her eyes not leaving the door, said, "We go together."

SEVENTY-SIX

Leah

THOUGH THE BOOKCASE that had held the door in place on their first visit was still there, someone—or some*thing*—had moved it to the side, allowing the door to swing open all the way when Leah pushed on it.

There was another difference, too. She sensed it as they moved inside, but she couldn't put her finger on it until Mike said, "Cold, cold."

The temperature.

The room was cold but not as cold as last time. And hadn't there been something else that was odd back then? Something like—

She stepped over to the center of the room and placed her hand in the space where the shaft of wind had been.

"The air's not moving," she said.

Joel joined her as she moved her hand around, thinking she might have misremembered the spot.

"It was moving," she said. "I'm not making that up, am I?"

"You're not," he assured her.

They worked their way to the wall where the air had disappeared last time. She half expected the opening at the bottom to be missing, too, but it was there. She and Joel slipped their fingers into the space and pulled.

As the wall swung into the room, the rest came back.

The door to the elevator.

The stairs she and Joel had taken down when they'd heard the scream.

The wind nudging them forward at first, and then all but carrying them to the bottom.

A dark, seemingly endless tunnel.

Oh, God! Help me!

Courtney hanging on to a light on the ceiling, the wind thrashing her as it worked to pull her free.

Please, help me!

And then she was gone.

Leah took a startled breath. The wind would've also taken her if it hadn't been for Joel.

She looked over at him and saw it had all come back to him, too.

She took his hand. "The Reclaimer's down there."

"I know."

"If we leave, she'll just keep using Mike and me. She'll probably use you again, too."

"I know."

"We need to stop her."

"I know."

"We need to go down."

Silence.

"Joel?"

"I know."

SEVENTY-SEVEN

Joel

JOEL HAD DREAMT of this, of the stairs and the wind and the spinning flashlight and the screams for help. He had woken so many times in a sweat not knowing what the dream meant, what it represented.

But it wasn't a dream at all. It was a memory.

And it represented nothing because it had been real.

He looked at Leah and then did what he should have done in Colorado Springs. What he should have done way back on the night hike when they were thirteen.

He pulled her into his arms and kissed her.

Because he had always wanted to.

Because he didn't want to die without his lips ever touching hers.

Because he wanted a reason to live through whatever they were about to face.

SEVENTY-EIGHT

The Reclaimer

THE DIAGNOSTIC HAD reach 97.83% when the Reclaimer received another alarm. So far, the test had uncovered only a few minor faults, none of which would account for a false reading. Since the chances were infinitesimally small that the final 2.17% would uncover any major issues, she canceled the rest of the diagnostic and initiated power up.

As each system was reactivated, her processing strength and access to her databases increased. Four hundred and thirty-seven milliseconds after the alarm was received, she had enough resources online to analyze the data. She learned that the alert had been triggered by the creatures entering the structure in the land above.

Programmed to experience certain emotions, she was perplexed as to why her sensors had yet to categorize the trespassers' biological type. Stranger still, the sensors had sent her contradictory data about how many there were. Two of her sensors even reported that everything was normal.

She accessed the data from her servant. It had located nothing that would have triggered the initial alarm. There was, however, one point of conflict in the raw data. The servant had made a detour on its return to the Reclaimer, venturing for several seconds toward the edge of the clearing, where it paused before returning to its original course.

She connected to the servant.

::EXPLAIN.

Task complete, complete, the servant replied. *No biologicals detected.*

The Reclaimer presented the data of the servant's detour.
::EXPLAIN.

The servant was silent for a moment, then, *I have no information about this. No biologicals detected. No biologicals, no biologicals.*

The Reclaimer knew the servant was nearing the end of its usefulness, and that its failing condition could have caused it to go off course before correcting its path. But based on the new sensor readings from the structure in the land above, she concluded there was a 66.71% chance the detour had not been a glitch, and had, in fact, occurred in response to the biological or biologicals that had entered the building. Why her servant had no information about this was troubling, but she could look into that after the current situation was resolved.

She activated the next most viable servant. Mechanically it was in worse operational condition, but it could ride the electric powered car to the top, where it should have no trouble rooting out what was going on. To ensure no missed data, the Reclaimer would monitor its sensor and see everything for herself.

"Task received," servant number two said, and then began crawling on its three still working limbs toward the access to the above.

SEVENTY-NINE

Mike

MIKE HAD ALMOST screwed up everything when the Doer crossed the meadow. He'd been splitting his attention between keeping the Doer in the dark about their presence and monitoring the Reclaimer in case she suddenly woke.

When the Doer started back toward the building, Mike was sure the danger it represented had passed, so he'd begun shifting his full focus back to the Reclaimer. He didn't realize the mistake until it was almost too late. Free of his attention, the Doer had detected Joel's voice and turned to investigate.

In a panic, Mike concentrated on the Doer, leaving the Reclaimer momentarily unwatched. Though he was able to stop the Doer, his work wasn't done. The thing would be returning to the Reclaimer with the knowledge it had sensed something, so he accessed its memory and dug out the data that would have betrayed them. It was easier to do than he'd expected. The Doer's storage system was very familiar. His years of sending data packets to the Reclaimer must have helped him know what to do and where to look.

Even then, he wasn't a hundred percent successful. Though he erased the reason why the Doer had turned toward the woods, he was unable to eliminate the memory of the course change itself. This was buried deep in a different part of the data. He decided it would be better to let the Doer go than keep it stationary while he rooted around for the rest.

Once their path was clear, his companions led him into the meadow.

He'd always had a special connection to the two of them,

and in the time they'd been in one another's company, that had only grown stronger. Now he could actually see everything they did and could have walked on his own, but he liked the feel of their touch, liked the sense that he was not alone anymore.

When he saw the rip in the side of the building, his heart beat faster. Never in the years he'd shared a room with the Beast had he thought he'd be back here again.

This was the Reclaimer's home. Sacred ground.

No. I can't think that way. Not sacred. Never was sacred. Never.

And yet, as he was pulled inside, he couldn't help but feel like he should drop to his knees and bow in subjugation.

He detected the Reclaimer's sensors almost immediately. He erased information where he could, and where he couldn't, he confused the data.

When he'd been here on that momentous night so many years ago, he had only ventured a few feet beyond the hole, so as he was taken deeper into the structure now, the rooms did not elicit any memories. He had no idea why Leah and Joel let go of his hands and began waving their palms through the air. He was surprised when they grabbed the wall and yanked open what turned out to be a hidden door, but then he instantly realized what they'd revealed.

Fear roiled in his chest as they stood on the precipice of the Reclaimer's warren.

When Leah took his hand and said, "This way," he considered resisting again, but knew it would serve no purpose. They had to go down. They had to, had to.

"Don't worry," she said. "We'll be with you the whole time."

He wanted to believe her, but he had a strong feeling that would not be the case, and his feelings were never wrong.

Nonetheless, he let her guide him onto the stairs.

THE END
&
THE BEGINNING

EIGHTY

THE MEMORY OF Joel's kiss stayed with Leah as they began their descent. She had not expected him to do that, but she was glad he had. There had never been anyone other than him. And given how different they were from everyone else, there would likely be no other in the future.

Initially they took the steps slowly to ensure Mike didn't fall. But while he was still in his trance, he seemed to intuitively know where each tread was and never lost his balance. Gradually they increased their pace.

They'd been heading down for well over a minute when Leah, through a hand on the rail connected to the inner wall, felt a vibration. Joel must've felt it too, because he stopped and put his palm on the cement surface. Leah did the same.

The vibration was strong, steady, and seemed to be moving upward.

"The elevator," she said.

Joel looked at her, worried.

"We need to keep moving," she told him.

Her flashlight revealed the bottom as they came around the final turn. Once there, she couldn't help but point the light at the ceiling where they'd last seen Courtney. The only thing marking the spot was the glass globe of the fixture their camp mate had been hanging on.

Leah aimed the beam down the tunnel.

EIGHTY-ONE

The Reclaimer

ONE MOMENT THE Reclaimer's consciousness was spread in over a thousand directions—overseeing systems still restarting, analyzing data packets, and monitoring sensors serving a variety of purposes. The next, her collective being was staring through a single sensor at the end of the long hall.

The darkness was not an issue. The sensor was designed to observe via multiple wavelengths, so the heat signatures of the three creatures who had exited the stairs were clearly visible.

There had indeed been trespassers in the land above. Humans, as they called themselves.

And now they were here.

Good.

Eighty-two

Mike

MIKE SENSED HIS friends tense as they reached the end of the stairs. Something about this particular spot disturbed them. He didn't know what it was. Their minds were too complicated by the changes the Reclaimer had made for him to probe without their knowledge.

When Leah turned her light toward the ceiling, however, thoughts of his friends' mental states disappeared as he felt the presence of the Reclaimer. He steeled himself for the onslaught of her wrath, but quickly realized she wasn't reaching out directly. She was using a sensor at the dark end of the corridor.

He concentrated on the device and sent it the same disabling code he'd used with the others.

EIGHTY-THREE

The Reclaimer

THE RECLAIMER FELT the harsh sting of something attacking the sensor. The image wavered and would have quit entirely if she hadn't quickly taken over direct control. With effort, she repulsed the attack and stabilized the input.

Somehow, one of the creatures had been able to tap into her system. That should have been impossible. Nothing could enter her system without her allowing it there.

The vermin's intrusion had gone on long enough.

She extended herself forward to take control of the beings' minds.

EIGHTY-FOUR

Mike

THE RECLAIMER SURGED into the sensor and began pushing Mike out. He fought for as long as he could, but soon enough she'd pried him loose.

He knew trying again was out of the question. She would be coming straight at them now.

Using every ounce of energy he had, he created a shield around his friends, hoping it would be enough.

EIGHTY-FIVE

The Reclaimer

IN THE NANOSECOND it took the Reclaimer's electronic impulses to reach the other end of the hall, an invisible barrier rose to encase the trio.

With rapid-fire jabs, she attempted to break through, but the shield blocked her every move.

She probed and prodded, assessing the shield's makeup. A surprisingly long 5.82 seconds later, she determined that the creature in the middle was generating the barrier. His strength was impressive. She would have never believed one of these creatures could do what he was doing if she had not seen it for herself.

As impressive as the feat was, however, these creatures were imperfect beasts, so she was confident the shield had a thin spot she could exploit. It took another 4.19 seconds before she finally detected a vulnerable section. It was tiny, not even a quarter millimeter in circumference—much smaller than she had expected.

Carefully, she pushed at the spot, but she'd barely started slipping through when her presence was detected. The creature immediately eliminated the weakness and cut her off.

Though her time inside had lasted but a fraction of a second, she had gained one piece of information so unexpected, it made her retreat all the way back into the Cradle.

The creature/generator was her own Translator.

While that explained how the being had been able to get into her systems, it did nothing to help her understand *how* it could be here, let alone how it had created the barrier. She knew her Translator's life from the packets it sent. Knew the building it lived in. Knew it could not leave even if it wanted to.

It should not be here.

It *could* not be here.

And yet it was.

The logical answer was that it must have something to do with the two beings accompanying it. Unfortunately there'd been no time to probe them for their identities.

She hastily constructed a program to cull a list of possible creatures from her vast data on the Translator and set it to run.

EIGHTY-SIX

"I'LL LIGHT THE way. You bring Mike," Leah said.

She turned, but before she could take a step, Joel said, "Hold it."

"What is it?"

"He's not moving."

She grabbed Mike's other hand and pulled, but he stayed rooted to the floor.

In the forest, Mike's refusal to move had been because the Doer was near, so she scanned the edge of the darkness ahead, wondering if it was close again. Maybe just beyond the reach of her light, or…

She shot a look back at the elevator, suddenly sure that whatever had gone up had returned. But nothing was there.

"Mike, I know you can hear me," she said. "We've got to keep moving."

He tightened his grip on her hand and pulled it closer to his side.

She frowned, and then peeled his fingers back and freed her palm. "Stay with him," she told Joel. "I'll take a look ahead."

Mike's hand shot out and snagged her shirt.

"Maybe you should wait," Joel said.

She looked at him, then at Mike. "Maybe you're right."

Mike's grip loosened but he didn't let go. Waves of stress washed over his face as he counted and counted. Suddenly the numbers stopped and his eyes opened.

"She knows I'm here." He blinked several times and

moved past them into the tunnel. "She knows I'm here! Hurry, hurry, hurry."

Falling in behind him, they ran down the corridor. When they reached the end, they found a new hall that curved off in both directions. Mike went left so they followed.

They came to a large, thick metal door that would have closed off the entire corridor if it wasn't already open.

Mike sped around it. "Hurry, hurry."

On the other side was a short elbow hallway that opened into a room so large, Leah's light couldn't reach the ceiling or the other walls.

Mike was already running across it, his echoing footsteps all but lost in the gigantic space.

"Wait for us!" Leah called after him.

But his pace did not lessen, and it took effort on her part to keep him in the far reaches of her light. Clearly, he was faster than he looked.

Then, as if hitting an invisible wall, he stopped dead in his tracks. For a second his whole body seized, and then he tumbled to the ground.

EIGHTY-SEVEN

The Reclaimer

THE RECLAIMER RECEIVED notifications in rapid succession as the Translator and its companions moved deeper into her fortress. When they neared the transition space outside her inner sanctum, she knew she could ignore the problem no longer.

She recalled the servant she'd sent to the building in the land above, then projected her consciousness toward the Translator. She expected to have problems with his shield again, but he had separated from the others and it was spread thin now, making it easier for her to penetrate.

As soon as she was inside, she clamped down on its mind. ::HALT!

Its forward momentum stopped and it crumbled to the ground like the delicate being it was. She probed it, trying to extract all its information so she could learn what had brought it here, but even in its restrained state, the Translator was able to project a limited shield around its thoughts and memories.

Again, the Reclaimer was baffled. The Translator had never shown any signs of being able to do anything so intricate and powerful before.

She squeezed harder.
::RELENT! TRANSMIT! MINE!

EIGHTY-EIGHT

Leah

AN ELECTRIC PULSE shot through the room, forcing Leah and Joel to double over, twenty feet shy of reaching Mike.

::RELENT! TRANSMIT! MINE!

Leah looked around, trying to locate the speaker.

::RELENT!

Her gaze whipped back to Mike. The voice was inside his head, she realized. But it wasn't his voice.

As she started toward him again, Joel grabbed her arm. "There's something out there."

"It's her."

"The Reclaimer?"

"Yes, now let me go."

He hesitated, and then did as she requested.

Leah raced ahead until she was only a couple of yards from Mike, set her feet, and shouted with both her mind and voice, "Leave him alone!"

The only response was the Reclaimer repeating, ::RELENT! TRANSMIT! MINE!

Leah tried again, but there was no sign her words were getting through. She wasn't strong enough. Not on her own, anyway.

She looked back at Joel. He had followed her and was standing a few feet away. She thrust out her hand. "Help me!"

He grabbed it. "What's going on?"

Before she responded, she heard the Reclaimer issue its orders again, and she could feel Mike weakening. To Joel she said, "Don't let go!"

She closed her eyes and worked her way into the part of Joel's mind she'd used to track him down in Mexico. It would've been better if the wall he'd built to keep her out was completely gone, but there was no time to deal with that now. She linked herself to him as best she could and refocused on Mike.

::RELENT! TRANSMIT! MINE!"

"Leave him alone!" Leah shouted.

The ball of energy that had been surrounding Mike retracted as if it had been smacked by a club. It didn't disappear completely, though. Leah could sense it nearby, immensely powerful, like nothing she'd felt before. And yet there was something intimately familiar about it.

The one who made us.

The end and the beginning.

She could feel the force surge forward to attack Mike again.

"No!" she yelled as she projected herself at it.

EIGHTY-NINE

THE RECLAIMER'S CONNECTION to the Translator terminated the moment her emergency protocols kicked in. These had been triggered by the surprise intrusion of one of the Translator's companions. According to her earlier risk calculations, the chance of that occurring was only 0.000181%.

She extended forward, intending to dive into the creatures' minds to find out how, twice now, they had overpowered her.

"No!" With the creature's shout came a pulse of energy that pushed the Reclaimer all the way back down the hall.

This was unprecedented. The Reclaimer had no data showing this species had anything close to this ability. Quite the contrary. Her information confirmed they were weak, petty animals undeserving of the atmosphere they breathed.

Unless...

Had the Translator been falsifying the information packets all along? That would account for the discrepancies.

Such a betrayal would set her program back years.

She conducted a rapid calculation. Though the majority of the information the Translator had sent her was probably legitimate, there was now an 84.3338% likelihood that false data was mixed among it.

She ran an analysis of all her potential responses. When the program finished, there was only one course of action that made sense. She had to assume the data was corrupt and would need to be discarded.

A more reliable Translator would have to be found, and a whole new data set—*accurate* data set—obtained. Schedules would need to be revised, and the day of reclamation she had thought was so close must be postponed for several more years.

Decision made, she turned her attention to devising a way of dealing with her former Translator and its vermin friends.

NINETY

"I GOT YOU," Joel said as he grabbed Leah and kept her from collapsing.

She blinked, disoriented, and then looked at him. "It was the Reclaimer."

"Yeah, I kind of got that."

Through the mental connection she'd made with Joel, he'd been able to witness the exchange. It had been like listening to a radio from another room—understandable, but distorted and distant.

"Is she still here?" he asked.

"No."

"Did you...uh..." He wasn't sure what word to use. Kill? Destroy? Defeat?

She seemed to know what he meant, though, because she shook her head. "Mike?" she asked.

With a steadying arm around her, Joel helped her over to where Mike lay curled up on the ground.

They knelt beside him.

"Mike, can you hear me?" Leah asked. "Are you all right?"

"You still with us, buddy?" Joel threw in.

For a moment, there was no response, then came a whispered, "Still...with you."

Grinning, Joel slipped a hand under Mike's shoulder, said, "Let's get you up," and carefully hauled him to his feet. He then glanced at Leah. She looked better but nowhere near a hundred percent. "We need to get you two out of here."

"No. We can't leave. We have to—"

"Whatever the hell that thing is, she's more powerful than us. At the very least we need to rethink our strategy. And it would be better to do that *any*place else."

They stared at each other for several seconds before she reluctantly nodded.

Joel put his free arm around her and started half walking-half carrying her and Mike back the way they'd come. Leah tried to keep her light pointed in front of them but she was exhausted, and every few feet Joel had to nudge her to lift it again.

Right before they reached the exit leading into the hallway, they heard the whir of an electric motor and then a heavy metal thunk.

They hobbled into the corridor, took the elbow turn, and stopped.

The giant door was closed. The Doer was there, standing at the nearby wall, shutting an access panel.

Not *the* Doer, Joel realized as he got a better look. This one's left lower appendage dangled uselessly below it.

Instead of turning and walking toward them, the Doer lowered itself to the floor and began crawling in their direction.

Being the only one currently capable of dealing with it, Joel leaned Mike against the wall and started to do the same with Leah.

"Oh, my God," she said.

Joel looked back down the hall. The Doer had stopped about fifteen feet away and was looking into Leah's light.

Every hair on Joel's body stood on end.

"Antonio?" Leah said.

Joel stared, hardly believing his eyes.

Despite the aging and gray, hairless, scar-covered body, Joel could see the Doer was Antonio Canavo, his old cabin mate. Antonio started moving again, so Joel let go of Leah and took a step toward him.

"Stop."

Antonio continued on, unfazed.

Joel took another step closer. "Antonio, please stop!"

No hint he'd been heard.

"I don't want to hurt you."

Antonio lunged forward, his good arm stretched toward Joel's leg. If Antonio's body had not been so damaged, he would have likely reached his target, but the awkward attempt was easy for Joel to avoid.

Antonio flopped onto the floor. When he looked up, he opened his mouth and a deep, rattling noise rumbled out.

It took a moment for Joel to realize it wasn't a single elongated sound but three different tones.

"Ooo, ahhh, ooouuu."

Over and over and over.

"I think he's trying to talk to us," Joel said.

"Yes, yes," Mike replied. "Talking to us."

"Can you tell what he's saying?"

"Not him, she."

"It's Antonio, Mike. He was with us on the hike."

"He was Antonio. Was, was. Not now. It's a Doer now. It speaks for her."

Joel looked at the broken body of the kid he used to know. He wanted to believe some of Antonio was still in there, but he also hoped Mike was right, that the person they had known was long gone.

"Ooo, ahhh, ooouuu."

Joel looked past Antonio to the door covering the passageway. Leah's light was barely strong enough to reach it, so he wasn't able to pick out the wall panel Antonio had shut, but he knew approximately where it was.

"Stay here," he said to Leah and Mike. "If he comes at you, just, I don't know, push him back."

As Joel leapt over Antonio, Antonio flung his arms up in an attempt to grab Joel's legs, but missed. Joel found the panel within a few seconds and popped out the cover. But his hopes of quickly opening the door again vanished when he saw the rows of switches inside. They were all identical and none were marked.

He flipped them one at a time but nothing happened. They must have required some kind of combination. With so many switches, he could be here for years and still not hit the right order.

They wouldn't be getting out this way anytime soon.

"There has to be another way out," he said as he ran back to them. "An emergency exit. We'll have to go back the other way."

"What about Antonio?" Leah asked. Their old friend was still trying to crawl within range of them.

Joel looked at him. "Right now we have to look out for ourselves. If we can do something for him later, we will."

He started to put his arm around her waist, but she gently pushed it away.

"I'm okay. Really. Mike needs your help more than me."

"You lead," he said to Leah as he propped up Mike. "We'll be right behind you."

NINETY-ONE

Leah

THE IMAGE OF the gray-skinned Antonio would be forever etched in Leah's mind. That he was still alive was mind blowing. She tried not to imagine what he'd gone through, but couldn't help having quick flashes of what could have happened. And if he was still alive, what about the others? Was the Doer they'd seen in the meadow another camp mate?

As they moved back into the giant room, her mind conjured up the possibility of one of the others who hadn't returned from the hike leaping out of the darkness and grabbing her with its gray arms.

She felt the desire to take Joel's hand but he was busy helping Mike. So she slipped her fingers into her pocket and touched the bag that held the folded Hershey's wrapper. The talisman calmed her.

They zigzagged through the room so Leah could shine her light on the walls and look for another way out. But all they saw were dozens and dozens of pipes running up the walls into the darkness.

They were several feet past the point where Mike had earlier collapsed when the far wall finally came into view. In the middle sat a door identical to the one Gray-Antonio had shut, only larger. This door was open.

She halted in front of the threshold. "Unless you spotted a way out that I didn't, then this is the only one."

"I didn't see anything else, either," Joel said.

She didn't step through it. "You know there's not going to be another way back to the surface through here."

"There's got to be," Joel said. "What if something happened that trapped whoever this place was meant for down here?"

"Look at it, Joel." She motioned at the door. "That's a *vault* door. The one Antonio shut, that was a vault door, too. There's only one way in and out of a vault. These were designed to keep whatever's down here down here."

The struggle between knowing she was right and wanting some way to protect his friends played out on his face. He'd lived the role of the savior for so long, she knew, it was part of his DNA now.

"Maybe you're right," he finally said. "But there must be an administration office or something like that. Someplace where we can find instructions on how to open the main door."

Now that was a possibility. Still, there was a bigger problem.

"She's in there somewhere," Leah said.

"I know. But it's not like she can't find us again out here, too. Look, I know it's a small chance, but maybe we'll be able to find out how to open the door and get out before she attacks again. If we don't, then we stand our ground."

Leah crept up to the doorway and shone her light inside. A hallway ran straight out, while another ran side to side.

"Mike, do you know which way she is?" she asked.

"Left…right…I don't know…everywhere."

"Not exactly the answer I was hoping for."

"Sorry. Sorry, sorry."

Leah crossed through the opening, and, with the mental flip of a coin, went left.

This part of the facility was not completely dark. Every thirty feet or so, a safety light threw a dim glow over a small section of the hall, like illuminated pools dotting a quiet midnight canyon. There were doors along each side, some with round, boat-type windows in the upper half. The spaces beyond these windows were uniformly dark.

They tried the doors as they passed. Many wouldn't open, and those that did revealed only work rooms filled with tables and equipment but no useful information.

The hall curved to the right so they could never see more than thirty or forty feet ahead. Leah guessed it encircled the entire facility, and if they kept going, they would end up back where they'd started. This thought was reinforced when they reached the junction of a hall that went straight off to their right. If she wasn't mistaken, this was the same hall directly across from the big door they'd come through, and bisected the circular route they were on.

As they continued around the curve, the rooms they came to now were different from those before. These were living quarters with beds and small desks and cabinets for clothes. Most of the beds were neatly covered with sheets and blankets. A check of the cabinets and small closets revealed clothes, some hanging, some in neat, folded piles. The style was really old, but none looked worn out. They were like costumes on a movie set just waiting for their actors.

Leah and her friends continued to find other living quarters until they reached the point where they had started. They looked down the bisecting hall.

It was the only part they hadn't checked, so if there was something in the facility that would help them open the door, it would be down there.

Along with the Reclaimer.

"Maybe I should go alone," Leah said. She'd fought the Reclaimer off once. If necessary, she'd do it again.

"We go together," Joel said, echoing Leah's earlier words.

"Together," Mike agreed.

NINETY-TWO

The Reclaimer

THE RECLAIMER APPROACHED the creatures in a planned progression from one set of sensors to another. She could have rushed to where they were, been there in nanoseconds, but after her previous experiences, caution was advised.

She would, of course, be terminating their existence. That had been a foregone conclusion once they'd left the land above, but her scientific curiosity had been activated, so a delay was inserted into her agenda.

Why had they come? What did they hope to achieve? The answer to these questions would help her avoid a repeat problem during the data collection redo. Failing again would not be acceptable.

Prior to reaching the intruders, she received a message from her second servant. The Translator and his companions had apparently attempted to flee. Fortunately, the servant had automatically invoked its lockdown protocol and sealed the door before they could escape.

As physically damaged as her servant might be, the Reclaimer was pleased its programming had operated at peak efficiency. She sent a targeted burst of energy that would stimulate its atrophied pleasure receptors in a show of appreciation.

Concerned that the Translator would sense her renewed attention, she merely accessed her sensor's data stream without taking active control of the device, and watched as one of the companions tried unsuccessfully to open the door. When it became clear to them that they would not be getting out that way, they headed back into the facility.

Previously the Reclaimer had focused solely on the Translator, so this was the first time she'd taken a good look at its two companions. She categorized the slightly shorter one as female and the other as male, both approximately twenty-five years old. Interestingly, both exceeded the normal physical specifications for their sex and age, based on not only the unreliable data the Translator had sent, but also information the Reclaimer herself had collected during her first years after activation.

As sub-routines automatically catalogued every piece of information possible about the two, the Reclaimer watched them make their way into the heart of her home. This pleased her. After her scientific observation node was satisfied, it would be so much easier to take control of them and program their husks to function as additional servants.

An indicator nudged her consciousness.

While still tracking the creatures' progress, she accessed her log. The information node had data on the companions it deemed important enough to alert her. She opened the report.

Shock was not a sensation written into her programming, but the 757-millisecond pause she took after she reviewed the file could be described as nothing else. According to the report, the female was Satellite One, and the male was the lost Satellite Two.

How could that be?

The Reclaimer had been extremely diligent when she set up the information network containing the trio. To avoid any problems, she had used protocols that had been adjusted after her failed experiments with her original test subjects. She had painstakingly built mental walls in their delicate minds that should have never allowed them to even remember each other, let alone figure out a way to come together.

She funneled all she had on the Satellites into her processors, correlating and analyzing timelines. Nothing pointed toward them remembering one another.

Was this also information the Translator had kept from her? Again, there was no other logical explanation.

Analysis indicated that fault ultimately fell on the Reclaimer. At some point, while she had prepared the three before releasing them back into the land above, she had made an error in their programming.

> **Solution:** *Obtain Translator. Catalog its true memories. Determine the nature of the fault. Terminate Translator. Rewrite protocols.*

> **Error potential:** *Possibility of Translator expiring prior to extraction of information—63.12%.*

> **Backup calculation:** *Probability of 51.83% that the nature of the error can be deduced from Satellites.*

> **Backup solution:** *Keep Satellites alive. If sufficient information is extracted from Translator, terminate Satellites. If Translator dies during data transfer, mine Satellites' memories and then terminate Satellites.*

The Reclaimer analyzed her choices, and selected the path that gave her the highest chance of success.

NINETY-THREE

Joel

MIKE NO LONGER needed to lean as heavily against Joel. Still, Joel kept a tight arm around him as they followed Leah down the bisecting hall.

Doors sat along the left wall every fifteen feet. Along the right, however, there was only a set of wide double doors located at the midway point. The first three doors on the left were labeled LAB A, STORAGE MAT 1, and LAB B. Leah opened each, shined her light around, and then continued on with only a shake of her head.

The fourth door was marked ACCESS AB.

"Stairs," Leah said as she looked inside.

"A way out?" Joel asked.

"They go down, not up." She turned to look at him and noticed Mike was staring off to the side, looking worried.

"Mike, are you all right?"

Mike didn't react. Joel gave him a gentle shake. Mike blinked and looked at him, confused.

"Are you okay?" Joel asked.

"I-I-I…"

"The Reclaimer?" Leah asked. "Is she close?"

Mike rocked forward and backward once. "Her home. She can be anywhere, everywhere."

"Do you sense her now?" Joel asked.

Mike rocked again but didn't say anything.

"I think we should probably take that as a yes," Joel said.

Leah looked back at the stairs. "I think we might as well go down and see what's there first, then finish up here after."

"Works for me."

The stairs went down only a single, albeit tall, floor, and exited into another hallway with the same dimensions and scattered lights as the one above. But here there were multiple doors on both the right and left.

The first several rooms they checked were labeled PROVISIONS, CAFETERIA, KITCHEN, JANITORIAL, LAVATORY FEMALE, LAVATORY MALE. As they made their way farther down the hall, the generic place names gave way to placards containing proper names: DR. CHAMBERS, DR. DANIELS, DR. KELLER, and DR. WRIGHT. They checked them all, hoping one contained the switch combination for the vault door.

The last two doors were separated from the others. The sign on the first read ASSISTANT DIRECTOR, DR. KOZAKOV and the one on the second, DIRECTOR, DR. DURANT.

Joel was sure these weren't medical doctors. He, Leah, and Mike had come across no hospital rooms or examination suites. What they had seen were workrooms and scientific labs that looked like older versions of the ones Joel had worked in during college.

Not for the first time, he wondered what this place had been.

They went inside the assistant director's office. Like the other offices, it looked as if its owner would be returning at any minute.

Joel led Mike to a chair. "Why don't you sit down and get off your feet for a minute?"

"Okay. Thank you...Joel."

When Mike was situated, Joel joined Leah at the desk. Several files were stacked in the corner, while one was sitting open as if Dr. Kozakov had been reading it.

"What is it?" he asked.

Leah flipped a page and shook her head. "Lab results of some kind. Nothing to indicate what it's measuring, though."

While she looked through the papers on the desk, Joel began opening drawers. He'd just finished the first and was opening another when—

"This is Dr. Magnus Kozakov, assistant director of Project Titan." The voice, already deep and drawn out, slowed with each word.

Joel and Leah shot looks toward it. It was coming from near Mike, who was no longer in the chair and now kneeling on the floor next to a cabinet.

"Before I say anything else," the voice continued, "if you are listening to this inside the Titan facility, stop now, take tthhiiss ttaappee aaannnddd gggeeettt ooouuuttt. Yooouuuu aaa...."

The voice stopped.

"What is that? Is that you, Mike?" Joel asked.

Mike glanced back and leaned to the side. On the ground in front of him was a metal box.

Joel and Leah hurried over and leaned down for a better look. The box was an old reel-to-reel recorder, like Joel had seen pictures of in college. It was extremely bulky by modern standard, but clearly designed to be portable.

"Sorry, sorry," Mike said.

"It's okay," Joel told him. "Where did you find it?"

"Under there." Mike pointed at the floor beneath the cabinet. "Under."

Joel gestured toward the box. "May I?"

After Mike nodded, Joel picked it up and carried it over to the desk. The PLAY switch was still depressed but the reels weren't moving, so he pushed STOP to release the button and pressed PLAY again. For a half second the tape began to move and "rrr" came out of the speaker. But then it stopped again.

Joel flipped the box over and opened a hatch on the bottom. He pulled out a large single battery of a type he'd never seen before. It looked as old as the recorder but seemed to be in surprisingly good shape. After popping it back in, he tried to play the tape again, but whatever juice the battery had was now completely depleted.

"Titan facility?" Leah said. "Is that where we are?"

"I guess," Joel said.

"Wasn't there a Titan missile program once?"

"Yeah, but I haven't seen a silo."

"Maybe we just haven't opened the right door yet."

"I don't know. This place seems more like a research facility than a Cold War missile bunker." He tapped on the reel-to-reel machine. "The warning would have been more helpful before we came down, don't you think?"

He turned the box around, examined the sides, and discovered a power input slot. "Was anything else down there?" he asked Mike. "An electric cord?"

"I-I didn't see one."

Leah, who was closest, lowered to her knees, peeked beneath the cabinet, and pulled something out. When she stood again, it wasn't a cord she held but an old-style notepad with spiral wire binding at the top.

She flipped it open and looked at several pages before saying, "Dr. Kozakov again." She looked at a few more pages and then turned the pad so Joel could see it. "Read this. It's the last entry."

Power has been out for three days now, and I'm down to my final set of flashlight batteries. I don't hear the others moving around anymore, though, so maybe the craft has gone back to sleep. I'll wait a few more hours and then try to get out. If it won't let me, I'll at least do what I can to make sure no one else can get in.

Dr. Magnus Kozakov. June 27, 1946

"Nineteen forty-six?" Joel said.

"The bookcase," Leah said.

Joel looked around, thinking she was talking about something in the room.

"No," she said. "In the cold room at the top of the stairs. The bookcase that blocked the door. He must have put it there."

"Didn't really keep us out, though, did it?"

She looked at the notepad. "Maybe it was the best he could do."

They searched the rest of the room for anything that might

help them, and then, taking the notepad with them, moved down to the director's office.

Joel was rifling through the desk when Leah said, "Where's Mike?"

He looked up and glanced around. Mike wasn't in the room. "Wasn't he right behind us?"

"I thought so."

They moved into the hall. No Mike. They sprinted back to Dr. Kozakov's office.

But it was empty, too.

NINETY-FOUR

Mike

MIKE FOLLOWED LEAH and Joel out of the office and down the hall toward the next door. His friends entered, but before he could do the same, the Reclaimer touched his mind.

::COME.

No.

::COME. REVEAL.

I won't.

::COME. REVEAL. IF NOT, THEN SATELLITES' TERMINATION GUARANTEED.

Mike began to rock. The Reclaimer's words weren't a threat. As far as Mike was aware, she was incapable of making one. So if he did not do as she asked, she would attempt to kill Leah and Joel. If she succeeded, it would be his fault. He could not—could not, could not—allow his friends to die.

If I come, you will allow my friends to return to the surface and-and-and guarantee they will not, will not be terminated.

The Reclaimer took a long moment before responding.

::IF COOPERATION IS TOTAL, THEN TERMS ACCEPTABLE.

You'll have my, my total cooperation.

::NEGOTIATIONS CONCLUDED. COME. REVEAL.

Mike wanted to see his friends one last time. To hear their voices. To feel them near. But he could not take the chance they would stop him from leaving, so he turned and quietly made his way back to the stairwell.

NINETY-FIVE

The Reclaimer

AFTER RUNNING AN analysis, the Reclaimer accepted the Translator's requests. Whether the Satellites died now or in the general extermination after data gathering was complete ultimately did not matter.

Backup solution—revised: *Keep Satellites alive. If sufficient information is extracted from Translator, release Satellites. If Translator dies during data transfer, mine Satellites' memories and then terminate Satellites.*

NINETY-SIX

JOEL AND LEAH checked every room on the floor, but Mike wasn't there.

"He must have gone back up," Joel said. "Can you reach him?"

Leah attempted to connect to Mike, but either he was blocking her or something else was because she couldn't find any hint of him.

They hurried up the stairs, burst into the hallway, and skidded to a stop. Standing twenty feet away was a Doer. Backlit by one of the safety lights, its face wasn't visible, but the mere fact that it was standing meant it wasn't Antonio.

"So I'm thinking Mike's that way somewhere," Leah said, nodding past the Doer.

As she took a step forward, the Doer raised a hand like a traffic cop, showing them its palm.

Leah continued forward, thinking they could scoot around the side of it, but the Doer raised its other hand—holding a heavy metal wrench. It drew it behind its head, preparing to throw, and in the process stepped back far enough so that the light shined down on its face.

Leah froze. "Courtney?"

Courtney's skin was as hairless and gray as Antonio's, and her eyes just as dead. A deep scar ran down her face, from her forehead through the corner of her mouth and onto her chin.

"Courtney, it's Leah. I know you remember me. Just put that down, okay?" She chanced another step.

The arm with the wrench cocked back an inch as

Courtney's mouth opened. "Ssssttttoooopppp." There was no emotion in her voice, only a drawn-out monotone.

"Camp Red Hawk. You slept in the bunk below me."

Not a twitch or tic.

Joel moved in behind Leah and whispered, "Whatever that is, it's not Courtney anymore. I'll grab her so you can get by."

"She might still be in there somewhere."

"We don't have time to find out. We need to find Mike."

He was right. She was about to nod when, out of the corner of her eye, she caught the swing of Courtney's arm. She threw her hand out and snagged the hurling wrench from midair, stopping it just inches before it would have split Joel's forehead open.

"Whoa!" he said.

Courtney moved toward them. Forward-pause-drag, forward-pause-drag, forward-pause-drag.

She had been the one in the meadow, Leah thought.

"Get ready," Joel said.

He rushed forward and grabbed Courtney around the ribs. The girl—Doer, whatever she was—slammed her fists into his back. *Thump-thump. Thump-thump. Thump-thump.*

Joel lifted her off her feet and swung around so that he was facing Leah. From his winces, Leah could tell Courtney's arms were much stronger than her legs. It didn't help that Courtney was squirming back and forth, making it difficult for him to hold on to her.

"The door," he said, jutting his chin toward the wall.

Leah, who'd been about to race past them, skidded along the concrete floor before readjusting her path to the door in question. After she yanked it open, Joel rushed by, barely getting Courtney inside before she wiggled free and fell onto the floor.

The moment he was out of the room, Leah pulled the door shut.

Still holding the handle, she said, "The wrench! Jam it under!"

Joel grabbed the tool and shoved it as far as he could into the narrow gap at the bottom of the door. Before he finished, the handle began to turn from the other side. Courtney moaned something too garbled to understand.

Joel stepped back from the door. "That should hold."

"Are you sure?"

He hesitated. "I think so."

As soon as Leah removed her hands from the handle, the door moved. She reached for it again, but then the underside finally caught on the wrench and the door ground to a halt. Courtney slipped her fingers through the gap and pulled.

"Let's go," Leah said.

They ran down the hall. Doors flew past on their left, but Leah was sure Mike wasn't behind any of them. The door she had in her sights was the solitary one on the right. Given that Joel was keeping pace with her, he'd clearly had the same thought.

When they reached it, they found that instead of having a simple handle like all the other doors, this one had a long flat bar, currently in the up position. Leah gave it a tug but it didn't budge.

"Locked," she said.

Joel quickly examined the door. "I don't see any kind of keyhole or anything."

Leah tried the bar again, this time using her superior strength. It groaned and started to move.

Joel added his hands to hers and they both pulled. The bar crept downward, then—

Pop!

Leah and Joel jumped back as the handle dropped all the way to the open position. She was sure they had broken the mechanism and now the door could be opened only from the inside. But when Joel grabbed the bar and pulled, the door moved.

NINETY-SEVEN

Mike

THE RECLAIMER HAD tried to cut off Mike's ability to see and hear, but while maintaining the façade of the obedient prisoner, he'd been able to retain enough of his senses to see shapes and hear dampened noises.

It was a small victory at best, however. His end was coming. He knew that. His only real solace was that Leah and Joel would be okay.

The Reclaimer guided him into a large room with a single object sitting in the middle. He couldn't get a good handle on the object's size or shape, but he couldn't miss the way the light shined off it, making it seem to glow.

He knew in that instant he was standing in the presence of the Reclaimer's true home.

Her sanctuary.

Her body.

Her...*cradle.*

::HALT.

As his body stopped moving, a flame flickered in the back of his mind. A mix of defiance and anger and outrage that would not allow him to just roll over and die.

Yes, he had made a deal.

Yes, he would submit to her probing.

And yes, he would give her what she wanted.

What he would not do is be a bystander during the process. No, he would do a little probing of his own.

::PREPARE FOR DATA TRANSFER.

Yes, Reclaimer.

NINETY-EIGHT

The Reclaimer

THE RECLAIMER DELVED into the Translator's mind.

Her first order of business was to retrieve the remaining packets the Translator had yet to send. There was a surprising number waiting in its buffer. Analysis indicated the Translator had been hoarding the packets to ration their arrival and mask the Translator's approach to her fortress, a tactic that clearly had worked. She flagged this information to include in the revised protocols for the next Translator.

The Translator's memories were harder for her to understand, as the raw data was formatted in the creature's biological patterns. Running them through the Translator's own translation programming was out of the question. The deceit it had no doubt sewn throughout the other packets would likely reoccur, thus negating the value. She wanted facts, not illusions. She would have to do the best she could without running its data through a native filter—a vital part of the translation process.

She activated the necessary programming, and began.

An alert went off. The Satellites had breached the door to the section of the structure where her chamber was located. Though they were annoying, there was little they could do to her now that she knew who they were.

She did, however, require a bit more uninterrupted time with the Translator, so she issued the appropriate commands and then returned the majority of her attention to the data.

NINETY-NINE

Joel

THE HALLWAY BEYOND the broken door went on for about thirty feet before ending at another door. Additional closed entrances lined each side, three on the left, two on the right.

The first door they checked opened into a room full of electrical equipment, but no Mike. The next door enclosed a workshop with metal tables and tools hung from pegboards on the wall, but again no Mike.

Rooms three and four were variations of room two.

As Joel reached for door five, he heard a metallic scrape from inside. He slowly turned the knob, but before he could ease the door open, it jerked inward, yanked by someone on the other side.

Joel stumbled forward into a tangle of gray hands. Two snatched his ankles while more latched on to his arms. Before he had time to react, his feet were pulled out from under him and he was dragged into the room.

He batted at the Doer holding his arms, knocking it into a metal table. He then drew his legs in and kicked out, sending the one near his feet skidding across the floor. By the time he was standing again, Leah had a hold on the Doer who'd crashed into the table.

"I don't recognize this one," she said.

While the Doer had the gray and the scars and the missing hair, the face was older, ancient almost. Man or woman, Joel couldn't tell. It seemed to sense his attention and reached out to grab him. It was far too weak, though, to break from Leah's grasp.

Joel turned toward the other Doer. At first he thought he must have knocked it out because it was still on the floor, but then he saw its legs were twisted to the point of uselessness from some long-ago accident. As it began pulling itself across the floor toward Joel, it looked up.

Joel cursed under his breath. Dooley.

Joel crouched in front of his former cabin mate. When Dooley reached for him, Joel grabbed Dooley's wrists and moved the gray hands to the side. Joel then looked into Dooley's eyes, trying to find some sign of his friend. "Can you understand me? It's Joel."

Dooley opened his mouth and groaned, but like with Antonio and Courtney, he showed no sign of recognition.

"What did she do to them?" Leah asked.

Though he knew the question was rhetorical, he said, "Made them hers."

"Like us."

"Yes, but different."

"We're not going to turn into this, are we?"

He didn't answer, because he didn't know.

Joel looked around and spotted a door at the back of the room. He gently pushed Dooley to the side and went over to it. No sound came from the other side so he pulled it open.

The inner room was pitch-black and filled with the smell of rot and decay. He felt along the wall next to the door for a light switch but found nothing.

"Can you bring your phone over here?" he asked.

Leah maneuvered the Doer she'd been holding onto the ground, stepped around Dooley's outstretched hands, and joined Joel at the door.

Shining her light inside, she whispered, "Holy God."

The walls were lined with chairs. While half were empty, others were occupied by piles of bones, gray mummified corpses, and, in a few cases, other functioning Doers.

At one time, the Reclaimer must have had over twenty slaves. Now, counting Courtney, Antonio, Dooley, and the old one behind them, there were seven. Of the trio still in the chairs, two were also ancient. The last was Kayla.

The reason she hadn't been sent after them was obvious. Her legs and arms had atrophied and wouldn't have even supported a child.

Bile churned in Joel's stomach as he imagined what had been done to these people, what they'd had to live through. The hijacking of his and Leah's and Mike's lives was nothing compared to this.

Leah played her light around the room again, stopping on a pile of clothes in the far corner. When she headed over, Joel followed. She rifled through them—slacks and dresses and shirts and underwear and shoes. There were also several dingy white jackets that appeared to be lab coats.

She looked back at the dead Doers. "They must have been the people who were working here."

"Back in the forties?" Joel said, remembering the diary entry by Dr. Kozakov. "That would make them..."

"Old," she said.

They dragged Dooley and the aged Doer into the inner room with the others, then closed the door and jammed it with one of the metal tables.

They returned to the hallway, where the only door left was the one at the end.

ONE HUNDRED

Leah

ONE MOMENT JOEL was reaching for the door, the next, he was soaring down the hall, carried off by a sudden, raging wind.

If not for Leah's superior reaction time, she too would have been sailing through the corridor. The instant she saw Joel's jacket begin to billow, she'd lunged back toward the doorway they'd just exited and grabbed the frame a split second before her legs were lifted into the air.

"Joel!" she called as she looked over her shoulder and watched him fly away.

She was sure he was going to smash into the walls, but the wind sucked him through the opening that had held the door they broke and into the bisecting corridor, where he disappeared.

She closed her eyes and reached out to him. *Joel, grab something!*

She received a panicked *what do you thing I'm trying to do?* before the connection was cut off. Not by Joel, though. It must have been the Reclaimer.

Leah looked at the last door. She needed to get beyond it but she couldn't just walk there in this wind. If she could pull herself through the entrance she was clinging to and into the room beyond, she could shut the door, get out of the wind, and have a moment to think.

Her body banged against the wall as she pulled herself around the jamb she was clinging to and back into the room where they had encountered Dooley. Though the wind whipped at the opening, little made it into the room before she forced the door closed.

She took a moment to catch her breath, and then looked around for something that could help her get to the last door in the hallway, a distance of about fifteen feet. In a cabinet, she found some tools and a sturdy, hundred-foot power cable. Unfortunately, she couldn't just throw the cable at the remaining door as a) it wouldn't attach itself at the other end, and b) the wind would send it sailing.

That's when she realized she was leaning on the answer. Three ten-foot metal tables were in the room. *Portable* tables.

She set to work.

First, she moved the table that had been blocking the door to the inner room into the back room itself, and positioned it length-wise across the doorway to hold it in place. She was concerned at first that the Doers might come after her, but they seemed to have lost interest. Or, more likely, the Reclaimer had assumed the wind would deal with her trespassers.

Leah tied one end of the power cable to the table's crossbeam, and moved another table over to the hallway door, where she flipped it so the top was on the ground. She measured off the power cable, adding in the extra length she'd need, and tied it around a leg of the table. She then sliced off the extra cable with the utility knife she'd found with the tools, tied one end of this second line to another table leg, and the other end around her waist.

Ready as she was ever going to be, she opened the door again.

The wind rushed inside, but not strong enough to knock her off her feet. She shoved the table out the door. As she knew would happen, the wind tried to push it down the hall, but with only the legs propped up in the air, the torrent didn't have much surface area to work with, and she was able to manhandle the table into position. When she was through, the tied-off end angled toward the other door, while the closer end was jammed against the doorframe she was standing in, the wind holding it in place.

She gave it a kick to be sure, and it didn't move.

Knowing she couldn't think about it too much, she

grabbed the table and pulled herself into the hall. Support piece by support piece, she worked her way to the other end of the table, the wind trying to rip her away the whole time.

She then braced her feet against the end and pushed through the wind until she was able to wrap her fingers around the handle of her target door.

She undid her safety line, and then, proving once more she was the fastest girl in the world, opened the door with one hand and, at the exact moment the door was out of her way, grabbed the jamb with the other.

The moment she pulled herself across the threshold, the wind ceased.

ONE HUNDRED ONE

Joel

JOEL WAS OFF his feet and flying before he had a chance to react. The wind was as strong as the one he and Leah had encountered when they were thirteen. He tried to look back the other way to see how far Leah was behind him, but she wasn't there.

The gale whipped him past the last door. He grabbed for the jamb but missed and shot into the other hallway.

Joel, grab something! Leah in his mind.

What do you thing I'm trying to do? he thought. He had no idea if she heard him or not because she didn't say anything else.

He looked side to side, desperate for something to latch on to, but the wind kept him in the exact center of the hallway, where everything was out of reach. He sailed through the giant vault door and into the large room, where he was swept toward the ceiling. Without Leah's light, he had no idea how far up it was.

He braced himself for impact, arm over his face, but then all sense of movement stopped. He could still feel the wind blowing against his back, but instead of thrusting him into the ceiling, it was holding him in place.

He looked down. The only thing he could see was the big doorway where light spilled out. But that was more than enough for him to see it was a long way down. If the wind suddenly stopped, he would not survive the fall, even with his superior recovery abilities.

Judging from the height, he must be close to the ceiling.

Carefully, he stretched a hand into the darkness above him. At full extension, his index finger brushed against a solid surface. He twisted his body to reach higher, and was able to place his palm against the top of the room.

Concrete. Smooth. Nothing to hold on to.

Panic started growing in his chest, but then he remembered: the bruised arm he'd woken with. He hadn't inflicted that injury on anyone yet. So unless the wind cut out and he dropped onto someone, he was destined to live a little while longer.

He concentrated on remembering what he'd seen in the room when they'd passed through before.

Pipes!

Dozens of them, running up the walls.

It had been too dark to know if they ran all the way to the ceiling, but some might.

He checked the door again, and judged that he was closest to the wall opposite it than any other. He pressed his palm as tight to the ceiling as he could, and then, calling on his considerable strength, started levering toward the back wall.

It worked. His body slid across the force of the wind, like a swimmer floating on his side under a dock.

Palm against the ceiling.

Pull.

Reset.

Palm against the ceiling.

Pull.

Reset.

ONE HUNDRED TWO

Mike

THE RECLAIMER PROBED Mike's mind, copying memories and questioning him.

::WHY RETURN?

::EXPLAIN RECONNECTION WITH SATELLITES.

::WHEN DID CORRUPTION OF DATA COMMENCE?

Mike answered her questions with as few details as possible, but never lied. She would know if he did.

As the culling went on, he sneaked along her connections back into her mind, or more precisely, what passed for her mind. He too began collecting data.

One of the first things he found was video from the night hike in 2005. He and Joel and Leah unconscious and being carried by Doers down into the facility and the very room where he stood now. He found logs detailing what the Reclaimer had done to them in the missing days. Though he couldn't understand all of it, he knew enough of her language to realize why she had changed them. He also learned about the purpose of the Reclaimer, and about the cargo she carried.

And for the first time, he knew what she meant when she called herself the end and the beginning.

There was no way he could let the Reclaimer take his life now. Not until he passed on what he knew to Leah and Mike.

One Hundred Three

LEAH PULLED HERSELF to her feet and looked around.

The room was huge, thirty feet deep and twice that wide, with a ceiling another twenty-five above. Mike was near the middle of the room, facing a large, ultra-reflective, rectangular box. The box was several feet above the floor, supported by four surprisingly thin legs. Sticking out of the top of the box were dozens of appendages—rods and discs and tongues, all of the same gleaming metal. The box was nearly as big as a small car—a Mini-Cooper or a Fiat.

This had to be the Reclaimer.

"Mike," she whispered.

He didn't move.

She took a few tentative steps forward. "Mike."

He made no indication of hearing her.

She took a breath and headed toward him, intending to drag him out of there if she had to.

She made it ten feet before a burst of energy slammed into her.

She dropped to her knees, black beginning to close in around her vision. A sudden memory appeared in her mind, she and Joel leaving the building on the surface and being hit by a similar burst. The next thing she remembered from back then was walking down the highway.

No! She could not let herself lose consciousness again.

She fought against her dimming vision until the black disappeared.

She climbed to her feet and looked at the metal box, her

eyes narrow.

"Let him go!"

ONE HUNDRED FOUR

Mike

MIKE SENSED LEAH a moment before the Reclaimer did. He wanted to warn his friend, tell her to get out of there, but what little control he had was focused on mining the Reclaimer's data. If he tried to extract himself now, the Reclaimer would know what he'd been doing and all would be lost. So he could only watch as Leah fell to the ground, presumably unconscious.

I'll get you out of this, he thought in the small bit of his mind that was still shielded. How, he had no idea.

First things first. He needed to collect as much as he could from the Reclaimer. He dug deeper and deeper and—

"Let him go!"

ONE HUNDRED FIVE

The Reclaimer

THE RECLAIMER REELED back as alerts sounded from several of her systems.

The Satellite's words carried a power many magnitudes greater than those from the earlier confrontation. The Reclaimer felt it *inside* her programming.

Emergency analyses indicated a 50.34% probability that this was due to the Satellite's proximity to the Cradle.

The Reclaimer activated her repair sub-routines to deal with the alarms and then chose protection mode 3, sure it would be enough to end the Satellite's threat.

While this was occurring, a newly corrupted piece of code entered her system and prevented her consciousness from being notified that her connection to her Translator had been severed.

One hundred six

Leah

THE ALREADY COOL temperature of the room plummeted. Within seconds, Leah's breaths hung like clouds in front of her, each denser than the one before. The skin on her hands and face burned with the growing cold.

She did her best to ignore it all, and kept her attention on the box in the center of the room.

"Let him go!" she repeated.

Did the decrease in temperature stop? It felt like it.

::YOU...SHOULD NOT...BE...HERE.

One of Leah's knees began to buckle as the Reclaimer's voice rang like a bell through her head, each halting tone a different strike of the clapper. But she willed herself not to fall.

"I'm not staying. Neither is my friend."

::HE IS MINE.

"I don't th—"

::YOU ARE MINE.

"No," Leah said, shivering. "I most definitely am not."

::EVERYTHING IS MINE.

The temperature dropped again, faster.

Leah shouted, "Stop it!" Riding her voice was a dense mental bullet aimed directly at the Reclaimer.

The freeze ceased and the room returned to its previous cool temperature.

::YOU CANNOT!

Leah felt the build-up of energy a half second before it pulsed out from the box. She dropped to a crouch and tried to build a shield around herself, similar to the one Mike had made.

But she was sure it wouldn't be strong enough.

Just before the pulse hit her, the power of her anemic barrier intensified, and the assaulting energy spilled around her without touching her.

A whisper in her thoughts, *You need, you need practice.*

Mike? She glanced toward where she'd last seen him, but he wasn't there anymore.

Another pulse gathered strength and then shot out, missing her again.

Are you all right? she asked.

I'm okay. A pause. *Don't move.*

Another pulse.

Where are you?

Under.

She almost asked, *Under what?* but then realized what he meant.

The shadow of a man—Mike—crouched under the Reclaimer. He seemed to be looking at the bottom of the box.

What are you doing? she asked. *We need to find Joel and get out of here!*

Another pulse, stronger than the others, but still unable to break through Leah's shield.

We can't leave. Not yet, not yet.

We'll die if we stay down here, Leah said.

Everyone dies, everyone, if we leave.

Mike suddenly filled her mind with images and information. It was far too much to take in at once, but he quickly led her to the most important pieces. The true nature of the Reclaimer. What it had done to her and Mike and Joel. Why it had done it. And what its ultimate plans were.

"Oh, dear God," she whispered.

Another, Mike warned, a moment before the strongest pulse yet streaked through the room.

You're right. We can't leave yet, Leah said. *But please tell me you have a plan.*

ONE HUNDRED SEVEN

The Reclaimer

THE RECLAIMER COULD not understand why the energy pulses weren't working. Even at the lowest setting, the pulse should have taken the Satellite down, and the Reclaimer was not using the lowest setting. Her monitoring system showed the pulse was working at optimum levels, so the creature should have been splayed on the ground, unconscious.

She upped the intensity by one level.

And then another.

And another.

Why was it not working?

She decided to forgo the attack and seize control of the Satellite's mind. It would mean nullifying her deal with the Translator, but the situation had changed.

She would have to proceed cautiously. While taking possession of a typical creature's brain was a simple task, it was abundantly clear that the Satellite was not typical. Misdirection was in order, something to cause the Satellite to drop its guard.

She listed the possibilities and then chose the one at the top.

Escape.

::SATELLITE. SPEAK...WITH...ME.

ONE HUNDRED EIGHT

Leah

LEAH SLOWLY ROSE to her feet, her shield extending with her.
"I've already tried talking to you."

::YOU WISH TO LEAVE.

"Yes. I think I made that pretty damn clear."

Careful, Mike whispered in Leah's head.

::THEN LEAVE. I WILL NOT STOP YOU.

"With Mike."

::MIKE?

"The, uh, Translator."

A pause.

::ALL RIGHT. WITH MIKE.

"And Joel," Leah said, adding, "The other Satellite."

::I HAVE NO NEED OF...JOEL.

"You'll need to open the door."

::I CAN PROVIDE YOU WITH THE COMBINATION.

"Great. Give it up and we'll be on our way."

::IT IS IN IMAGE FORM.

Be ready, Mike said.

Leah shot him a quick, *Don't worry about me*, and then said out loud, "I don't care what form it's in. Let's have it."

ONE HUNDRED NINE

The Reclaimer

THE RECLAIMER GRABBED the image of the door combination from the stored memories of one of her initial test subjects from over half a century before. Within it, she embedded a command to disable the Satellite's shield and allow the Reclaimer in.

She made the image available.

::TAKE IT.

ONE HUNDRED TEN

Leah

ARE YOU READY? Leah asked Mike.
Ready. Are you *ready?*
I hope so.
That doesn't sound—
Yes, I'm ready.
"Thank you," Leah said to the Reclaimer. She accepted the image into her mind.

For a brief moment nothing changed, and she wondered if Mike had been wrong. Perhaps the Reclaimer was going to let them go after all. But then the barrier she had built with his help suddenly dissolved and the Reclaimer rushed in.

Instead of trying to blast the Reclaimer out, Leah wrapped her essences around the assault, pinning the Reclaimer's strike in place so that it could neither forge ahead or retreat with ease.

::RELENT! REVEAL! MINE!
The hell it is! Leah thought.

::MINE!
The Reclaimer pulled and pushed, trying to break free. It was like trying to hold on to a giant snake.

Hurry, Leah thought, but did not send to Mike.

He must have been listening in anyway, because she heard him say, *Just a few more seconds.*

::MINE!
The Reclaimer rocked Leah to her knees. With one hand on the ground, Leah tried to push herself back up, but it was too strong. It would only be a moment before it gained control of Leah's mind.

Almost there, Mike said.

Leah wanted to warn him she was nearly out of time, but she needed every last bit of energy to keep the Reclaimer at bay.

Then, as if a switch had been flipped, the Reclaimer's attack ceased.

Leah nearly dropped all the way to the floor. Breathing deeply, she looked toward the center of the room, thinking Mike had done it.

He had, but not in the way he had planned.

Leah jumped to her feet and ran toward the gleaming metal box.

ONE HUNDRED ELEVEN

The Reclaimer

THE SATELLITE DEFENSES were beginning to fail. The Reclaimer could sense it. She upped the intensity of her assault to maximum level, knowing the creature's mind would soon be—

She had not heard an alarm so loud since the day she'd arrived and one of her relays had broken off the Cradle. Per protocol, her contact with the Satellite ceased instantly, and her total attention was refocused on the Cradle's underside, where an access hatch had been opened. Sitting below the opening was the Translator.

Here was yet another item to add to the list of things it should not be able to do.

A microsecond review of the logs revealed where the error had occurred. The Translator had been siphoning information from her as she was siphoning information from it.

She set her defenses at maximum, too.

ONE HUNDRED TWELVE

Leah

MIKE LAY ON the ground below the box, his body trembling. Above him hung the panel door he'd opened while Leah had distracted the Reclaimer.

"Mike!" she screamed as she ran.

Ten feet from the box, an invisible electric bolt smashed into every cell of her body, throwing her backward onto the ground. She pushed through the searing pain and struggled back to her feet.

"Leave him alone!" she yelled.

The Reclaimer attacked again but Leah was ready this time. Though the bolt was as painful as before, she did not lose her footing.

"I said leave him alone!"

Leah sensed the Reclaimer shifting its main focus back to her, and then she felt the onslaught as it tried again to overpower her mind.

Get out of there! Leah thought, hoping Mike would hear. But his body remained prone.

::RELENT!

"No!" she screamed, weaker now, finding it harder to hold off the attack.

::RELENT!

"I said no!"

The Reclaimer's tendrils closed in on Leah. She could almost feel them touching her mind.

::RELENT!

"Go to hell!"

Using what power she had left, Leah pushed outward. The Reclaimer moved back, but not nearly as far as Leah had hoped, and in no time it was encircling her mind again.

::RELENT!

Something slipped into Leah's hand.

"She will not!"

As she glanced toward the voice, a surge of power rushed through her.

Joel stood at her side, his hand in hers. "We do this together, remember?"

Leah gave him a thankful smile and turned back to the box. With an avalanche of her and Joel's combined strength, she flung away the Reclaimer's attempt to dig into her mind.

::RELENT!

The Reclaimer's voice boomed, and should have drowned out all other thought, but now it interfered with nothing.

Leah fired off another burst, pushed the Reclaimer farther away.

She saw that Mike was no longer shaking and was pushing himself back up.

As he started to reach into the alien machine, Leah shouted, "You will leave us alone!" and sent another debilitating bolt of energy.

::RELE—

Leah and Joel attacked again.

And again.

And again.

ONE HUNDRED THIRTEEN

The Reclaimer

THE RECLAIMER'S PROCESSORS were working at top speeds, trying to figure out how it was possible the creatures could have so much power. It was *incompatible* with everything she knew. None of the creatures she had observed up close had even a fraction of this ability.

It simply did not make sense.

Every time she tried to retaliate, the creatures struck again.

An alarm notified her that something was wrong.

Everything was wrong, of course, but the emergency value it carried demanded her immediate attention.

ONE HUNDRED FOURTEEN

Mike

MIKE HAD HIS arm inside the Reclaimer all the way to his shoulder. His eyes were closed as he matched the movements of his hand to the map he had extracted earlier of the machine's interior.

He could feel Leah and Joel doing all they could to distract the Reclaimer. So far it was working, but at some point the Reclaimer would realize what Mike was doing. He needed to work fast.

Obviously the designers of the machine had never considered the possibility of someone gaining unauthorized access, a task Mike would have never been able to achieve if not for his years of working closely with the Reclaimer. And now that he was inside, he knew what he needed to do.

He moved his hand a few more inches to the left, past a glass dome and around a curved bar until his fingers hovered over several rows of small spheres. The receptacles held microscopic seeds of life—embryos of the Reclaimer's creators, an ancient race of beings that had long ago claimed the galaxy as its own. The beings had never been to Earth before, but in their mind it was theirs and they wanted it back.

The Originators, that was what the Reclaimer called them. Hundreds of times they had built vast civilizations, only to die out and be rebirthed by other Reclaimers. This was to be the beginning of a new wave, and humanity was in the way.

Mike quickly worked the end of his jacket over his hand and raised his forearm as high as he could.

As he started downward, the Reclaimer tried to take

control of his mind.

::DO NOT!

Too late.

Not all the spheres broke under his blow, but those that remained intact dislodged from their receptacles and flew throughout the interior of the machine.

As he yanked his arm out, he smashed whatever else he could along the way. He then scrambled out from under the Cradle, expecting all the while for the Reclaimer to attack him again.

Then he felt it—not an assault, but a sense of resignation cloaking the machine, and something else. Something more…permanent.

He jumped to his feet and shouted at his friends, "Out, out! We need to get out!"

He ran toward the exit. They started running, too.

They were fast, faster than anyone had ever been, but Mike didn't know if it would be enough.

ONE HUNDRED FIFTEEN

The Reclaimer

10.221 SECONDS. THAT'S all the time the Reclaimer had between realizing her mission had failed and catastrophic shutdown.

10.221 seconds.

The first 1.487 seconds were spent dismantling the wall behind which her failsafe program was kept. This program then spent 6.419 seconds preparing a final information packet—one the Reclaimer herself would send. The packet departed 1.279 seconds later, allowing 1.036 seconds for her to activate her self-destruct and ponder all the things she could have done.

ONE HUNDRED SIXTEEN

Joel

LEAH REACHED THE door first and turned out of sight. Joel slowed just enough to let Mike get by him, but as his friend reached the threshold—

Whomp!

If Joel had been anywhere else in the room, he'd have rocketed into one of the walls, and would have likely died the moment his head crashed into the cement. Instead he flew through the doorway and clipped Mike in the arm with his shoulder. The contact spun Joel sideways so that he hit the corridor wall with his leg and hip.

The spin helped reduce the speed of the contact, but it didn't make it hurt any less.

Lying on the ground, he could feel heat coming from somewhere. Through squinted eyes, he looked back toward the room where the Reclaimer had been and saw it now glowed orange like a furnace.

That couldn't be good.

He hobbled to his feet, his hip howling in pain. Mike was crumpled a few feet away, seemingly unconscious. The heat was intensifying. Joel grabbed one of Mike's arms and started pulling him down the hall.

Once they had gone far enough away, he maneuvered Mike to his feet.

"Hey, can you hear me?" Joel said.

A groan.

"Mike, come on. I need your help."

Mike's eyelids fluttered and opened. "My…arm hurts."

He breathed the last word more than said it.

"I know it does. Trust me, it'll be fine."

Joel put an arm around Mike's back and they headed down the hall.

"Leah?" he called.

There was no sign of her.

"Leah!"

They struggled to the end of the hall and limped through the giant door into the large room where minutes before Joel had been hovering under the ceiling. It and the conduits on the wall he'd climbed down weren't visible through the darkness, however.

"Leah!"

They walked as far in as the light from behind them allowed. Joel called her name again.

From somewhere ahead, he finally heard her shout, "This way!" A moment later the glow of her phone appeared. "Straight to me."

Behind them, Joel heard the crash of something large falling. He guessed that the floor in the Reclaimer's room had fallen onto the level below it.

"Hanging in there?" he asked Mike.

"Hanging."

Joel smiled. "Yeah, me too."

They shuffled through the darkness toward the light. When they reached Leah, she headed into the exit hallway.

"Slow down," Joel said, needing her light.

She pointed it back so he could see the floor, and in the process lit up the gray body lying against the hallway wall.

"Antonio?" Joel asked.

"I checked him," Leah said. "He's...dead."

"All dead," Mike said. "They're all dead. Without, without the Reclaimer, they could not...sustain."

Joel wasn't sure what to feel. For all intents and purposes, Antonio and the others had been dead for years. Maybe it was time for their physical selves to follow. Should he mourn them? Should he be happy they finally had peace?

"We need to keep moving," Leah said.

As they rounded the bend, Leah's light shined on the big door Antonio had closed. But now it hung open.

Leah, seeing the surprise on Joel's face, said, "The Reclaimer gave me the combination. I'm sure she didn't think we'd be able to use it, though."

More rumbles came from back toward the laboratories. They picked up the pace.

ONE HUNDRED SEVENTEEN

Leah

THEY RODE THE elevator to the surface, and then made their way through the abandoned building and out into the meadow.

Twilight. The faint sizzle of the finished day touched the western horizon, but the rest of the sky was painted with the star-encrusted blue-black of night.

Leah took a deep breath and closed her eyes. She knew the Reclaimer was gone, but it was strange not to feel its touch. She'd been sensing it since the day she'd first been here, she now realized. Every moment of the intervening years, the thing had been there, hovering in the back of her mind. But now—

"It's really gone," she said.

Joel moved up beside her. "Yeah."

"So what do we do now? Tell someone?"

"Tell them what? That there was a mind-reading crate hidden in a secret mountain bunker?"

She looked at him, confused, then it dawned on her. "You don't know."

His brow furrowed.

"What she really was?" Leah said.

"Uh, no. Are you saying you do?"

She ran a finger through the hair over his ear and caressed his cheek. *Let me show you.*

She opened her mind to him and guided him through the same information Mike had shared with her.

When she finished, no one spoke for several moments.

Finally Joel said, "So we were the information gatherers."

"The Satellites."

"And-and-and the Translator," Mike said.

Leah smiled. "And the Translator." She took Joel's hand and then Mike's. "I think it's time to get Mike home." She looked over at him. "How's that sound?

He looked tense all of a sudden. "I'm not going back there. No more. I...I don't need them."

"I was thinking your parents' house."

"Oh. Well, okay. Yeah. My parents. That's fine."

"They're not going to be happy with us for kidnapping him," Joel said.

"When they see the way he is now, I think they'll figure out a way to forgive us."

They started walking toward the woods.

"Can we, can we get something to eat?" Mike asked. "I'm hungry."

Leah and Joel laughed.

"That sounds like a great idea," Leah said. "We can stop at that café down the road."

They walked on for a few more seconds, then Mike said, "But, um…"

Leah cocked her head. "But what?"

"Joel promised me Chinese food."

EPILOGUE

THE CUSTODIAN CONTINUED along his arcing path, the star he orbited a distant pinprick in the black of space. Out there, at the very edge of this solar system, his existence was a quiet one, but such was the nature of his job.

On that particular segment of his journey, however, the quiet was about to be broken.

When the Custodian's antenna received the packet, it had already been traveling for nearly three rotations of the planet from where it originated. The information contained within was extracted, processed, and analyzed. There was no rush. Time was not an issue.

Though the Reclaimer failed to complete her mission, her time on the third planet had not been a complete waste. The data she returned was detailed and provided a clear picture of what had gone wrong.

Utilizing this information, the Custodian drafted a revised mission plan, rewrote protocols, and put into place new emergency measures. After these tasks were completed, he downloaded the entire operational system into the next Reclaimer unit.

The optimum separation point would not arrive for another four years, seven months, and twenty-three days (target planet standard). After that, the journey would take fifty-one years, two months, and seven days.

The Custodian powered up the Cradle to run all the predeparture tests.

::ARE YOUR CHANNELS OPEN? he inquired.

::YES.

::ARE YOUR RECEPTORS WORKING?
::YES.
::ARE ALL LINKS INTACT?
::YES.

The Custodian initiated the long countdown for launch.

Made in the USA
San Bernardino, CA
03 September 2016